Drop the Mitts

CANADIAN PLAYED
BOOK SEVEN

CYNTHIA GUNDERSON

BUTTON PRESS

With Gratitude

Editing and Critique
Jordan Truex, Scott Gunderson, Sue Prince

Cover Design
Mitxeren

Assistant and Sanity Support
Stacey Wilson

CHAPTER
One

GRACE

THE EMPTY HALLWAY swallowed the sound of Grace's heels, the sharp clicks softened by layers of drywall dust. She should have scheduled another walk-through with her contractor this week, but what was the point? Every time she stepped into this building, another problem surfaced.

She entered the first condo on the right, the door still missing a knob. The plumbing needed updating, and it seemed to have been installed by a Yukon dead set on burying those pipes so deep in the walls they'd never be one cold snap away from bursting.

She sighed. It could've been worse.

Troy Bowen knew exactly what he was doing when he left her this place, and if she ever had any doubts that he loved her, this put them to rest. Who was she kidding? She knew he loved her, but that had never been the problem, had it?

Troy loved everyone. Specifically women. More specifically, women with hourglass figures and asses you could bounce a quarter off of. Hers had qualified five years ago, but she was quite certain she'd been kicked out of the coin-flicking club sometime after her thirty-second birthday.

Grace crouched and inspected the new baseboards, running a finger along the sharp, clean edge. Flat-profiled, five inches high, with a crisp, modern finish—they were the kind of understated but intentional detail that made a space feel polished without drawing attention to itself. The contractor had pushed for something trendier, maybe a shaker-style or craftsman cut, but she'd shut that down immediately. The goal wasn't to make a statement.

She stood and straightened her slacks. Troy may not have been willing to commit romantically, but he'd left her this Kensington condo building in his will. It was the only complex of its kind in this part of the city, a unicorn in Calgary's real estate market. The architecture alone made it valuable, and once she got through months of permits, renovations, and legal headaches, it would be worth a small fortune.

A part of her wondered if this was his way of winning after all. Finally convincing her to move to Calgary when she'd refused to years prior.

The joke was on him. She wasn't going to keep this building. Grace had all the know-how to hire a management company and put these units up for rent, but she'd never wanted to be a landlord. She wouldn't start now in a city across the country from home.

She strode back into the hall and pushed open the next unit, inspecting the new drywall and finished tile on the kitchen backsplash. The units on this floor could be used to make a time-lapse video of the renovations, all in varying states of disarray. But blowing up at the contractor wasn't on the table. At least not until people took their Christmas lights down.

Grace's phone buzzed, vibrating in her purse. She pulled it out and glanced at the screen. Jenna.

She grinned, already prepping herself for the gushing and

unadulterated bliss Jenna doled out these days. Whoever said a woman has to be pregnant to emit glowing life energy never met a new adoptive parent.

"Checking in to make sure I haven't been buried alive under drywall?" Grace answered, wedging the phone between her ear and shoulder as she paced toward the window.

Jenna's laugh was bright. "Thought I'd remind you there's life outside that mess you keep calling an investment."

Grace snorted, glancing at the city stretching out beyond the glass. "You say that like I don't have a *very* full social calendar with my contractor."

"Wait, are you sleeping with him?"

"No! I meant—"

"I know what you meant, I was only hoping."

Grace scoffed. "Have you met Matthew?"

"What, is he gross?"

"Not gross, just extremely married."

Jenna blew out a breath. "Well, what the hell are you doing, spending all your time with a married man?"

"It's a strategy. That way, I don't have to hang out with single men."

Jenna laughed out loud. "Well, you're probably not going to like my proposition then."

"Which is?"

"We have an extra ticket to the Blizzard game tonight. A "thank-you" for all the legal wizardry you did with Hope's adoption."

"Is that . . . reverse bribery?"

"You'd know the legal term."

Grace pretended to consider it, tilting her head toward the ceiling. "Is this where I remind you that last time I went to a game, I spent the first period checking my emails and the second cleaning beer off my Fendi bag?"

Jenna burst out laughing. "Okay, to be fair, that was an accident. Country isn't normally that clumsy. Ooh! And we have a suite this time. With food." She paused for a moment. "Am I swaying you?"

"It's not a terrible offer."

"Hm. Excellent. That's what I was going for."

"But I'm exhausted."

"You're also boring."

Grace scoffed. "That . . . is not true. I have a career and—"

"You're a workaholic with the social life of an old library book. Which I can say because you're hot as hell and make more than Country and I put together. So. You can't win 'em all, I guess."

Grace sighed. "Jenna, I love you, but I genuinely don't know if I have the energy to—"

"You could analyze the arena's commercial real estate value between periods. Or discuss the legal ramifications of Henley breaking his contract." Jenna must've sensed her resolve cracking because she went in for the kill. "You only have a few more months here. Don't you want to hang out with your best friends?"

Grace groaned. "You're my only friends."

"My point exactly. Come out with us and meet *new* friends. And I promise, Country's a great bouncer. He can keep the feral single men away from you. I won't even let him hold his beer. He'll have to keep it on the counter like a toddler."

"Ugh, fine. I'll come. What time?"

Jenna shrieked into the phone, and Grace pulled it away from her ear. "Seven. I'll meet you at the front."

"Bring Hope. That's the only reason I'm agreeing to this."

"Well, of course."

Grace shook her head as she hung up, staring out at the Calgary skyline. One night wouldn't kill her. And, if she was being honest, her rental was feeling a bit lonely.

She turned from the window and found her bag. Might as well clear up a few loose ends before heading out for the evening. She pulled out her laptop and scanned her emails, only to pause halfway down her scroll.

Her brows pinched. The subject line hit like a punch to the sternum.

Petition to Revoke Consent for Adoption.

Grace's hand hovered over the mouse, suddenly useless, her fingers numb as she clicked the email open. The words on the screen blurred at first, then sharpened into something cold and undeniable. The birth mother was trying to get Hope back.

Her stomach plummeted.

No. No, this wasn't possible. This was done. This wasn't some half-baked agreement or rushed paperwork—it was iron-clad. She'd made sure of it. She didn't make mistakes.

But here it was. A legal petition. A challenge.

The paragraphs swam before her eyes, but she forced herself to focus. She ran through everything she knew about Alberta adoption law, ticking off every safeguard she'd put in place.

The birth mother had signed away her rights.

It was a closed adoption.

Jenna and Country had full custody.

Unless…

Grace scanned further, her stomach turning.

"Material change in circumstances . . ."

Oh, hell. That's what they were arguing. A birth parent in Alberta could challenge an adoption post-finalization under extreme conditions—abuse, fraud, coercion. None of those applied here. Absolutely none. But then she saw the argument.

"The petitioner was in a vulnerable state at the time of relinquishment and was not of sound mind when consenting."

. . .

Bullshit. Absolute bullshit.

Grace dug her nails into her palm, grounding herself in something other than the sheer fury tightening her chest. This wasn't about fraud or coercion. This was about regret. A mother who changed her mind, and the court would let her try?

That pissed her right off. Not because the mother had feelings—of course she did. But because there was no way this woman had gotten her ducks in a row in the past month. She wasn't doing what was best for Hope, and Grace had plenty of professional experience with that kind of maternal selfishness.

Could this even get traction? The standard for overturning an adoption was insanely high. The birth mother would need evidence—medical records, psychiatric evaluations, proof of instability at the time of consent.

Could this woman have faked it? Or was there something she'd missed?

A sick feeling crawled up her spine. She'd left family law for a reason. It had been too personal, too draining, too rife with other people's pain that then bled into her own life. Property law didn't cry on the phone at midnight. It didn't come with gut-wrenching, life-altering stakes.

She had walked away from this kind of emotional wreckage years ago. And yet, here she was, drowning in it again.

Did she screw this up?

Her brain hissed at her, tearing apart every step of the process, every document signed, every witness present, every single moment she had assured them it was done. She was careful, meticulous.

She squeezed her eyes shut and forced a deep breath. *Stop spiraling. Solve the damn problem.*

Fine. Worst-case scenario: The court agrees to hear the petition. That doesn't mean they win.

Step one: Call the adoption agency first thing in the morning.

Confirm the mother's state at signing. Make sure there's zero ambiguity in their records.

Step two: Find out if this judge is sympathetic to these cases. Some were sticklers for legal precedent, and some were more emotional. If they got the wrong judge, this could drag out longer than it should.

Step three: Do not tell Jenna and Country. Not yet. If this case got legs, she'd tell them with a plan in place. Not a second before.

Her hands were steady again. The fear still coiled in her chest, but it wasn't running the show.

She glanced at the clock and swore under her breath. The game.

She needed to leave now if she was going to arrive home in time to change. How was she supposed to sit through a hockey game and pretend everything was okay?

But if she didn't go, Jenna would only be more insistent. She needed to show up to avoid giving any indication that things were *not* fine.

Grace shut the laptop, grabbed her blazer, and walked out the door.

CHAPTER
Two

ANDRÉ

THE SADDLEDOME WAS alive with the usual game-night chaos—beer sloshing, screens flashing, and the heavy bass of the arena music vibrating through André's chest. He barely heard or saw any of it.

He lounged in one of the suite chairs, feet kicked up on the railing, grinning like a man who had already won. Because tonight? He was playing a different game.

Grace was coming.

Country sat across from him, arms crossed like he was waiting for André to realize what kind of shitstorm he'd created. He did. He just wasn't sorry about it.

"You should be thanking me." Country nodded toward the entrance where Jenna had disappeared to meet Grace.

André dragged a slow hand over his mouth to cover his smirk. "I'll write you a poem about it later."

Country shook his head. "Don't be an ass. Don't hit on her

here. Jenna told me she didn't want to come because of guys like you."

"Hm. I'm one of a kind, so—"

"That. Don't do that."

André tipped his beer in Country's direction. "And what if she wants me to?"

Country grinned. "Bud. She's not going to want you to. You step out of line, and I'm going to pretend we never had this discussion."

André dropped his feet and sat straight. "Right. Jenna will never know that I'm into Grace. I just happen to be here."

Country blew out a breath. "This is going to bite us in the ass. I can already feel it."

"How so? You wanted to ask her about the charity game. That's a plenty good excuse—"

"Jenna doesn't know about that either. She's weirdly protective of Grace. She acts like if anything goes wrong where she's concerned, we'll anger the gods and lose Hope or something."

André frowned. "The adoption's final."

"Yeah. That's what I keep saying. I—" Country looked up, and André turned his head. The door to the suite opened, and everything in his body locked up.

Jenna stepped in first, her eyes darting between Country, him, Emma, and Tyler, and the other guys filling their plates in the back. Then Grace appeared behind her.

And shit.

As much as he'd been anticipating this, he wasn't prepared. The last time he'd seen her in person was at the adoption party. She'd only been there for a few minutes, but it was long enough to scrawl her into his brain with Sharpie. Seeing her now, in real-time, in his space, looking like a Wall Street goddess? It knocked the air straight out of his lungs.

The arena lights caught the sharp edge of her jaw, the gold in her hair, the faint pinch of irritation in her brow that made him want to see her come undone. He wanted her to slice him open with her words. To eviscerate him. Just so he could snap back and break down those walls and find out what she looked like underneath.

André's gaze drifted lower, hungry, involuntary. She was all sharp lines and tailored perfection—the kind of woman who made blazers look weaponized. Dark green, cinched at the waist, fitted to the point of obscenity. He imagined slipping his fingers beneath the lapels, popping open the single delicate button with nothing but the edge of his knuckles.

And those pants? Black. Cut within an inch of their damn lives.

His brain short-circuited. That high waist? It begged for his hands. The clean, sleek line from hip to heel? A masterpiece. And he had no business imagining what those legs would feel like wrapped around his hips, pressing into his back, pinning him in place with the kind of control he knew she had.

His fingers twitched. Jenna was going to know he wanted her. One look, and she was going to read it all over his face.

"Pick your jaw up off the floor," Country hissed.

André stood, slow, like he had all the time in the world and wasn't sporting a massive boner. He kept his body turned toward the ice as Jenna introduced Grace to everyone. She'd seen Suraj, Curtis, Brett, and Penny at the party, but he doubted she remembered anyone's names. Except for Emma and Tyler, whom she'd known since she first came into town. He'd already given Tyler crap for not bringing her around to a game back then.

André gave a small wave when Jenna introduced him, but when Grace started looking for a place to set her purse and blazer, he couldn't help himself. "Here." He stepped past Country, took the stairs up the central aisle two at a time, and reached for her things.

Her eyes flicked to his, sharp and assessing. She hesitated a moment, then slipped out of her blazer and handed both items over. Her blouse was cream-coloured and delicate, with thin straps over her shoulders.

"Sorry, didn't have time to change." She smiled at Jenna, but it didn't reach her eyes.

"You can have my shirt if you want." André folded the blazer over his arm and nearly tripped as he stepped back on the stairs.

Grace's mouth quirked. "And you would wear . . ."

"Nothing." He deadpanned until Jenna smacked his shoulder.

"What the hell, André? Country!"

"Yeah." Country started up the steps behind him, but André turned and waved him off.

"It was a joke. Geez." He turned to look back over his shoulder and winked at Jenna. "But even you wouldn't complain."

She glared at him, then blew out a breath and turned to Grace. "He's always like that. Just ignore him."

André grinned as he laid Grace's blazer over the seat back beside his and set her purse on the upholstery. Perfect. He hadn't triggered any alarm bells.

At least not with Jenna.

He barely had his butt in his seat before the chirping started.

Curtis leaned forward from the row behind. "So, uh . . . you want to tell us what that was?"

Suraj grinned and crowded in from the left. "The moment she walked in? You looked like a rookie getting his first shift in the show. Wide-eyed. Breathless. A little sweaty."

André rolled his shoulders back. "Just the curry I had for lunch."

Brett, who'd just taken a bite of nachos, finally swallowed and grinned. "Bud, I haven't seen you move that fast since you noticed Fly standing behind you in the showers."

André snorted, stealing one of Brett's nachos just to chap his ass. "I didn't know him then. Now, I'd consider it."

Country sat down with an exhale just as Jenna appeared in the aisle. She crouched, bracing herself on his knees. "You planned this, didn't you?" Country started to shake his head, but

Jenna didn't pause for half a second. "Brett? Suraj? Curtis? All in committed relationships. You told me you were inviting the guys—"

"It's not my fault they were the only ones who said yes!" Country threw out his hands, and Jenna motioned for him to lower his voice. "I tried to get Ryan and Aelin to bring the girls, but they had some commitment at the school."

"I promised Grace there would be no single guys hitting on her."

André scoffed. "Why are you looking at me like that? You brought a guest, and I acted like a gentleman. Can we no longer help a woman without her thinking we're trying to sleep with her?" He nudged Country. "What's the opposite of misogy—"

"Ugh, you two are the worst." She pushed up from Country's lap and pointed at Grace's jacket. "I'm telling her she doesn't have to sit there."

André shrugged, trying to keep the grin off his face. "I think Grace is a grown woman—"

"So nice of you to notice." Grace dropped to the step behind Jenna, one hand holding her plate and the other a full cup of beer. The foam slipped over the side of her cup, dripping over her fingers. "Anything else you'd like to discuss? Bone density, cholesterol levels?"

Jenna stepped back. "I was just telling André it was presumptuous to put your things in the seat next to him."

"It was." Grace cocked her head to the side. "I'm not going to sleep with you. If that's what you were hoping for."

Suraj snorted behind him, and Country's eyes flew wide.

André's grin widened as he gestured to the purse chair. "Damn, Grace, you sure know how to crush a man's dreams. I was already mentally designing our wedding invitations."

Brett choked on his soda. Country just shook his head like he regretted every decision that had led to this moment, avoiding Jenna's eyes like the plague.

Grace didn't so much as blink. "Let me guess. Black tie affair, open bar, you show up late if you show up at all—"

"Why wouldn't I show up?"

She raised an eyebrow. "You don't exude 'husband material.'"

André put a hand to his heart. "I feel so seen."

Grace wet her lips, then slid past Jenna and Country. She paused when she stood directly in front of André, the waistband of her hot-ass pants brushing his thighs. "I'm too old for you." She looked up into his eyes, her jaw set.

"That sounds like a limiting belief."

Grace released a small puff of air, slid past, picked up her purse, and sat.

"I know a good therapist. She'll take you on as a favour to me if you want to work through that." André watched her settle in–the precise way she placed her beer in the cupholder, the way she tucked her legs beneath the seat, her posture stiff like she'd been trained out of letting her body take up space.

"I don't need a therapist. Especially not one you've slept with."

He scoffed. "You're a lawyer. Don't you know you need evidence before accusing?"

She didn't take her eyes off the ice. "You said you knew a therapist, not that you had one, and you led me to believe you can influence her behavior. So, either she owes you money or she's somehow still interested in you. Either one seems wildly unlikely, to be honest, but I'm going off of what information I have."

"She's my sister."

Grace blinked, her eyes flitting briefly to his. "Well. A shot and a miss."

André grinned. "Or I met her in grad school, and she definitely still wants me." He winced when something hit him in the back of the head. Turning, he found Jenna with another Peanut M&M pinched between her fingers.

André pretended he didn't know why she was pissed and spread out like he owned the damn row. "You don't have to scrunch up. There's plenty of room."

"Mmm. Thank you for telling me how to sit in my seat to watch a hockey game."

"Here to help. If you need instructions on getting the appropriate amount of dip on those celery sticks or making sure your fingers aren't sticky from the beer—"

"I have a napkin."

He shrugged. "They'll still be sticky."

She turned her head. "Let me guess, you'll lick them off for me?"

He swiped his tongue over his lips. "No. I'll watch while you lick them."

Grace didn't break eye contact. "Is this how you talk to every woman you meet?"

André exhaled and leaned back in his seat. "Only the ones who enjoy it."

She rolled her eyes and dipped a celery stick. Way too much ranch. André tried to focus on the game, but Grace pointedly licked dressing off her finger. Slow. Turned toward him. Daring him to turn his head. His nostrils flared, but he didn't give her the satisfaction.

He cleared his throat and leaned forward, resting his arms on his knees. The Blizzard controlled the game, cycling the puck in Winnipeg's zone, their top line shifting seamlessly. Warren took a shot, and it clanged off the post. The crowd groaned as the Jumbotron showed the replay.

André barely noticed any of it. Which was insane, considering hockey was his entire life. Grace was like a TV in a sports bar. He kept wanting to glance over and see what was playing.

She hadn't relaxed an inch. Not even a single casual shift in her seat, no slouch, no settling in. Just perfect posture, legs crossed tight, hands resting carefully on her lap.

André reached for his beer, which he'd conveniently placed

in the left cupholder, and Grace's eyes flicked down to his hands. She paused. Her nose scrunched.

"What?" he asked.

Grace didn't answer. She narrowed her eyes, her gaze flicking from his fingers back up to his face. The expression was pure, concentrated judgment.

André drew from his beer, waiting for her to say it. He knew exactly what she was looking at. The nicotine stain on his fingers. Yellowed at the edges, just barely there, but enough for someone like her to notice. Someone who paid attention to details.

He should have cared. Should have been embarrassed, maybe. But he wasn't. Because this wasn't some new, bad habit. This was muscle memory. This was waking up after a road game and lighting up before his first piss of the day. This was learning to breathe through it because it was the only thing that ever made him feel steady.

The first time he smoked a cigarette, he was sixteen, sitting on the porch to avoid another drunken outburst. His brother, Luc, handed it to him.

André had taken it without thinking because the alternative was looking at the way Luc was staring blankly at the concrete, blood dried at his temple, mouth set like he wasn't sure he still had all his teeth.

"Coach is going to be pissed," André had muttered, rolling the cigarette between his fingers as if he knew what to do with it.

Luc hadn't looked up. So André lit the cigarette, took his first drag, and hated it. It burned, tasted awful, made his lungs seize. But Luc exhaled, smoke curling in the air, and said, "It helps."

And that had been enough of a reason to try again. Again and again. Until he didn't hate it anymore. Until it became routine. Until he needed it.

He tried to quit once. He'd been successful for exactly three weeks and two days. It was after his second season in Juniors when his conditioning coach made an offhand comment about his lung capacity dropping.

By week two, his hands were shaking before practice. By week three, he was snapping at teammates, grinding his teeth, buzzing out of his skin. He caved, sitting in his car outside his apartment, lighting up with shaking hands.

"For someone who seems to have a high opinion about his body, I'm surprised. That's all." Grace turned back to the game.

André smirked. "Looking good naked has nothing to do with my vices."

Grace's lips twitched. "No judgment here."

"Hm. It feels like judgment."

Grace took a sip of her beer. "I'm not the one who has to kiss you. Or apply for life insurance."

André set his beer in the cupholder. "You've never kissed a guy who smoked?"

"No, I have. That's why I can speak with authority."

André's jaw tensed. The chirps from his teammates? Easy. The lectures from trainers? White noise. But this? Not sharp, not cruel. Just flat. Matter-of-fact. Like he'd already lost points he didn't even know he was playing for.

Her words crawled under his skin. "Turns out I'm a fan of poor decision-making."

Jenna sighed loudly. "We're aware."

Curtis clapped him on the shoulder. "Don't know the context, but that was never up for debate."

André turned, feigning offense. "What did I do to deserve this?" He cleared his throat and swivelled forward. "First of all, I'm in peak physical condition." Grace arched a single, devastating eyebrow. "Second, I don't smoke that much."

Curtis let out an actual cackle. "Bud. You have two separate gas stations that know your order."

"He's a franchise," Tyler called out from two rows up.

Penny grinned. "Marlboro probably sends him a Christmas card."

André threw up his hands, grinning despite himself. "Wow. We done?"

Emma thankfully changed the subject, and André somehow forced himself to focus on the game. It had been getting chippy for a while. The refs were letting them play, letting the sticks ride high, letting the little extra shoves after the whistle slide.

Sure enough, halfway through the second period, it finally boiled over. Lindholm, a Blizzard winger, got buried along the boards—a clean hit, but heavy. One you feel in your bones.

Then the gloves came off.

"Here we go," Curtis muttered.

André sat forward, grinning as Appy and Monohan put elbows up at centre ice, dropping their gloves like they'd been waiting for an excuse.

The fight started like all of them do. A little hesitation, circling, waiting to see who throws first—then boom, first grab, first shot, first real connection that makes the crowd go feral.

André loved a good tilt. Not for the violence, but for the mechanics. A real hockey fight was an art form. One player controlled the collar grip while keeping his head tucked, and the other used footwork to stay just out of reach, the little tugs and balance shifts to keep the other off-centre.

Then came the big shots. Monohan threw a heavy right hook —missed, but it kept the pressure up. Appy landed a sharp uppercut, knocking his helmet loose. They went back and forth throwing bombs in front of thousands of screaming fans, knowing damn well this was more about the code than the actual outcome.

Eventually, Monohan hit the ice, and the refs broke it up, pulling them apart while the crowd rose to their feet, screaming approval.

André grinned, shaking his head. "That was solid."

Grace exhaled sharply, crossing her arms tighter. "That was ridiculous."

"What? You don't like a little old-fashioned conflict resolution?"

Grace's lips pressed together. "That wasn't conflict resolution. That was two idiots giving each other concussions for no reason."

André turned. "There's always a reason."

"There isn't."

Hilarious. He doubted Grace had played a day of hockey in her life, and here she was, lecturing him. "There is. It's about respect."

Grace let out a small, incredulous laugh. "Respect? Earned by punching a guy in the face?"

"There's an order to it. You don't fight because you're pissed off. You fight because someone has to answer for a dirty hit, or a guy's been running his mouth all game, or the boys need a momentum shift. It's part of the game."

Grace shook her head. "Part of the game. Right. And I suppose brain damage is just a fun little side effect?"

And just like that, everything inside him went still. The noise of the crowd dulled, faded into the background.

Brain damage. The words spun like a top in his head. He should answer. Should laugh it off, chirp back, keep it light. Instead, his throat locked up.

"Hey, speaking of which, I had something I wanted to talk with you about." Country leaned forward, snagging Grace's attention. He gave André a small nod, then smiled wide. "There's a charity game our team is putting on. To raise money for Heads Up Alberta. They support kids and families dealing with traumatic brain injuries."

Grace straightened in her seat, if that was possible. Considering she already seemed to be sitting on a metal rod. "Oh. That's amazing."

Country nodded. "Yeah, it's something we've been trying to get off the ground for a while now. We've got a lot of guys backing it, but we need help on the legal side."

Grace pursed her lips. "I'm not sure that's my area of expertise." She crossed her legs, curling into herself. She crossed her arms like she was trying to hold herself together.

Something twinged in André's middle. He cleared his throat, his breathing beginning to normalize. He owed Country for the distraction. And for what was about to come next.

Country continued, "It's just contracts, sponsorship agreements, liability waivers."

Grace nodded but didn't bite. André silently willed her to ask more questions, to seem even the least bit interested, but she was buttoned up.

Country leaned back, forced into straight-up asking. "I wondered if you'd be interested. It would only be a few hours a week, and while we don't have much of a payroll budget—"

Grace turned, that pinch back in her brows. André wanted to reach out and smooth it with his thumb. "I wish I could, but I'm already overcommitted." She uncrossed her legs and stood. "Excuse me." She scooted past the two of them and climbed the stairs, exiting the suite.

CHAPTER
Three

GRACE

THE FINAL BUZZER screamed through the Saddledome, and the crowd roared in response. She'd half planned on leaving when she left the suite to go to the washroom, but didn't want to explain that to Jenna and Country. They probably would've blamed André, which could've been worth it.

She was glad she'd stayed. Not only because of the baby cuddling and conversation with Jenna, but the game was a barn burner. The Blizzard scored a last-minute goal, sealing the win against Winnipeg, and everyone in the arena lost their ever-loving minds.

Grace stood with them, clapping and shouting. It felt good to get lost in the energy of it for a moment, even if it didn't last.

She tried. She really did. But even as she smiled at Jenna, even as she acknowledged the deafening excitement around her, the weight in her chest hadn't budged or lessened all night.

The email sat over her heart like a lead brick. After Country brought up the charity game, it seemed to crush her spine.

It would be a miracle if she went back to work in the morning, let alone take on more projects. If she screwed this up, what else was she overlooking?

All night, it felt like she was playing a part. She spent the last two hours forcing herself to stay present, nodding in the right places, laughing and cheering when appropriate. Had she done well enough? Had she seemed normal?

The whole game was a blur. At least her snark had been on point with André, which made her a teensy bit proud. For most of the third period, she'd played with Hope. That's what she needed. A baby at all times so she had an excuse to avoid any adult social interactions.

"Warren should've buried that five minutes ago. Never should've come down to the wire." Country threw himself back into his seat, shaking his head.

"Unreal," Brett crossed his arms over his chest. "He had an empty net and still managed to put it wide."

"Okay, but the angle of that pass—" Suraj started.

"The angle was fine!" Tyler cut in, gesticulating. "He panicked. You could see it. His footwork was all off."

André scoffed. "Monohan was getting double-teamed in the corner. He did everything right with that push."

Jenna rolled her eyes. "It wasn't bad, but Warren played like he had fifty-pound weights strapped to his ankles."

Country pointed at her. "See, Jenna gets it."

Tyler laughed as he stood. "Smart man. Take your wife's side."

Jenna's eyes flared as she switched Hope to her other arm. "Only if I'm right."

"You really should be filming right now. Your channel would love this." Grace stood and smoothed her slacks. André hesitated a moment, his face inches from her crotch. His throat bobbed, and something swooped low in her belly when he looked up. She stepped back, pretending she didn't notice.

"Could you do an 'on location' YouTube stream?" Emma asked.

Jenna shrugged. "The audio would be shit."

Country rubbed his jaw. "I don't know. We could get those mics with the little grey puff balls—"

"Don't start on the cute mics again." Jenna laughed, then sobered when Hope mewled in her arms. She pulled the blanket up over her ears. "It's too loud in here. I'm going to get her back to the truck."

Country saluted the group, then rushed to gather Jenna's purse and the diaper bag. Grace's hand tightened over the strap of her handbag. They were so adorable it hurt, right at her sternum. It wasn't that she was looking for someone. She was glad to be single after Troy, but the novelty was beginning to wear off.

The crowd was still buzzing, a mix of people lingering to watch the post-game interviews on the jumbotron while everyone else filed to the exits. Grace half-listened to the rest of their banter as she slipped into her blazer and slung her purse over her shoulder. Check 'being social' off the list. Now she needed to get home and work on damage control.

They all left with Jenna and Country, pushing into the crush of bodies streaming through the concourse. A wave of Blizzard fans buzzing with post-game adrenaline as the crowd funneled toward the exits. The heavy scent of pulled pork clung to the air, mixing with an obscene variety of cologne brands. What was it with men and sports events? They sprayed themselves like they were fighting off mosquitos in the Amazon.

André, Tyler, and Country busted up laughing in front of her, parting the seas with Country's full set of baggage on his arms. André made some outlandish hand gesture, but she couldn't hear what they were saying. Not that she wanted to. He'd been over the top since the second period, and she'd been mostly successful at ignoring him.

She'd seen it all before. He was playing to an audience, just like Troy used to. It was nearly impossible not to be sucked in by his charisma, but her divorce had been the most effective inoculation money could buy. Not paid for with her savings. Troy's. He'd at least had the decency to pay all the lawyer fees. It meant they could be friends in the end, and she was grateful for that.

Jenna fell into step beside her, nudging her with an apologetic smile. "For the record, I didn't know André would be here."

Grace exhaled. "It's fine."

Jenna sighed, adjusting Hope against her chest. "No, it's not fine. Country is in the doghouse."

"I'm sure he just invited his friends—"

"No, uh-uh. I initially told him I doubted you'd be interested at all in coming to the game, and he was the one who told me to push for it. Don't get me wrong, I wanted you to come, but I was planning on setting up a brunch or something. The second I saw André jump up like a ball boy, I knew they'd set this up."

Grace squeezed herself past a group of inebriated women to continue the conversation. "He plays on Country's team?"

Jenna nodded. "He's good. Joined a couple of years ago."

"He looks barely old enough to rent a car."

"He's thirty-one, I'm pretty sure. I think he barely qualified for the league when he joined the team."

Grace's eyes widened. She'd thought he was at least ten years younger than her, but that was only five. "What does he do?"

"Wait, are you interested?"

Grace scoffed. "No, just curious."

Jenna raised an eyebrow. "He's a welder."

That explained the burn scar on his knuckle. Not that she'd noticed everything about his hands. It was just *there*. "I didn't— you don't think he got the impression—"

"No, no. You weren't giving off vibes. He basically forced you to sit with him."

"I probably owe him an apology."

Jenna gave her a quizzical look. "Why?"

Grace shrugged. "I barely know the guy. I wasn't very gentle."

Jenna laughed. "You don't know André. He loved it, I'm sure."

"Are you saying I should've fawned over him? That would've turned him off?"

"I don't think anything turns André off."

They laughed and made their way through the now-obsolete metal detectors. Truly, Grace couldn't be pissed about André because he'd been a perfect distraction. With him peacocking and Hope being adorable, the spotlight hadn't been on her. It was the best gift she could've asked for.

Grace glanced toward André again as he threw his arm around Brett's shoulders, dramatically explaining some play. Big, loud, cocky. He'd been over the top all night, but . . . there had been a moment. What had she said? Something about head injuries. Yes, it had been immediately before Country invited her to join the team for the charity game. He'd gone strangely quiet.

She didn't think too hard about it because, just then, a rush of cold hit her flushed skin as they stepped out of the Saddledome. She'd left her winter coat in the car and now regretted it. At least she'd paid for preferential parking.

"I'll see you soon. Brunch is still happening." Jenna gave her a hug, then hurried to catch up with Country. Grace waved at Emma, Penny, and the others, then tried to orient herself since they'd exited from a different door.

Before she could find her lot, André turned and pulled Jenna into his arms, careful not to crush Hope as he pecked both her cheeks. "Don't be mad. It was my fault, not his."

"Mmhmm." Jenna gave him a skeptical look, but her eyes lit up when Country wrapped an arm around her waist.

Grace caught herself staring and averted her eyes. *Awkward.* She needed to get moving before she had to say goodbye a second time.

Car horns blared, and fans hooted and hollered, still riding the high of the Blizzard win. Ah. There it was. She found the sign for the preferred parking and started off, then jumped when something landed on her shoulders.

Grace stuttered a step and almost lost her footing in her heels.

Two hands clamped around her arms. "Sorry, I thought you saw me coming."

Grace looked back. André. She shivered at the warmth from his coat. "My car's right there—"

"I'll walk you." André's hands dropped, and he started forward. Grace didn't move. When he realized she wasn't following, he slowed and turned. "Is something wrong?"

She shrugged his coat off her shoulders. "I don't need this, and I don't need you to walk me to my car." She stalked toward him, holding out his coat like a sacred offering. Obviously she was going to need to be more blunt.

André's mouth quirked. "I didn't ask what you needed. What kind of man would I be if I let you walk alone in a dark parking lot?"

"A normal one?" Grace pointed to the thousand other fans. "Also, not exactly alone." André shoved his hands in his pockets, but before he could make another inane argument, she continued, "If it wasn't obvious back there, I'm not interested. Kudos for waiting to make your move until after Country was occupied, though. Real ballsy."

"Sarcasm?"

She pressed the coat against his chest. "See? You can read social cues."

André watched her with amusement. He didn't take the coat. She had half a mind to let it drop to the concrete. He blew out a breath. "Alright. Let's get it out in the open. Yes. I want to sleep with you."

"Excuse me?"

"Aren't you proud of yourself? You were correct in that assumption. But it shouldn't be anything new for you." He turned and threw out a hand, grabbing a guy who looked like a former linebacker and pointing at Grace. "Would you sleep with her?"

The man blinked, then said, "Hell, yeah." His friends cheered behind him.

"André —" Grace tried to grab his hand, but he was too quick, snagging a couple with face paint and light-up necklaces as the men walked on.

"Threesome tonight? With her?" André held out his hands in front of her like he'd just pulled a door open to reveal a free car.

The woman giggled and nodded, and the man's eyes widened. He pulled out his phone.

Grace flushed. "No, thank you! He's just—" She gave an apologetic wave and yanked André out of the river of people winding toward the parking lot. His behavior was so ridiculous, her mind was wiped clean and all she could say was, *"What the hell?"*

He grinned. "I'm proving a point. You're a beautiful woman. So don't get all pissed and self-righteous when people notice."

Grace scoffed. "I'm not an object for your enjoyment, asshole." She pushed past him, stalking toward the parking lot. This was why she didn't go out socially, why she said no to invitations to hockey games, and why she didn't hang out with single men. She'd never seen herself as having old spinster energy, but cats, tea, and crochet were looking fantastic right about now.

"Exactly." He jogged after her. "I'm telling you I'd love to take you home right now and do every dirty thing that ran through my head the first time I saw you walking into that adoption party. *If* you wanted me to. But since you're obviously not interested, I'm offering to walk you to your car. That's the least asshole thing I could do, no? You told me you don't want me to pleasure you into the wee hours of the morning, and I'm still being a gentleman. I could've walked away. Cut my losses."

Grace whirled on him. "And there was no part of you that thought if you played your cards right—"

"Every part of me thought." He stood so close, the spearmint on his breath cooled her cheek. He didn't smell like a smoker. "One part, specifically." André pulled the coat from her hands and dramatically draped it over her shoulders a second time. "If you didn't notice, I'm French. I love art, and I love pleasure."

The skin on his biceps and forearms prickled from the cold, but it didn't seem to bother him in the least. He stepped back and pulled a cigarette from his pocket. "Do you ever do things for fun, Grace?"

She rolled her eyes. "Am I supposed to walk into that? I say 'sometimes' and you say, 'would you do *me* for fun?'"

"Hm. That's funny. I'll remember that. You know, for other women who don't have sticks up their asses."

"Ha. Ha."

André grinned, walking backward. "I don't think you had fun tonight." He pulled out his lighter and flicked it.

She followed him, her eyes flashing as she pulled the coat tighter around her. If he wasn't going to take it, she'd at least use it until she got to the car. "And you would know?"

André exhaled slowly, the cigarette glowing between his fingers as he gave her one of those infuriating grins. "I observe," he corrected, tapping ash onto the pavement as he turned toward the rows of cars. "I'm guessing you parked in the least convenient place possible? Didn't want to scratch your nice car?" She let out a slow breath, unwilling to admit it. André slowed his stride, glancing at her sideways, smirking like he was putting pieces together.

"Let me guess." He gestured toward a row of sleek, mid-tier luxury sedans. "You're the black Lexus. Safe, practical, but still a power move."

Grace didn't blink. "No."

His grin widened. "I like this game."

"You're playing by yourself."

"Mm." He took a slow drag of his cigarette, exhaling into the cold night air before pointing to a Range Rover parked under a streetlamp. "That one. Big, intimidating. Perfect for overcompensating."

She let out a sharp laugh before she could stop herself. "I have nothing to overcompensate for." Fake bravado. Not a good look, but she couldn't help herself. An SUV had been on the table for a few minutes two years ago when Honda came out with a hybrid.

André nodded. "Interesting. So you make big money, but you don't spend big money."

She picked up her pace. "I didn't say I make big money."

"Based on that purse, either you do or Daddy does. But you don't strike me as someone who would take handouts." André tossed his cigarette onto the asphalt and stomped it out with the heel of his shoe.

Grace searched for a smart-ass rebuttal on that one, but his comment stung. Her parents both made good money, but they were never flush. They'd saved up for years to go to Europe for the first time, and the purse André noticed? Her parents gave it to her for her thirtieth birthday.

André stopped and scanned the lot again, then pointed at the back corner. "It's the Volkswagen, isn't it?"

Grace strode past him and reached into her purse to click her key fob. The lights flashed.

André jogged to catch up. "Classy. Reliable. A little boring, but that tracks."

She narrowed her eyes at him. "Call your therapist. Maybe she'd have some insights." She pulled open the driver's side door. "Maybe when you get a little older, you'll understand the need for comfort in a vehicle."

André laughed out loud. "Yes, you're practically geriatric." He leaned against the car, his eyes sparkling as he watched her.

Grace swallowed hard. "While this has been a delight, I'm safely at my car."

André's mouth quirked. "That you are. I apologize for keeping you out so far past your bedtime. Did you miss your nightly dose of Metamucil?"

Grace rolled her eyes. "Goodnight."

"Goodnight." He straightened, then nodded once and sauntered off through the parking lot, keeping right to avoid the stream of cars waiting to exit. Grace slid into the driver's seat, and it wasn't until she set her bag down that she realized she was still wearing his coat.

CHAPTER
Four

GRACE

GRACE'S COFFEE mug sat on the desk in front of her. Full. It cooled in the ceramic mug that said, "None of your emails are finding me well"—a gift from her law school friend Alexis—while she stared at her laptop screen. No new messages from anyone but her regular contacts.

Grace drummed her fingers against the rim of the cup. The lawyer representing the birth mother still hadn't responded. Over twenty-four hours. Which, fine. It was a legal matter, not a five-minute customer service request, and it was the weekend. But every hour of radio silence felt like a thousand.

She exhaled, finally lifting the cup to her lips and turning her focus back to work. She had a text from her assistant.

Sent you the contract notes. Let me know if you want to tweak the language before the call.

. . .

The text message blinked, but she could barely process it. Her brain felt like it was being dragged through molasses. She clicked into the document, scanning the flagged sections with the developer's latest demands.

They wanted less liability, more loopholes, fewer guarantees. Classic. On a typical day, she could carve through this in ten minutes. Today, though?

Grace leaned back against the lumbar-supported office chair, blowing out a breath. What if this petition was legitimate? What if the birth mother had a case? She cycled between being pissed off that she hadn't received any clarifying details and hopeful that the lack of information meant they were stalling.

Work. Right.

She spun in her chair and stretched, adjusting the waistband of her joggers. Normally she forced herself to dress for work even if she was remote. She couldn't refute the research correlating productivity and uniforms, but that morning, she didn't think a pencil skirt was going to magically lower her cortisol levels.

Grace stared up at the blank wall opposite her. She'd never meant to stay in Calgary long, but she was starting to regret not hanging something. Perhaps a canvas from Home Sense or a colour other than greige would've made her feel a little less desperate.

Her gaze flicked to the time on her laptop.

9:17 a.m., which meant it was 12:17 p.m. Eastern Standard.

Perfect. She tapped the call button before she could talk herself out of it. The phone barely rang twice before her mother answered.

"Well, hello, beautiful daughter of mine."

Grace huffed a laugh. The sound of her mother's voice was like a fluffy blanket in the middle of a snowstorm. "Hey, Mom."

"What's wrong?"

Grace blinked. "Who says something's wrong?"

"You're calling me in the middle of the day."

"Maybe I just wanted to chat."

Her mother hummed. "Great, let's chat."

Grace pinched the bridge of her nose as her mind went blank. "Uh . . . okay. So there's something wrong."

"Spill."

So Grace did. She ran through the situation with Country and Jenna, how she became friends with Troy's son, Tyler, and found out they were having trouble fostering to adopt and how she only wanted to help. She told her about the petition, how she didn't have any information, and that she was spiraling wondering whether it was her fault and what in the hell she was going to do if that sweet, perfect baby was stripped from Jenna's arms.

By the time she finished, her mother was quiet.

Finally, she sighed. "I'm so sorry. That's terrifying."

"It is."

"I can't even imagine what would've happened if your birth mother tried to take you back."

Grace pushed out of the chair and started pacing. It had been hard enough for her to track down her birth mother so she could get information on her genetics when she was in her early twenties. Her mother had passed away, overdose, five years prior.

"But . . . "

Grace stilled. "But what?"

Her mother proceeded with caution. "I also can't imagine giving up a child. I'm forever grateful that your mother chose adoption, but . . . I guess I can't blame any mother who second-guesses that decision."

Grace started to sweat. "But she had time to make that decision, Mom."

"How much time is ever enough time? We're only human, Grace. We grow and change from one hour to the next. Most days, I second-guess the choices I made for breakfast."

Grace plopped back down in her chair. This was exactly why she'd gotten out of family law. There was rarely a cut-and-dry answer, and finding a solution that satisfied everyone was like trying to catch a glimpse of the Northern Lights. Just when you thought you'd found the perfect night, clouds rolled in.

"It's such a different world now. Adoption wasn't the same back then. It was closed, and records were sealed. If a birth mother changed her mind, she had no recourse."

Grace frowned, staring at the sparkling city skyline through the window. "And you think that was better?"

"Not necessarily," her mother admitted. "The system back then was harsh. But I do remember feeling great relief when the whole process was final."

Final.

That word sat heavy in Grace's chest. Hadn't she been the one to use that word with Jenna and Country? After the ten days had passed since the birth mother signed the paperwork?

Tears pricked her eyes. "What if it was my fault? Maybe I was careless. Maybe I—"

"No," her mother said sharply. "You were not careless."

Grace inhaled through her nose. "You don't know that."

"I know you." She paused. "None of us are above making mistakes, but it wasn't carelessness. You know, when you were little, you were so observant. Always watching, always assessing. Do you remember when you saw Aunt Carol for the first time in years and you noticed immediately that she'd had a mole on her neck removed?"

Grace laughed. "I don't remember that."

"It was a little creepy, to be honest. You were only six."

"Maybe the mole was creepy, Mom."

"I grew up with her, and I didn't notice! I think it's why you're so good at what you do. Your brain is like a supercomputer. But that also means you blame yourself when you can't predict everything."

Grace exhaled, squeezing her eyes shut as André's comments

from the night before flashed through her mind. Uptight. Boring. It was the same thing Troy had said at the end of their relationship, albeit in more flattering terms. *You're so smart, you operate on a different level. I just can't keep up.*

Was that how people saw her? Some robot with input in and input out? Unrelatable? With a stick up her ass?

There wasn't anything wrong with preparation and predictability. She worked hard to keep her life running smoothly, and that kind of foresight had skyrocketed her in her industry. She was known for her prompt communication, her attention to detail. So how was that a ticking time bomb when it came to relationships?

"There are some things we simply can't control, no matter how hard we try, Grace."

Grace nodded, working to swallow the lump in her throat. "I know that." She drew a deep breath and tried to exhale away from the speaker. "So what do I do?"

"You wait."

Grace groaned. "That's the worst advice you've ever given me."

Her mom laughed. "I know. But it's the truth. This is one of those things. You don't have enough information, but at some point, you will. You have to find a way to weather this storm until you get some answers. Can you jump into a hobby? Go out with friends? Do something to take your mind off it?"

No, no, and no. Her friends here were all connected with Jenna and Country, and while she'd survived the game the night before, she didn't relish the idea of playing pretend a second time.

"You could go out dancing—ooh!—or take a Zumba class! I just did one with Lori for the first time the other day. I didn't think my hips moved like that anymore."

Grace laughed. "Yeah, not doing Zumba." The last time she'd danced at a club in her twenties, she'd nearly taken out a guy's eye. She had less rhythm than Michael Cera in Superbad. "But thank you, Mom. I'll figure it out. I know you probably need to eat. Lunch is over at one?"

"It is, but if you need to keep talking—"

"No, I'm good." She wasn't good, but no amount of conversation would solve that.

"Alright, well keep me updated?"

"I will."

"What's the worst case scenario, Grace?"

She blew out a shaky breath. "That it's all my fault and I ruin my friends' lives forever?"

"Or you saved a mother from losing her baby. There are always different angles, and sometimes it's hard to see all of them. People are more resilient than you think. Just look at us if you need proof."

Grace nodded, her throat tight. "Love you, Mom."

"Love you, too." She hit the red button to end the call, then swivelled back to her computer, and her heart lurched to a stop. There, at the top of her inbox, was a brand-new bolded message.

CHAPTER
Five

ANDRÉ

THIS WAS THEIR RINK. Their damn house. And yet, here they were, tied three to three in the third period against Mills Hoodie, a team that had no business hanging with them this long.

André dug his blade into the ice, heart hammering with every rattle of the boards. This was when hockey got good. When the game stopped being about systems and started being about who wanted it more.

The Snowballs were on the kill, twenty seconds left on a bullshit hooking penalty against Ryan Vargo. Mills Hoodie had their top unit out, their big defenceman quarterbacking from the point, waiting for an opening.

Sean anchored the PK like a brick wall, stick active, eyes locked in. Mike was with him, covering the low slot, ready to eat a shot if he had to. Country and André were up front, running the chaos.

The puck cycled back to the point with a bad bounce, and

that was all Country needed. He read it like he was sniffing out a storm. Country jumped the lane, chipped the puck past their D-man, and suddenly, they were flying up the ice—two-on-one, short-handed.

The crowd exploded. André caught up fast, the rush unfolding perfectly. Country had the puck, dragging the defender toward him, waiting, waiting—

Then he flipped a saucer pass over the guy's stick. It rolled head over tits to the top of the net, but André caught it on the tape and flicked it back. Their goalie snatched at it with his glove, but it ricocheted. He dropped and lunged right, Country flicked left.

The red light flashed, and the crowd roared. André collided with Country against the boards, grunting when Mike and Sean joined the huddle.

They skated back to the bench, Country pumping his fist. Up one. Now they only had to lock it down.

They played out the next ten, but with five minutes left, Mills Hoodie was getting desperate. Their forecheck had gone full kamikaze, throwing everything at the net. Boyd was blocking faster than a twenty-two-year-old blonde on Hinge. Brett chirped a guy in front of the net, cross-checking him lower than the refs could see.

André loved this shit.

Finally, Mills Hoodie pulled their goalie, and in the chaos, he poked the puck free. Tyler grabbed it. No hesitation—he launched it from just past their own blue line.

The puck glided in slow-motion perfection. Dead centre.

Five to three. Game. Over.

The buzzer sounded, and the benches emptied onto the ice. They smacked backs and rapped their sticks against each other's shin pads as they rushed Boyd.

Electricity flooded André's veins. He turned toward Country, who was laughing as he shoved his helmet back, sweat dripping down his face.

"Shit, Maddox," André panted. "You ate your Wheaties this morning."

Country grinned. "Farm fresh eggs, bud. I'll get you some."

"Don't announce it or you'll trigger a tariff." Ryan slapped his back as he glided past.

"Don't ruin my good mood!" André called back. On the ice they didn't have to think about real life, and he wanted to keep it that way.

As they skated off, the high started to wear off, the adrenaline settling into a low buzz. They poured into the locker room and stripped off their gear. Boyd stopped mid-change to pound on the walls, adding percussion to Country's victory chant.

André grabbed his towel, but when someone started playing Thunderstruck over a Bluetooth speaker, he couldn't help himself. He climbed up onto one of the benches on his way to the showers, slung his towel over his shoulder and free-balled it in an air guitar solo.

Curtis groaned from across the room, pulling his jersey over his head. "Hell, Leclerc, can we go one game without seeing your dick?"

André lunged deeper. "Don't be jealous, Curt. Your balls will drop sooner than you think."

Tyler laughed as he towelled off his hair. "Someone film this and send it to Grace."

André straightened and gave his best "The David" pose. "Just wait a second. It needs to get—"

Country snapped his ass with a towel. "Take your own boudoirs. Or hire Polk. I hear he gets great angles."

"You would know." André laughed as he stalked to the showers. He waited for the water to heat, then stepped in and threw his head under the stream. Grace. He'd thought about her non-stop since the night before. He hadn't meant to rile her up as well as he had, but everything he did seemed to rub her the wrong way.

That scratched an itch. Maybe he was a glutton for punishment, but he'd never been interested in the girls who wanted him. He liked the chase. The challenge. And as much as Grace pushed back, she'd gotten into her car wearing his coat and hadn't even noticed.

She might've been cold.

Or she might've liked it.

He was going with the latter. "Tyler, can I get Grace's number?" he yelled.

"Hard pass," Tyler called back from the locker room.

"She took something of mine. I need to get it back!"

"Hate to tell you, but you can't ever get your virginity back, bud!" Ryan shouted.

André grinned. He soaped up and rinsed, then towelled off and strode back into the locker area to change.

Tyler slung his bag over his shoulder. "You walked with Grace to her car after the game?"

André nodded, the metal door creaking as he pulled open his locker.

"You better not have done anything Jenna's going to find out about." Country shoved his arms into a cotton pullover.

"Nope. Perfect gentleman."

"That's what worries me," Country muttered.

André pulled on his boxer briefs. "Grace doesn't know what she wants."

Brett laughed. "So you're going to show her?"

"She needs to loosen up." André straightened his jeans and stepped in. "She's here for another couple of months. Jenna should be grateful, she's been worried about her holing up in her condo—"

Country snorted. "Jenna made one comment."

"And I listened. I'm a sensitive, thoughtful, altruistic—"

"Panty chaser." Tyler shook his head as he walked past them to the door.

"And you can talk?!" André gave him an incredulous look. "You're with Emma now, and suddenly you're a saint?"

Brett grinned. "That's what love does, bud. The whole world you knew tips on its head. It's the death of the old self."

"Ah, thank you, Dr. Jung. I'm so glad you stopped by to enlighten me."

Tyler shrugged and ran his fingers through his damp hair. "I get it. I didn't think I'd ever settle down. But when it's right . . . I didn't know what I was missing."

André pulled his shirt over his head, then opened his bag and started shoving in his gear. Over the last two years, he'd watched half his teammates drop roots. If he was being honest, he resented it a little. Their celly's after wins looked different now. Especially since Country and Jenna got married and adopted Hope. He was happy for them, but he missed their nights at The Dusty Rose. He missed his wingmen.

"If this is an intervention, I'm going to need beer and a recliner." He zipped up his bag.

Country leaned against the lockers. "If you want Grace's number, you're going to have to come up with some reason to get it. One I can justify to Jenna."

André chewed on this. "What if I get her to sign up for the charity game?"

Country shook his head. "She shot that down already."

"Maybe she didn't have enough information."

———

By the time André pulled up to the curb, the post-game high was wearing off, replaced by the usual ache settling into his muscles. He dragged his bag from the backseat of the truck and walked up the steps to the house, let himself in through the front door, then dropped his hockey bag near the front closet. He unzipped it and hung up his gear to air out. The skates went on the rack, and his game jersey went straight into the washer with the rest of his stuff.

His eyes flicked out the window to the detached garage that he'd turned into a workshop. Housing prices in Calgary were brutal, but this place had been worth every penny. Having a heated space to work had doubled his productivity in the winter.

He wandered into the kitchen and sat down at the counter to check his messages.

J. MITCHELL

> Did you get a chance to adjust the hinge layout? Need to confirm before we finalize the post dimensions.

André rubbed a hand over his jaw. He needed to finish that custom gate by Monday, and he'd left Sunday wide open besides Sunday supper to do it. He sent a quick text back, promising measurements and pictures by the next night.

He set his phone on the counter, circled the island, and pulled chicken out of the fridge. He heated a pan with olive oil on the stove, seasoned the chicken, then tossed the chopped veggies he'd prepped that morning—sweet potatoes, zucchini, and red peppers—onto a tray with a drizzle of oil. He slid it into the oven and cooked the chicken. He plated everything and walked to the living room, then pulled out his phone, dialed, and propped it up on the coffee table.

The screen flashed, then connected.

"Tiens, le voilà!" Luc's voice boomed through the speaker, and the knot in André's chest immediately loosened.

His older brother was propped up on the couch in his apartment back in Montreal, wearing a hoodie way too big for him, his dark curls a mess.

"You eating?" Luc eyed André's plate like he could smell it through the screen.

André smirked, holding it up. "Real food, no takeout."

Luc whistled. "Damn. What's the occasion?"

André shrugged, shoving a bite of chicken into his mouth. "Don't need one. Just fueling a masterpiece."

Luc laughed. "A Picasso, maybe."

André gave him a cheesy grin, then took another bite. "You go to therapy today?"

Luc's eyes dropped. "I slept in. Had a bad headache."

There was nothing he could say to that. All of the therapies he'd encouraged Luc to sign up for were experimental. They didn't have enough data to prove that they worked, and both of them knew it. He couldn't blame him for being unmotivated.

"How's work?" André asked.

Another shrug. "I missed a few days last week. I should go in tomorrow, but now I think they're mad—"

"They're not mad." He didn't know if that was fully true, but he did know they wouldn't fire him. Legally, they had to work with him because of his disability status.

André stabbed his chicken hard enough to scratch the plate. It had been years, but the anger still lived in him, simmering under the surface. One bad hit. That's all it took. One blindside, one reckless charge into the boards when Luc was playing Juniors, and just like that, his career was gone.

Worse than that? So was a part of him. The migraines never stopped. Neither did the memory problems or depression.

André hated it. Hated how unfair it was. Hated how Luc, his big brother and hero, had been robbed of everything he'd worked for.

But he'd become an expert at hiding that over the years. Tonight was no different. André smirked, pushing away the heaviness in his chest. "Don't tell me you've gotten soft. You're not scared of a boss, are you?"

Luc snorted. "I'm not scared of my boss."

André grinned. "Then get your ass to work in the morning."

"Yeah." He nodded. "Yeah, okay."

André filled his fork with roasted veggies. "Mom and Dad come by this week?"

Luc nodded. "Mom did. Dad was on a work trip."

André had to work hard not to scoff. It was always a work trip. At some point, he'd have to get more creative with his excuses. "Did she look good?"

"She brought me cookies."

"You little bastard, you didn't send me any?"

Luc laughed, dragging a hand through his curls. They bantered back and forth for a few minutes more, and when Luc ended the call, André sat in silence, staring at his empty plate. He hated that he couldn't do more. That he couldn't fix this.

He was running a charity game and doing all he could to raise money for Heads Up Alberta, but that seemed like it was too little too late.

André took his plate into the kitchen, that old guilt niggling at him. He should be there. He should bring Luc here, let him stay in the guest room. He'd chased both of those arguments round and round like a dog chasing his tail, forgetting every time why neither option would work.

He turned on the faucet, and the water ran warm over his hands. He rinsed and scrubbed the sheet pan, then moved on to the other dishes. He worked until the only evidence of his dinner was neatly stacked in the drying rack. He liked clean counters, an empty sink, and everything in its place. It made his head feel less cluttered—or at least, that was the theory.

He wiped down the stove, slung the dish towel over the oven handle, and stretched, rolling his shoulders. The game left his body aching in the best way. Not sore, not tired—just deep, bone-level satisfaction.

He stalked into his room and pulled his shirt over his head, tossing it into the laundry hamper in the closet. His socks and jeans followed, leaving him in just his boxers as he brushed his teeth. He then dropped onto the edge of the bed, reaching for his phone on the nightstand.

The screen's glow lit up the room, the only illumination now that the kitchen lights were off, the city outside muted behind closed curtains. He scrolled out of habit, then flipped over to his calendar, thumb hovering over the screen.

Sunday supper at the Thompsons. Monday, ten a.m. training session. Optional, not a full team practice, but one he planned to attend. Tuesday, poker night at Country's. Then Wednesday he had a meeting with Heads Up Alberta to hammer out a few logistics.

He stared at the calendar entry, the wheels in his head spinning. They didn't need a lawyer present, but it sure as hell wouldn't be a bad thing. Maybe Grace didn't want to be involved in the entire process, but would she consider coming along as a consultant? A one-time advisory favour?

André exhaled, flipping his phone over in his hand. He swiped to his messages and pulled up Jenna's number. Couldn't hurt to ask.

CHAPTER
Six

GRACE

GRACE'S KNUCKLES flashed white on the steering wheel. Her stomach had tried to turn itself inside out at least twice since she left the house, and the roads were just icy enough that she couldn't speed. Driving forty kilometres per hour was veritable torture.

She could handle high-stakes negotiations and multimillion-dollar corporate disputes no problem, but driving to a small, private law firm first thing on a Monday morning was about to send her into cardiac arrest.

The moment she pulled into the parking lot, her pulse lurched. The building was unremarkable, a small, two-story office complex with Patel Family Law labeled on the sign at the entrance, tucked between a dental clinic and tax advisor.

Grace parked, then drew a few deep breaths to steady herself. Apparently, there was a discrepancy in the social worker's paperwork. It wasn't necessarily her fault. She just needed to walk in there and be curious. Ask plenty of questions.

She would've much preferred if the lawyer would've simply sent the evidence over email, but if she were representing the birth mother, this is exactly what she would've asked for. An in person meeting was more, well, personal. Tapping into the emotion of it could only help their case. Which was why she had a picture of Hope with Jenna and Country on her phone.

She strode through the glass doors, and a rush of warm air washed over her. The sign on the wall made it easy to figure out where she was going. She turned left down the hall, then entered Suite 2B.

The office was cozy but dated, the reception area neatly arranged with a small coffee station, worn armchairs, and an overstuffed shelf of parenting magazines with curling edges.

Not flashy, but functional. Elton John singing "Can You Feel the Love Tonight" took her back to her elementary school classroom when her class earned a Friday movie afternoon. She could practically smell the popcorn.

A woman behind the desk—mid-fifties, wearing a navy blazer and gold studs—looked up and smiled. "You must be Ms. Fairbanks."

Grace blinked. "Yes. I'm a bit early."

"Not a problem. Mr. Patel is expecting you." The receptionist rose, leading Grace down a narrow hallway lined with framed photos of smiling children and families. Grace's stomach coiled tighter.

They reached the last door, and Grace saw her through the glass. The birth mother. Amey. She was younger than she'd expected. Maybe nineteen? Barely twenty? Thin. Pale. Dark circles beneath her eyes.

Her hair was strawberry blonde, and she wore a hoodie that swallowed her frame. Their eyes met for one brief, electric second, and Grace felt everything at once.

The receptionist opened the door and gave a gentle nod. Grace exhaled and stepped into the room.

"Good morning." The lawyer, Neel Patel, was a calm,

measured man in his forties with kind eyes. He jumped up and rounded the table to meet her. "Thank you so much for coming down this morning."

"Of course." Grace shook his hand, then sat at the table across from Amey.

Neel motioned between the two of them. "I'm sure you've gathered, but this is Amey. Amey, this is Ms. Fairbanks."

Amey nodded once.

"Let's get right to it, shall we?" Neel reached for a folder and slid it across the table to her, then sat in the rolling chair beside Amey. "The issue is simple, Ms. Fairbanks," Neel said smoothly, folding his hands on the table. "The consent my client gave may not be legally valid because she wasn't properly informed of her right to revoke within ten days."

Grace exhaled slowly. "You're saying the social worker didn't tell her?"

Neel nodded. "Correct. There's no record of that conversation taking place. No signed acknowledgment, no audio, no written note in the case file. Nothing."

Grace turned her gaze to Amey, studying her. The woman didn't look malicious. She looked . . . raw. Grace couldn't blame her for the regret. But that didn't mean she was right.

"Amey, you signed a legally binding document." Grace kept her voice steady, even. "You acknowledged that decision in front of a witness. You held Hope, kissed her goodbye, and said you knew this was best for her."

A flicker of pain crossed Amey's face. Neel didn't react.

"But if the court believes you weren't properly informed of the revocation period, that could change things," Grace admitted, keeping her tone neutral even though everything inside her was screaming.

"That's the argument we'll be making," Neel said smoothly. "That Amey was not given full and proper information before consenting, which could render the adoption invalid."

Grace's fingers curled against her notepad. This was bad. Not impossible, not a guarantee of loss—but bad. If the judge bought this argument, even just enough to consider a full review, it could drag Country and Jenna into months of legal battles, uncertainty, and worst of all, the possibility of losing Hope.

Because Grace knew one thing for sure. No matter how airtight she made her counterargument, no matter how solid her legal defence was, no judge wanted to be the one who took a child away from their birth mother if they could find a legal reason not to.

"So what are your next steps?" Grace asked, her voice flat. She wasn't going to mince words. It was easy to assume how they'd proceed, but she'd learned long ago that it was beneficial to make people state it out loud. They wouldn't be in this situation if the social worker had done that.

But had she missed something? She was sure she'd double-checked the paperwork before filing. How had she overlooked this? Her palms began to sweat.

Amey swallowed hard, her fingers tightening around the edge of the table. "I just . . . I need to know if I have a chance. If I can get her back."

Neel answered for her. "We're filing a motion to vacate the adoption on the grounds of improper counseling."

Grace clenched her jaw. "That motion won't be easy to push through. Even if we assume the court agrees to hear this case, they will focus on one thing—Hope's well-being. Not just what you want, but what's best for her."

"I know," Amey whispered.

Grace nodded. "She has a family. A home. Stability. Are you ready to walk into that courtroom and argue that it's in her best interest to leave all that behind?"

Amey's expression wavered.

Neel didn't flinch. "We'll let the judge decide that."

Grace leaned back, inhaling through her nose. "Then I'll be expecting your official filing."

Neel gave her a small, knowing smile. "You'll have it by the end of the week."

CHAPTER
Seven

ANDRÉ

> Grace, this is André .

> If you're pissed Jenna gave me your number, I stole it off her phone. If you're not pissed, she gave it to me under only mild duress.

> Had a quick question for you

GRACE

> If your question involves "fun" or "pleasure," don't ask

> The opposite, actually. Intense boredom. Numbers. Lots of numbers. It's why I thought of you

> I can't help with STD panels

Damn it. Okay, well, in that case, maybe you could at least help me out with a consultation

Please don't send me a dick pic

Another time. My current lighting is terrible

I have a meeting with Heads Up Alberta on Wednesday, and no, that's not a euphemism. Wondered if you'd come with. Nothing official or on the books

This is for the charity game?

Correct. I'm fine with you turning it down. Country is crushed, but he's a little soft now that he's a dad

I'm going to assume you're finally doing something fun, and that's why you haven't responded (stranger things have happened). Not that my last message offended you

Now I'm thinking I offended you.

Can't do the meeting. Sorry

CHAPTER
Eight

GRACE HAD NEVER WANTED to knock on a door less. Just a few weeks ago she'd been here celebrating the ten-day mark after the adoption papers were signed. Now she had to walk in there and . . . say what?

Ugh, how could she do this to them? She clutched her midsection and whirled on the porch, walking across the deck boards to curl over the railing. This wasn't fair, none of it. And the worst part was, there was nobody to blame. Amey was convinced she didn't know the timeline. The social worker was sure they'd had the conversation, but there was no documentation.

She couldn't blame the therapist for reporting—that was her job—and she couldn't blame herself, either. The paperwork had looked like it was in order. Why would she have ever thought to second-guess any of the other professionals?

The whole thing was a mess.

But how could she do this to Jenna and Country?

Tyler had told her their story one night when she'd visited him and Emma. That night, she'd gone down the rabbit hole on Turner's syndrome, and that weekend, she'd gone out to lunch with Jenna.

She loved her immediately, and she loved the idea of doing something meaningful.

Not that property law didn't matter, but it was often the opposite of heartwarming.

Property law equaled contracts and clauses, negotiations that went in circles, and clients who fought over easements and land use regulations like their lives depended on it. It was development disputes, last-minute financing collapses, and municipal bylaws that never seemed to favour anyone. It involved powerful men in suits with too much money and not enough patience, and investors looking to squeeze every last dollar out of the land beneath them.

It was tangible and high-stakes in a financial sense. But it wasn't this. It wasn't a child's future.

Grace inhaled deeply, straightened her spine, and turned toward the farmhouse. The air was crisp and sharp, biting at her skin as she adjusted the collar of her coat. Alberta winters had a way of waking a person up whether they were ready or not.

She smoothed her hair, clenched her jaw, and knocked firmly on the door as her breath curled around her.

A beat later, the door swung open.

Jenna stood there, messy ponytail, wearing an oversized sweater, Hope resting against her hip. Hope's chubby fingers tangled in the fabric of Jenna's shirt, her little face pressed into her mother's collarbone, still groggy from sleep.

The sight made Grace's chest ache so fiercely she almost had to take a step back.

"Grace!" Jenna moved aside, ushering her in. "Hope woke up at five, and I couldn't get her to go back to sleep. Normally, I fly solo for a couple of hours while Country is out doing chores with Polk, but since we knew you were stopping by—"

"I made breakfast." Country appeared behind her, his massive frame filling the doorway. He rubbed a hand through his unruly morning hair, already dressed in jeans and a T-shirt. "You hungry? We've got pancakes."

Grace's throat tightened. She tried to smile, but it barely held. The farmhouse smelled like coffee and maple syrup, the kind of warm, familiar scents that belonged to slow mornings and safe places.

It was homey, lived in, loved.

And Grace was about to drop a bomb in the middle of it.

The wooden floors creaked under her step as she shut the door behind her, shrugging out of her coat. She kicked off her shoes at the door, the cold from outside still clinging to her legs as she followed Jenna and Country into the kitchen.

Jenna moved on autopilot, settling Hope into her swing, then grabbing a clean mug from the cupboard. Country moved to the stove, flipping thick golden pancakes, the scent of butter and cinnamon curling through the air. A plate of crispy bacon sat on the counter beside a bowl of scrambled eggs, piled high, steam still rising off of them.

It was the kind of scene that should've been comforting. It made what she had to say so much worse.

Jenna poured a cup of coffee and looked up, her brow furrowing slightly at Grace's expression. "You okay?"

No. She wasn't. There was no amount of small talk that was going to make this easier to say, so Grace ripped off the Band-Aid. "I got an email yesterday from Neel Patel, Amey's lawyer."

The air shifted. Country's movements stilled, spatula hovering over the frying pan for just a second too long before he set it down. Jenna's hand tightened around the handle of her mug.

Grace drew a breath, forcing herself to push through. "She's petitioning to revoke the adoption."

Jenna's face went completely blank. Country exhaled slowly. Grace could almost hear him counting to ten.

"What do you mean she's revoking it?" Jenna's voice was steady, but barely. "She signed the papers. We waited the ten days."

Grace nodded. "I know. But Amey's arguing she wasn't able to give full informed consent."

Jenna's expression froze.

Country crossed his arms over his chest. "What the hell does that mean?"

Grace sat at the kitchen table, her stomach twisting. "In Alberta, birth parents have ten days after signing to revoke their consent. But the law states that they have to be explicitly informed of that window." She met Jenna's gaze. "The social worker didn't document that conversation."

The colour drained from Jenna's face.

Country's voice dropped to something dark and low. "Are you telling me this entire case comes down to one missing piece of paperwork?"

Grace clenched her jaw. "It's not just paperwork. It's procedure."

Jenna shook her head. "But she knew. Right? She had to know."

Grace hesitated. Because she didn't know. Not for certain. She'd gone through every record she had, and there wasn't anything that could disprove Amey's assertion. "That's what we have to prove."

Jenna ran a shaky hand through her hair, exhaling hard. "She knew. There's no way she didn't know."

Country's hands braced on the counter. "So what happens now?"

Grace had spent all night reviewing case law, reading every precedent she could find. None of it felt good. "The judge will determine whether she was given all the information necessary to make an informed decision. If they believe there was a failure in procedure, they could allow her case to move forward."

Jenna stared at her. "And if they do? If they think she wasn't informed?"

Grace forced herself to say it. "They could vacate the adoption." The words hung in the air, cold and brutal.

Jenna let out a sharp exhale, eyes wide.

Country nodded once, his voice tight. "So what do we do? How do we fight this?"

Grace fell into lawyer mode because it was the only thing keeping her together. "I'm going to challenge the petition. I'll argue that she received the proper information and had every opportunity to revoke within those ten days and did not." She rubbed her temple. "I need to review everything. The social worker's case notes, the agency's. I don't have access to everything yet. Any emails or texts Amey sent during that period. Anything that could indicate she knew."

Jenna nodded sharply. "Whatever you need. Just tell us what to do."

Grace curled her hands in her lap. "Thank you. I'll keep you posted. I'm hoping this won't get traction, but if it does, we're going to court."

Another silence. Then Jenna let out a breath that sounded too much like a sob. Country pulled her in, wrapping an arm around her, pressing a kiss to the top of her head as they both stared at little Hope in the swing.

She hadn't planned to stay, but when Country handed her a plate of pancakes, eggs, and bacon, she didn't have the heart to turn it down. She picked up her fork, absently swirling a piece of pancake through a small pool of maple syrup. She wasn't hungry—her body was too wired, too tense—but she forced herself to take a bite.

Jenna joined her, handing her a cup of coffee, and eventually, Country turned off the stove and sat with them, too. They chatted about the ranch, their property rentals in the silos out back, and the season outlook for the Snowballs. Grace didn't know hockey, but she was glad to listen and eat.

When she finished, she thanked them profusely and stood to take her dishes to the sink. Country jumped up and insisted on doing it for her.

"You probably have to get going for that meeting." Jenna smiled and took a sip of her coffee.

Grace blinked, scouring her head for context surrounding that comment.

"Babe, she said she couldn't help with that." Country slid her plate into the dishwasher.

Jenna frowned. "Oh! André asked for your number the other day. I assumed he invited you."

Grace's stomach dropped. Ah. Right. The text conversation with André replayed in her mind.

"Sorry if he badgered you with that. Told him you had enough on your plate." Country dried his hands on a dish towel.

Jenna stood with her mug. "Yes, please. Not a big deal. I'm sure he'll be able to—"

"I'm going," Grace blurted, guilt slamming into her full force. This charity game was important to them, and while the idea of giving any kind of legal advice made her want to rub sandpaper over her eyeballs, it was something she *could* do.

Jenna's face lit up with relief. "Oh, I'm so glad. We've been worried about ensuring the sponsorships and player contracts were set up correctly. I know you said you weren't available to do all the paperwork, but even being there to point us in the right direction will be so helpful."

Grace nodded. "Of course. Happy to help."

Jenna and Country walked her to the door. She embraced them both as Jenna promised to send over all the communication she had regarding the adoption, then stepped out onto the porch.

Grace pulled out her phone as she walked to the car, her boots crunching over the hardened snow.

· · ·

GRACE

> Where's the meeting?

She silently pleaded that André would see her message. She should've asked Jenna, but that would've required her to admit that she'd initially declined.

Her phone buzzed as she settled behind the wheel.

ANDRÉ

> You can just say you miss me

She ground her teeth, inhaling sharply through her nose.

> The meeting, André

Three dots appeared.
  Disappeared.
  Appeared again.
  Finally, the response came through.

> 9 a.m. Heads Up Alberta. I'll forward you the address. Meet you in the parking lot

She typed the name into her GPS, then pulled out of the driveway. Mist had settled overnight, coating every bare branch in frost that shimmered like crystal in the rising sun.

It was breathtaking. Like a winter wonderland.

Morning traffic was surprisingly calm, which made settling her nerves a tad easier. She tried to take her mother's advice as she drove into the city.

She couldn't control this. She had to wait.

Grace drifted as she followed the navigation on her dash, but as she turned onto 6th Ave, something caught her attention. Her shirt was bubbling over her chest. She frowned and felt around, realizing one of her buttons was undone.

At the next red light, she tried to push it through, and the button came off in her hand. She groaned, flicking the fabric to see just how much of her black bra was visible through the gaping hole.

Most of it. Fantastic. "You've got to be kidding me." She flipped the button between her fingers as she pulled into a parking spot and did a quick, frantic inventory of her car.

No extra shirt. Anything in her purse? Glove compartment? Napkins, old receipts, a pen with no ink.

The first aid kit her mother bought for her ten years ago when she purchased her first car. She lunged for it, shoving aside tire gauges and old granola bars, finally landing on a single safety pin.

She murmured a silent prayer of thanks, then fumbled with the tiny metal clasp, trying to maneuver it one-handed over her chest, but the angle was awkward.

She gritted her teeth, glancing around. The lot was full of other cars, but there didn't seem to be any signs of life. She'd be fast.

Grace inhaled, stripped off her coat, and pulled her shirt over her head. She shivered and laid it out over the steering wheel, making the seams lie flat. She inserted the pin, trying to hide it under the first layer of fabric, then jumped when a tap sounded on her window.

She yelped at the prick of pain in her thumb as her head snapped up.

André stood at the driver's side, hands shoved in his pockets, watching her like she'd just handed him an early Christmas present.

CHAPTER
Nine

ANDRÉ

ANDRÉ HAD SEEN a lot of unbelievable things in his life. A line brawl so vicious that a guy left the ice missing half his front teeth. A goalie scoring from the other end of the rink, the puck floating in like it had divine intervention. Hell, he'd even seen a fan throw a fully cooked rotisserie chicken onto the ice in the middle of a playoff game.

But nothing—nothing—had prepared him for the sight of Grace Fairbanks sitting in the front of her car wearing khaki slacks and a black lace bra, her blond hair curling over her bare shoulders.

André stopped dead in his tracks. His brain stalled, lagging like a bad WiFi connection. She was stunning. This was what men wrote poems about. The way the light hit her skin, the curves of her body. He could only see snippets through the car window, and it was enough to make him start thinking in rhyming couplets.

His heart sped so fast, his hands tingled. When Grace lifted her head, he panicked. Since he didn't want to get caught staring, and he was sure any movement on his part would draw her attention at this point, he went with the default. Play it off. Make the whole thing a joke. Be the asshole.

He strode up to her window and tapped, plastering a grin to his face and forcing his eyes to stay fixed on hers even though they screamed to drop south.

Grace startled, her head whipping up, her eyes wide. She looked completely, utterly horrified, her navy blouse bunched in her hands like she was debating whether to throw it at him or choke herself out with it.

For one long, excruciating second, they just stared at each other. Then, in a motion that looked physically painful, she rolled down the window.

André bent over, leaning his arm on the top of the door. "So, is this a morning ritual? Or a special perk I get for inviting you to a charity meeting?"

Grace made a strangled noise, draping her shirt over herself. "Can you give me some privacy, please?"

André tilted his head, biting his cheek to keep from laughing. "If you need help with whatever is—"

"I don't need help." Her jaw clenched. "It's a missing button on my shirt, okay? I'm not having the best morning, so—" Her voice cracked, and she turned her head.

She flipped the shirt, opening the safety pin, her fingers shaking as she fumbled with the fabric. And just like that, his amusement flickered into something else. She wasn't laughing. She wasn't even yelling at him the way she usually would.

Grace ducked her head, swiping at her face like she had a stray hair bothering her, and he realized she wasn't only frustrated. She was on the verge of tears.

Shit.

His stomach twisted. Maybe it was his fault. Maybe it wasn't.

Either way, he didn't like it. Didn't like seeing her like this. Didn't like not knowing what the hell to do about it.

So he did the only thing that made sense. Without a word, he reached for the hem of his shirt, pulled it over his head, and handed it to her. "Here."

Grace blinked at him, confused. "What—?"

"Trade me."

Her mouth parted slightly, but for once, she didn't argue. Just passed him her ruined blouse, fingers barely brushing his.

André sucked in a breath, working to ignore the jolt of energy zinging from his hand to his thighs. Without another word, he turned and headed back to his truck. Because if he stayed any longer, if he kept looking at her like that, he would do something stupid.

He barely made it five steps before Grace scrambled out of her car, his shirt hanging loose over her frame. "I can't go in there like this."

"Do you have the button?" he asked over his shoulder.

"What?"

"The button, Grace. The one that abandoned ship on your shirt."

She jogged up to walk beside him. "Yeah. Right here." She held it out.

He reached out and took it from her. "Thanks."

Before he could pull on his truck door handle, Grace grabbed his elbow and pulled him to a stop. "What are you doing?"

André worked to fill his lungs with air, his nipples pinching against the cold. And . . . other things. She was wearing his shirt, and he wasn't prepared for what the sight of that did to him. The faint scent of her perfume or body lotion tinged the air. He cleared his throat. "Fixing it."

Grace's eyes dropped, but she quickly snapped them back to his. "I have a safety pin."

"Well . . ." He pulled free and yanked on the door, then opened the glove box. "I have a sewing kit."

He climbed into the passenger seat. He was willing to sew on a button, but not freeze to death in a parking lot. Grace wrapped her arms around herself, watching for a moment, then jogged around the front of the truck and slid into the driver's seat.

Grace Fairbanks climbing into his truck wearing his shirt while he sewed the button back onto hers was not on his January vision board. But he wasn't going to say he hadn't manifested it. He'd imagined Grace in a bra. A lot. But in those daydreams, she was usually berating him, so he had work to do on that front. He had yet to admit to himself that he found that part disturbingly hot.

"How do you know how to do that?" Grace asked, watching him thread the needle with black thread. He figured black was better than the royal blue included in the kit.

"Because hockey gear is expensive as shit, and my mom got tired of fixing it for me."

Grace let out a puff of air. He glanced up. That almost sounded like a laugh. He couldn't tell if she was laughing at his answer or laughing at him. Something inside him withered. It wasn't like he was painting his nails or anything, but his dad had given his thoughts freely when he'd seen him with a needle and thread. *Your mother's raising a helluva pansy. Maybe you should take up figure skating.*

"I was a disaster with equipment when I was a kid," he continued, looping another thread through the button. "Ripped my jerseys, busted the padding in my gloves, wore holes in my socks."

"Well, that's not a surprise," she quipped.

André's hand froze as he looked up with a grin. "I'm sorry, was that a masturbation joke?"

She scoffed, her hand flying to her chest. "No, I would never insinuate such a thing! It's just believable that you'd be rough on your socks."

André watched her a moment. Was she flirting with him? He didn't want to assume. He'd been wrong before, and he didn't especially feel like getting slapped first thing in the morning. He dropped his head and put the final loop in the knot he'd sewn into the backside of Grace's shirt. "It's true. I'm rough on a lot of things actually."

"Hmm. Good to know." Grace didn't ask him any other questions. She sat there still beside him, her eyes burning holes into his hands, the side of his face. She may as well have been holding a magnifying glass up to the sun.

He finished crisscrossing the thread over the button and through the fabric, then wound a few loops of thread between them to keep the button loose and easy to use. He tied off the end and brought the shirt to his lips to bite the thread since he didn't have scissors.

"There you go." André held up the blouse, fully intact, button secured.

Grace didn't take it right away. She just stared at him. It only took him half a second to realize why. She wasn't looking directly at the blouse. Sure, her eyes were aimed the right direction, but they were off by a few millimeters.

His lips curved before he could stop them, because Grace was staring, just a little, at his bare chest. André wasn't the kind of guy to waste a moment of ego padding, so he let her. He didn't move, didn't speak, trying not to spook her.

Her throat bobbed slightly, her fingers tensed around the hem of his shirt, like she'd just remembered she was still wearing it. "This is yours." She blinked and drew in a breath, quickly dropping her eyes.

"I'd be happy to wear this, but I don't think it would close." André gestured at the blouse in his hand.

Grace laughed, a little too high and bright. "Uh, no. I can—" She paused, her hand gripping his shirt, halfway up her abdomen.

André's heart slammed against his ribs. He dropped the blouse in her lap. "Better take that to your car."

Grace's lips twitched. "Why?"

He wet his lips. "Because I've been a gentleman, Grace, but if you change here, I'm not going to be able to stop myself from watching."

Grace froze mid-motion, his shirt bunched around her ribs, revealing just the smallest strip of bare skin. Her gaze locked with his. There was a flicker of hesitation and then a blush. Soft. Barely there. But it still lit up her cheekbones, crept down the delicate line of her throat.

André clenched his jaw. She was thinking about it, and for just a second, he imagined what would happen if—

But then any fantasies evaporated because Grace pulled his shirt over her head. She moved slow. Relaxed. Not tense like she had been when he'd caught her at the window. She pulled her hair free and smoothed it, then tossed the shirt into his lap before picking up her own blouse.

She didn't rush. Didn't fumble. Grace held out one arm and pulled on the shirt, bowing her head as she pulled it across her back and slipped it over her other arm, then freed her hair caught in the collar before straightening it.

It sat open like a jacket, and the sight of that was somehow hotter than when it was all the way off. She started at the lowest button, working her way up. She took her time with the button he'd just sewn on, fingering it before slipping it through the hole. He couldn't hear anything over the blood rushing in his ears.

When she finished, she looked up. "That's better."

André forced his mouth to close. He frowned and pulled his own T-shirt on, the image of her still seared onto his retinas, playing like a movie teaser. He didn't know what this meant. Was that her idea of a gift? A thank you for the button fix? If so, she was a sadist.

"We should probably get in there." Grace nodded toward the building.

André dragged a hand over his face, tilted his head back against the headrest, and exhaled. "Yeah. I'm going to need a minute."

Silence.

He glanced over just in time to see a small curl of Grace's mouth before she turned and reached for the door handle. "See you inside, then."

CHAPTER
Ten

THE BOARDROOM at Heads Up Alberta was functional, nothing flashy—grey carpeting, a long oak table, a TV mounted on the wall, and a few framed photos of past events hanging neatly in a row. They clearly weren't some massive corporate operation. It was a small office with few staff. Grace read the mission statement on the wall.

"Provide emotional, physical, and monetary support for families dealing with the lifelong effects of traumatic brain injuries."

The director, Michael Russo, stood and introduced himself as she entered—mid-fifties, solid build. She wouldn't have staked her life savings on it, but she was betting he was a former hockey player. He looked the part. Well, all except the missing teeth.

"Hi." Grace shook his hand, then stretched her arm to greet

the woman sitting beside him. Michael introduced her as Lucy, their fundraising coordinator. She had sharp eyes, dark curls tied back in a bun, and a laptop already open in front of her.

"I'm Devin, the community outreach manager." The second man stood and rounded the table to shake her hand. He looked young, maybe in his mid-twenties, and had round wire-rimmed glasses reminiscent of a character from Harry Potter.

"Did André ditch you?" Michael grinned as he sat back in his rolling chair.

Grace laughed. "No, he—"

"Was just parking." André swept into the room with a grin. He was fully dressed now, his jacket on over his T-shirt. Grace groaned internally. *She hadn't brought his winter coat.* That was not an oversight, she just hadn't planned on seeing him this morning.

Michael pressed his hands into the table top. "André, thanks for putting this together. And Grace, we appreciate you being here." He sat and opened the folder in front of him, glancing around the table. "First off, I want to thank you all for making this happen. I know the logistics of something like this can get complicated, but if we do it right, it's going to make a real impact."

Lucy leaned in, her excitement obvious. "Have we talked funding goals?"

Michael shook his head. "Not formally."

She turned to André. "I'm not sure if this is in the ballpark, but my goal would be to raise at least two hundred and fifty thousand, ideally more. That will make a big dent in our annual goals."

André nodded. "I think it's high but not unrealistic. We've got some big names. We'll have player interviews, some media spots leading up to the game. We'll also auction off jerseys, equipment, signed memorabilia—all of that goes straight to the foundation."

Michael turned to him. "And you're good with managing that?"

André nodded. "Yeah, I've already got contacts for it. We've already got verbal agreements for sponsorships, we're in the process of getting local businesses involved. Ticket sales will be a major factor too, so we need to make it a real event—something people want to show up for."

Grace steepled her fingers. "This is happening when?"

"End of March. Leading into playoffs. Take advantage of the hype."

Grace sat back, arms crossed loosely as she observed. André wasn't here as a representative, he was fully involved in the organization of this event. He was well-versed. Confident. A very different version of the flirty André she'd met at the hockey game and had seen in the truck that morning.

She fingered the button he'd sewn back on her shirt. André noticed. His eyebrow lifted, and Grace quickly dropped her hand to her lap, trying to banish the image of him sitting shirtless in his truck with his teeth over the thread.

Michael tapped his pen on the table. "Sponsorships are great, but our main concern is making sure all proceeds benefit the foundation. We don't want things getting tied up in unnecessary overhead."

André nodded. "Yeah, that's why we're keeping the sponsorship structure simple. Any corporate partners donating directly to the charity get a tax deduction, like any other charitable contribution. But the sponsorships tied to game promotions—jersey logos, rink boards, ads—those need to be classified differently to avoid hitting the taxable advertising threshold."

Lucy sat up straighter. "You've looked into the tax classifications?"

André shrugged. "Yep. Sponsorship revenue can be considered a business expense instead of a donation if it's promotional, which means they write it off differently. But if we package it right—tie the exposure to a fundraising pledge instead of straight-up advertising—it keeps us in the clear. And keeps the donors happy."

Grace wanted to ask why André thought he needed her there. He knew what he was talking about. She had nothing else to contribute, which was not what she'd anticipated, and that gave her pause. Something pinched behind her ribs. She'd judged André. Hard. Now, here he was sewing on buttons and organizing charity events.

But . . .

She thought of Troy. He was successful, wasn't he? Capable? Smart? And he was still a bit of a misogynistic asshole, if a frustratingly loveable one.

Michael crossed a leg over his knee. "That's exactly the kind of foresight we need. The last thing we want is a paperwork nightmare after the fact."

André ran a hand over his jaw. "I'll work with our contacts to make sure every business understands the benefit structure before they sign on. If we make it easy for them, we'll bring in bigger sponsors."

Lucy nodded. "And the auction? Any concerns there?"

André shook his head. "Not if we run it properly. We're setting up a silent auction, both online and at the event. Auctioned items are donations, so there's no tax obligation on our end, and winning bidders don't get tax receipts since they're technically purchasing an item. The key is making sure everything's documented correctly so we don't run into compliance issues later."

Grace blinked. What. The. Hell. This was the same man who'd grabbed a random couple outside the Saddledome and asked if they wanted to have a threesome with her. Now he was breaking down tax-exempt sponsorship structures like he moonlighted as an accountant?

He didn't seem like the same person at all.

She shifted in her chair, subtly catching a whiff of his cologne and the faintest hint of cigarette smoke. Wearing his shirt had cemented that scent in her brain, and it catalyzed a warm, tingly sensation coursing through her. Grace took an unsteady breath, leaning in the other direction to avoid drinking in more of that laced air.

Michael smiled, satisfied. "Sounds like you've got everything in hand. We're lucky to have you running this."

André flashed a lazy grin. "Don't say that yet. Let's see how much money we actually bring in first."

Michael chuckled, nodding. "Fair enough."

Devin turned to her. "Grace, is there anything on the legal side we should be aware of?"

She straightened in her seat, the sudden attention sharpening her foggy brain. She paused a beat, waiting for instinct to kick in. *Structuring. Organization. Right.* "You're already set up as a registered nonprofit, so the structure for tax-exempt donations is in place. As long as all sponsorship and ticket proceeds are documented properly, there shouldn't be any issues."

Devin nodded. "We've got an accountant handling the donations and tax paperwork. But I actually had a question about sponsorships. Some of the companies donating are involved in sports medicine and training. They want their branding visible at the event."

Grace crossed her legs, falling into the natural rhythm of a conversation she knew how to navigate. "That's standard, but be mindful of how you structure the sponsorship agreements. If you're giving any direct promotional space to a business—logos on jerseys, for example, or company banners in the arena—that needs to be classified separately from pure donation revenue."

André turned to her. "What about if they want their name on the charity game itself? We had one company floating the idea of a full sponsorship."

She frowned slightly. "That's where it gets trickier. If a business wants to sponsor the event outright, that starts to look less like philanthropy and more like a marketing expense. They can still write it off, but the tax treatment is different. Your team should ensure those details are clear in the contract so there aren't issues later."

Devin scribbled something in his notebook. "That's good to know. What about the players? We've got some high-profile guys lined up. Any potential legal issues there?"

Grace arched a brow. "Define high-profile."

André shrugged. "We've got Jack Harrison from the Blizzard. He's a friend of mine."

Grace blinked. "Jack Harrison? As in the Jack Harrison who's engaged to Delia Melise?"

André laughed. "The one and only. He used to play on our team before he was called up."

Grace worked to keep her expression even. How had Tyler not mentioned that? Had he not been playing when she was working with Troy? Or maybe he wasn't on the Blizzard yet. Apparently, she hadn't been paying attention. "Okay. Who else?"

André listed them off. "Mikhail Volkov from the Edmonton Titans. Colin Fraser from Toronto. Cade Bishop out of Vancouver."

She nearly choked. "Cade Bishop?"

André grinned. "Big fan?"

She worked to keep her eyes from rolling. Cade Bishop was hot, yes. She wasn't going to pretend she wasn't aware of his Calvin Klein underwear ad, though she also wasn't going to admit that she'd been tempted to save a picture of it on her phone. She cleared her throat, officially putting on her lawyer hat. "He's under a massive contract extension right now. His team might have concerns about injury risk. Do you know if his agent signed off?"

"You know a lot about him for someone who isn't a hockey fan." André twisted the cap of the pen that sat on the table in front of him.

Grace scoffed. "Who says I'm not a hockey fan?"

"You didn't seem to be. At the game the other night."

She shot him a look. "What is a fan supposed to look like?

Did I not put on enough body paint?" Devin coughed, and Grace glanced up, a flush jumping to her cheeks. "Sorry. Just a joke." She straightened in her seat. *What the hell was that? Totally unprofessional.*

Devin waved her off. "We haven't spoken with Bishop's people. We assumed since it's a charity game, it wouldn't cause any problems."

Grace tapped her fingers on the table, forcing herself not to look at André even though his eyes seemed to be heat seeking missiles. "That depends. NHL contracts have clauses that prohibit certain activities outside of official league games. If a player gets hurt in an unsanctioned event, his team could claim he violated his contract."

Devin paled slightly.

André nodded. "It will be sanctioned. We'll have every participating player sign a liability waiver."

"Ideally, they should run it past their agents first," Grace added. "Otherwise, if someone gets injured, the team could come after both them and the charity."

Devin nodded. "We can get that in place. Anything else?"

Grace glanced at André, who was still watching her. She cleared her throat. "Just make sure all agreements are written, not verbal. Otherwise, things can get messy fast."

André smirked. "Dammit, I was going off handshake deals."

That time, she did roll her eyes. "Hilarious."

His grin widened. "That's all very helpful." He paused, his gaze wandering over her face, stopping on her lips before dragging back to her eyes. "Thanks for coming, Grace."

Her blood heated. "You're welcome."

Michael planted his hands on the table. "Well, I love this plan. What do you need from us?"

André broke their connection and turned, launching into ideas for marketing and hype. Grace felt like she was underwater for thirty seconds, and when she tuned back in, she heard, "I'm not sure if he'd be on board, but I think sharing your story could make this personal. In a good way. Hockey is all about getting back on the ice, but we need players and fans to know how imperative it is to take player safety seriously." Michael watched André, his eyes kind as he waited for a response.

André ran a hand through his hair. "Yeah. I could ask him. I don't think he's opposed to it, but travelling here wouldn't be an option."

"No, of course. But maybe a video or something? The two of you together?" Michael suggested.

André considered this, and Grace held her breath. What were they talking about? She used context to piece things together, but it was all assumption. Someone André knew had experienced a traumatic brain injury? Was that why he was so passionate about this event and this charity in particular?

"I'll work on it." The grin was gone from André's face, and the muscle in his jaw jumped as he stood. "I'll be in touch."

CHAPTER
Eleven

ANDRÉ

THE SHARP SCENT OF SWEAT, rubber mats, and menthol filled the Snowballs' locker room as André pulled his jersey over his head, shaking out his shoulders. The team was in good spirits, but their conversation had an edge tonight. That always happened this time of year. A buzz at the edge of their game and their celly's at the pub. All of them were too superstitious to say anything out loud, but they were winning. And they wanted that damn Rose Cup.

The past three years, they'd come close without taking home the prize. After everything that happened with Pucks Deep over the past six months, they only wanted it harder. There wasn't outright animosity between them like there had been—Rhonda's smackdown at the pub had put them all in their place where that was concerned—but on the ice, they still wanted revenge.

They were playing them over the weekend.

Tyler tossed a roll of tape to Vargo, who caught it midair and started wrapping his stick. "Feeling good out there."

"Looking good out there," Brett winked, tugging on his shin pads.

André read between the lines. *Tyler: I'm ready to kick the shit out of Pucks Deep. Brett: I'm ready to watch.* He grinned, shaking his head as Sean, already half-dressed, laced up a skate and looked up. "No dumb penalties, eh? No hero plays. We keep playing our system, wear them down shift by shift. We play heavier in the neutral zone and cut off their rush chances before they get momentum."

A series of grunts echoed around the locker room, and warmth swelled in André's chest. He hadn't always seen himself here. The Snowballs weren't the NHL, weren't even the AHL, but this team, this league? It meant everything to him.

André had been that kid on the fast track. Growing up in Montreal, hockey was religion. And he had it—the skill, the drive, the raw, untamed hunger that separated the good from the great. At sixteen, he went top ten in the QMJHL draft. By eighteen, he was lighting it up in juniors, leading the league in points for three straight months, playing with an edge that made people talk.

But André had a reputation. The scouts liked him, but they didn't love him. Cocky. Hot-headed. Too much attitude, too much showmanship, too much damn personality for the front offices who wanted robots on skates.

Still, his numbers spoke for themselves and at nineteen, he got the call. Signed a three-year entry-level contract with the Bruins. Not a first-round pick, not a franchise golden boy, but a kid with talent who could carve out a spot if he worked hard enough.

He spent a year grinding in the AHL, showing up, putting in the work. Then it was one bad hit. One freak collision at centre ice, a knee bending the wrong way, a ligament tearing so fast he barely had time to register the pain before he was on the ice, clutching it, knowing in his gut that something was gone.

He missed the rest of the season. Rehabbed. Fought like hell to come back, and when he did? The organization had moved on. Because in hockey, there's always someone younger, just as fast, just as hungry, but without the injury history, rehab schedule, or risk.

Front offices didn't bet on risks.

His contract expired, and there was no extension. No new offer. No more chances, just a door closing. He was twenty-two and already past tense. No one said it outright, but he knew what they were thinking. Another kid who almost made it.

But André wasn't wired for that. He wasn't wired to quit. He played wherever they'd let him. He bounced through minor pro leagues, overseas teams, random offers that barely covered rent but kept him on the ice.

And then, by some act of God, he landed a first-role contract with Les Diables Rouges de Lyon. He played there for three years, making triple what he made in the AHL and a name for himself in Europe.

And damn, did he light it up over there. Played three years, stacked points on points, took in revenue from marketing collabs and sponsorships, building the kind of financial security that most guys in his position never saw. He still had residuals coming in from ad campaigns he'd done during his time there.

André grinned thinking about Grace's reaction to hearing the name Cade Bishop. He'd had half a mind to email her the pictures of him in Polo underwear lying in bed with model Melanie Tress. That image still sat thirty-feet tall on a billboard in Paris.

While everyone else was blowing their money on cars and bottle service, André was investing. Real estate. Startups. A couple of stupid crypto mistakes that actually paid off. When he landed in Calgary after his contract was up, he was set, especially with the exchange.

So he did what he wanted. Started Leclerc Custom Metalworks. He'd always liked working with his hands. Liked the feeling of creating something solid, something lasting. He took his dividends, found a couple of artists and fabricators who actually knew what they were doing, and set up a custom metal-working business catering to high-end clients.

It started with ornamental gates, luxury fixtures—things that rich assholes liked to flex about. But when a well-known architect in Geneva who'd been a fan during his time in Lyon commissioned a series of sculptural railings for a château, the business blew up.

Now he only took on the clients he wanted and trusted his team to run the contracts and shipping. Once he found the Snowballs, it was exactly the life he wanted. He got to play on a team in a league that wasn't flashy, wasn't rich, but the teams were fast, physical, and competitive.

This wasn't just a beer league full of washed-up guys trying to relive their glory days. The Snowballs played to win. And this year? They were the best damn team in the league.

Sean finished taping his stick. "Everyone's in for the tourney, yeah?"

Curtis raised a hand. "I'm good. Sorry I couldn't commit 'til yesterday."

Sean waved him off. The rest of the guys nodded, and it was then that André noticed Country quietly packing his gear. His wide grin and stupid-ass jokes were glaringly absent.

André dropped his gear and walked over, slapping a hand on his shoulder. "You good, bud?"

Country looked up, looking like a startled rabbit. "Yeah. Sorry, just in my own world over here."

"Focused. That's hot."

Country blew out a breath, not looking up as he packed his gear. "Super hot."

André's grin dropped. The other guys went about their business, packing up, so André leaned in. "You want to talk about it?"

"Not especially."

André nodded. "Got it. Well, if you need—"

"Hope's birth mom filed a petition." Country kept his voice low. "Wants to revoke the adoption."

André stilled, his blood curdling. *What the hell?* "When?"

"This week. Grace came over. Before the meeting you went to with Heads Up."

André replayed that morning in his head. How Grace had looked when he'd found her in the car. How she'd nearly been in tears. "Holy f—"

"Share with the class, boys?" Mike reached out and mussed both their hair.

André was about to turn and shove him against the locker, but Country grabbed his arm. "All good." Country dragged in an unsteady breath. "Probably good they all know because I'm going to be a mess for a bit."

The locker room quieted as Country turned to face them. He announced the petition, then explained that Grace was working on it and they didn't know what to expect.

There was silence for a long moment.

Ryan was the first to speak. "Shit, man."

Country just nodded once. "Yeah."

"How's Jenna holding up?" Sean asked.

"Better than me, honestly." Country ran a hand through his hair, then reached for his bag. "I don't think she can afford to be worried." He flexed his fingers. "It'd crush her."

André watched him for a long moment. Then his thoughts shifted to Grace. "Was it a problem with the paperwork or something?" It was a roundabout way of asking if they thought she was responsible.

The look on her face when he'd shown up at her window snapped back into his memory. Her red-rimmed eyes, the way she'd tried to hide that she was emotionally compromised. It wasn't only about the button.

Country exhaled. "It was a problem with the social worker. They didn't document a conversation that needed to happen with the birth mother."

André's hands clenched. Grace had looked over that paper-work, hadn't she? Even if it wasn't her mistake, he could guess she'd been beating herself up for days. Plus, she didn't have the same foundation here. She didn't have family around or a social network outside of the people she knew on the Snowballs.

André stepped back and picked up his bag while the other guys moved in to offer gruff hugs and back slaps.

Sean's voice was quiet. "You guys aren't alone in this. What-ever you need, we've got you."

Brett nodded. "Yeah. Anything, man. We're in."

Country's jaw was tight. Keeping his emotions in check looked painful. When he was alone again, André picked up his bag and walked over. "I had no idea you were shouldering this on your own."

Country shook his head. "I've had Jenna and our families. Polk's been jumping in and helping so I have more time to be with Hope. Oh, and Grace. She's working behind the scenes as our own Benny Cooperman. Searching through emails and texts. She's slammed with work and her renovations, so I honestly feel the worst for her." He slung his bag over his shoulder. "It's not like I have any skills to offer, though."

André nodded, his brow pinching. "I was thinking the same thing."

"That I have no skills?"

"Oh, definitely." He flashed a grin. "But also the whole Grace thing." He schooled his face into a neutral, nonchalant expres-sion before asking, "Do you have her address, by the way?"

Country's brow furrowed. "Why?"

"She has something of mine. With everything going on, I thought I'd stop by and grab it instead of adding another thing to her list."

Country's eyes narrowed. "What does she have of yours?"

André held up his hands. "My coat. From the other night when she walked to her car after the game."

"Your coat. That's it."

"Correct. But what happened? You were on board with helping me set this whole thing up."

"Yeah. Before I saw how pissed she and Jenna were."

André dropped a hand on Country's shoulder. "I'm not going to make this worse for you."

"You didn't promise."

André squeezed. "Sometimes I make it worse without knowing it, so it's better to underpromise and overdeliver."

Country wasn't close to being convinced. "Why don't you text her?"

André blew out a breath. "Hey, if you want to explain why she has to spend time texting about a missing coat and make her feel bad about taking it—"

"Fine. But I will pull a Sean and punch you out on the ice if you do anything asinine." Country pulled out his phone and swiped up.

ANDRÉ

ANDRÉ HAD NEVER LOST A FIGHT. Sure, he'd been beaten a few times—once so bad he woke up in a trainer's room with his left eye swollen shut and the distinct memory of a guy named Korchinski treating his face like a speed bag—but he'd never lost.

He wasn't about to start now.

Not that Grace was some cup to be won, but he couldn't leave things the way they were between them. Half the time she was biting his head off and the other half she was showing him her bra. He needed to up that second portion to at least eighty.

André parked on the curb and grabbed the paper bag sitting in the passenger seat. He would ask for his coat. But he'd also drop off the best tacos in the city. Their spiced meat, fresh tortillas, and house-made salsa had been known to make grown men weep. Probably because Alberta had such shit Mexican food, it restored their faith in their fellow countrymen, but that was beside the point.

He walked up the drive, climbed the steps, and rang the doorbell. The camera eye stared at him as he shifted his weight. He was suddenly self-conscious. Was he standing too close? Wrong angle?

After a couple of minutes with no answer from Grace, André frowned, glancing at the Volkswagen parked in the driveway. She was home. A light was on inside, a faint glow filtering from some room at the back of the house through the front window.

So she was either avoiding him—which, yeah, fair—or didn't hear the doorbell. Except Grace didn't seem like a person to ignore her notifications. He also highly doubted that she hadn't connected this camera to her WiFi network.

Grace was a woman who liked things in order. That was what she wanted, and she'd curated her life to get exactly that. But André couldn't help but wonder, after seeing her so worked up and anxious Monday morning, if it was what she needed?

André smirked, rocking back on his heels. She could see him, and she was making him wait.

Fine.

He dropped onto the front porch steps, stretching his legs out like he had all the time in the world. She could sit inside, watching him like he was some overly persistent Uber Eats driver, but he wasn't leaving.

He had nowhere to be, and he had tacos. Maybe if he ate one—

"What are you doing here?" Grace stood in the doorway, barefoot, her yoga pants hugging the curve in her calf and lower thigh before disappearing under her oversized sweatshirt.

André's throat went dry. He'd never seen her like this. So casual. So . . . normal. Even if she didn't quite pull off "relaxed."

"André. You're sitting on my porch." Her voice was flat, unimpressed.

He shrugged and stood, grabbing the bag. "You didn't answer your door."

Her arms crossed. "You didn't take that as a sign?"

"Could've meant a lot of things." He stood, easily stepping into her space, letting her feel him there. "Maybe you didn't hear me. Maybe you were busy."

Her eyes narrowed. "Or maybe I saw you on the camera and decided I wasn't in the mood for whatever this is." She gestured at the bag, but also toward all of him generally.

André grinned. "Hey, I'm good with eating these tacos myself, but—"

"Tacos?" Her ears perked up. "From where?"

"Añejo."

Grace's eyes flared. "They're downtown."

"Yes. They are."

Grace fiddled with the door knob, then finally stepped back, just enough for him to pass to the entryway.

Not into the house. Not an invitation. Just out of the cold.

She reached for the bag, but he didn't immediately hand it over. "I got a few for me, too." That whole week it'd felt like he was playing chess. Taking his time to make a move, then committing and holding his breath until she responded.

She was unpredictable. Frustrating. A code he couldn't crack. And that was probably why he wanted to keep playing.

Grace made a small noise as she pulled the cuff of her sweatshirt over her hand. Why was that so hot? It was coy, almost schoolgirl-ish.

As if sensing his thoughts, Grace dropped her shirt and straightened. "I can get a plate and take mine—"

"Am I that repulsive to you? You can't even eat a taco with me?" Screw the game. He was breaking the fourth wall.

Grace blinked. "You're not—I've had a bad couple of days, and I'm not even dressed—"

"You're more dressed than you were in the car the other day, and yeah, I'm aware of your shitty days. Country told the team what's going on with the adoption, so I sat in 17th Ave traffic to get you some damn tacos, and now you're acting like I came here holding a condom in my teeth."

Grace opened her mouth, then snapped it closed. She drew a deep breath, then exhaled and drew another. "I—I can't do this."

"Do what? Spend time with me? Because—"

"No, I can't make another decision, okay?" Grace stalked into the living room, threading her hands in her hair. "I'm in charge of everything right now. The renovations, the permitting, one of the largest purchases with my company that I've ever managed, and then all of this with Country and Jenna. I can't get the damn therapist on this case to call me back, the birth mother's lawyer is cock-blocking me, and I just—I can't do it. I can't be in charge of hosting you for tacos, André, okay? I can't think about whether I should offer you water or Coke or the bottle of tequila I've been too scared to bust out in case I drink the whole damn bottle, and whether you'd be okay with paper plates, because that's what I'd be using for tacos tonight since I don't have a spare second in my day to run the dishwasher, and—"

"Right, got it," André snapped, kicking off his shoes and striding into the room. He stopped in front of her, momentarily distracted by her pulse fluttering in her throat.

He wet his lips. "So here's what we're going to do. I'm going to put my arm around your waist. I'm going to take you into the kitchen, and then I'm going to tell you exactly what to do. No decisions. Just tacos."

That damn flush rose to her cheeks again. She swallowed hard. "No decisions."

"Right." Something flickered behind her eyes, and André caught her wrist. "Not because you're incapable, but because you're so damn capable your brain needs time to shut off. I'm going to give that to you, okay? And if you don't like it, you can tell me to go, and I'll—"

"Don't go," she whispered, her shoulders finally dropping an inch.

André took in the deep circles under her eyes, then did exactly what he said he would. He slid his arm around her waist and pulled her toward the kitchen. Her body stiffened for a heartbeat before melting into the contact. She moved with him, barefoot on the hardwood, her long legs brushing his as they walked.

"Hands on the counter." André planted her next to the stools at the island. "You can sit when I tell you to."

Her brows lifted, but she didn't argue. He didn't want to take this too far, but that desperate look in her eyes made him bold. If he was too passive, this wouldn't work. Human brains weighed information and made choices nearly every second. Grace was so burned out, she needed to let go of all of them, even the subconscious ones.

André opened the cupboard on his right.

"Good guess." Grace watched him pull two plates from the middle shelf.

André unpacked the food with slow precision. He rolled back the foil, and the scent of warm corn tortillas and slow-roasted pork filled the air. He arranged the tacos on the plates, added the salsa and lime, then slid her portion across the counter. "Sit."

Her lips twitched, and she obeyed. André leaned over the counter, picking up a taco. "Eat the one on the right. You're going to pick it up and make a mess. You're not going to think about it or give a shit if juice drips over your hands and wrists because I'm making a mess, too. I'll clean you after."

Grace's eyes flicked to his. Okay, maybe that was too much, but a small part of him wanted to see what he could get away with. Her cheeks flushed a deeper shade of pink as she reached for the taco.

"One more thing. You're going to enjoy this. You're not going to eat it only to eat. You're going to eat it for pleasure. This is food you didn't have to cook or buy yourself. You have friends here. You're not in this alone, and that means you can take a breath and savour it."

Grace watched him with wide, glistening eyes. She quickly looked away and sniffed before taking a bite. Sauce dripped over her palm and down the inside of her wrist. Her eyes fluttered, and there was a small, audible moan in her throat.

"Exactly." André bit into his al pastor. Even though the tacos had been sitting in the bag for close to half an hour at this point, the double corn tortillas kept them from falling apart.

They finished their first tacos together. André rinsed his hands at the sink, then pulled two glasses from the cupboard. He filled them both with water and squeezed in a little of the extra lime. André rounded the counter and set Grace's drink beside her plate. "You're going to get the glass dirty, but you're not going to care because it's easily washable."

Grace nodded once, then hesitated for a split second before picking up the glass from the counter and taking a drink.

"That's good," André murmured. Grace set the glass back on the counter. André returned to his place across from her. He nodded at the opened foil in front of her. "Eat the second one."

Grace dropped her eyes, but not before André saw the tears welling there. They ate together, then André threw out their trash and hand-washed their glasses after Grace cleaned up at the sink. He set them to dry, then turned to find her leaning against the island, watching him.

She swiped at her cheek. "Thank you."

André dried his hands on the tea towel she had sitting beside the sink. "You're welcome."

She pursed her lips, then released them. "Is it over?"

"Is what over?"

She let out a small embarrassed laugh. "I—there are a lot of calls I need to make. I should probably—" Grace paused when her phone lit up on the counter. André glanced down and saw the caller without meaning to. Elodie Shaw.

He frowned, wondering if it was his phone he was seeing for a moment until he felt the outline of it in his pocket.

"Oh, I need to get that." Grace hurried over and snatched the phone from the granite. She answered the call with a chipper, "Hello!" then mouthed, "I'm so sorry" to André.

Elodie Shaw. Grace was talking to Elodie Shaw two feet from him. It wouldn't have felt strange at all if he'd spoken to Elodie besides a brief hello at Christmas in the past two years. But since he hadn't, the fact that Grace was shooting the breeze with his sister made his stomach twist.

Why were they talking?

Had it really been two years?

André did the mental calculations as he strode to the door. Grace was already walking down the hall and lowering her voice—obviously something she didn't want him to overhear. Which made it even easier for him to get the hell out of her condo. For both their sakes.

André strode out of the kitchen, his pulse racing. He slipped on his shoes, opened the front door, and stepped out into the night. By the time he descended the steps, he was already reaching for his phone.

CHAPTER
Thirteen

GRACE

ON FRIDAY MORNING, Grace stood in the gutted hallway of the Kensington building with her arms crossed. Matthew, her contractor, flipped through his notes, discussing permits, delays, and a structural issue they didn't recognize until they pulled up the flooring in unit 3C.

His voice droned on, but she barely heard him. She didn't want to be standing in this freezing, half-finished building when all she could think about was tacos.

After finally receiving a phone call from the therapist working with Amey, Hope's birth mother, she'd walked back out into the living area to find André gone. She couldn't blame him. She'd been on the phone for at least ten minutes, though she hadn't accomplished much.

All week, she'd been trying to get in contact with Elodie Shaw. She hoped they'd be able to set up an in-person meeting, but Elodie skirted the request twice on the phone. She wasn't interested in discussing anything with her, even off the record. It wasn't as if Grace was asking her to break therapist-patient confidentiality. She only wanted to encourage Elodie to get written consent from Amey for her to have a conversation and, if this thing did go to court, for her testimony to be included.

Amey's mental state needed to be determined. Based on the texts and emails she'd read, Amey had consistently desired adoption. So why would she change her mind now?

Surprisingly, the frustration she felt after Elodie ended the call was eclipsed by the disappointment of leaving and finding her living room empty. Which was concerning on multiple levels.

Heat rushed to her middle as she remembered André pulling plates from her cupboard. How he'd pressed his hands against the counter and told her to enjoy the food, and she'd mentally superpositioned herself in the rounded space between his arms.

That wasn't what she wanted. André was charming, yes, but he was reckless and crass—he was a smoker—and there was no universe where pushing boundaries with another smooth-talking womanizer went well for her. Not to mention, André was young and hadn't even started to figure out his life yet. He probably ate ramen four days a week and had a healthy amount of credit card debt.

And yet.

She couldn't stop thinking about those tacos. About André standing in her kitchen. About

"Grace?"

She blinked, snapping back to reality. "What?"

Matthew gave her a look. "I was asking if you wanted to hold off on the electrical in unit 3C until we reassess the subflooring."

She forced herself to focus. Nodded. "Yeah. Hold off. Just keep me updated."

Twenty minutes later, she was back in her car, heading home. She had to keep in mind the property's resale value. Otherwise, it was starting to feel like a trap.

Everything about Calgary was stifling at the moment. She wanted out. She wanted to go back to Toronto, where things were manageable, predictable, where she could accept cases and ignore the crap she didn't want to deal with. That was the benefit of seniority, wasn't it? She never thought she'd yearn for paperwork, but electrical problems? Subfloors? *I'll pass, thanks.*

By the time she got home, her brain was already switching gears. She tossed her bag onto the counter, kicked off her heels, and made a beeline for the dining table for her laptop, where she had over fifty tabs open in her browser.

Half of them contained everything Country and Jenna had sent and the records she had on file from the social worker and the adoption agency. Half were references and resources for her caseload at her actual job.

She rolled up the sleeves of her blouse, sat down, and started with tab number one, combing through the next twenty plus emails. Message by message. Date by date.

She scanned every conversation, every signed document, every notation that should have covered them. None of it led her to believe the social worker hadn't followed correct procedure or that Amey was being manipulated or coerced.

Her gut told her she was missing something, but that was more confusing than anything. Why hadn't her damn gut told her she'd missed something in the first place?

Grace rubbed her temples, then lay back on the couch and let her eyes drop closed. She should have been working on the opposite twenty-five tabs. She had multiple submission deadlines coming up, but she couldn't bring herself to care. What was more important than keeping a baby in a home?

But all of this was a dead end. Every time she looked for confirmation that Amey had been properly informed of her revocation rights, she found nothing. No notation. No proof.

A vibration on the table made her heart leap into her throat. She scrambled for her phone, adrenaline rushing through her veins. The message on the screen only made her heart beat faster.

JENNA

Running five minutes late. Sorry!!

Five minutes late—?

Brunch. Shit.

Grace checked the time and cursed again under her breath. She had forgotten entirely.

She closed the laptop, grabbed her coat, shoved her feet into her boots, and rushed out the door.

———

Calgary's winter morning air was crisp, a thin mist still clinging to the streets as Grace pulled onto the main road. The car was still warm from her earlier trip, but she blasted the heat regardless. She'd long suspected that she had some kind of circulatory issue since her feet and hands were freezing in the winter and swollen in summer. No doubt something that would require an amputated limb in her sixties.

Grace lamented that she didn't have a self-driving car that would allow her to work on her drives. Technically, you were supposed to have your hands on the wheel, but she'd seen enough YouTube videos to convince herself her knees were a suitable substitute.

She neared the brunch spot, Elm & Ash. It was one of those

trendy-but-cozy places, nestled between an independent book-store and a boutique coffee shop. From the main picture on their website, it had exposed brick walls, warm pendant light-ing, and mismatched vintage tables that looked effortlessly curated.

She'd been legitimately excited when Jenna sent the invita-tion, which only made her feel more like an idiot as she parked ten minutes late. How often had she silently judged people who couldn't make the effort to be on time? It seemed karma was calling in all her past dues as of late.

Grace exited the car, locked the doors, and strode through the front glass door. Inside, the scent of freshly brewed coffee and warm pastries wrapped around her, cutting through the last of the cold. It was already buzzing with conversation, waitstaff weaving between tables, balancing plates piled high with french toast and eggs benedict.

Jenna waved at her from a table by the window. She was bundled in a thick sweater, her blond hair pulled into a high ponytail. Grace exhaled, rolling back her tension as she made her way over.

Jenna grinned as Grace slid into the seat across from her. "You made it."

Grace gave an apologetic smile. "I'm so sorry I'm late. Did you already order?"

Jenna shook her head, quickly peeking under the blanket of the curved car seat nestled beside her on the bench. "Just got us both water with lemon."

As if on cue, their waitress stopped by and dropped off their water, then took their orders. Black coffee and avocado toast for Grace, a vanilla oat latte for Jenna along with the breakfast hash.

"Okay, before I forget . . ." Jenna took a sip of water. "Thank you for everything you're doing. I know it's been a mess."

Grace waved a hand. "It's kind of my mess to clean up."

"Umm, no, it's not."

Grace moved her water to the side as the waitress set down

her coffee along with a bowl holding small packets of cream and sugar. "I'm not moping about it, I just should've caught it."

"How would you have noticed a tiny detail like that? The social worker said all procedures were followed. Are you supposed to micromanage every last detail? Second-check all their work?"

Ideally, no, but Grace had done more scanning than she would've liked to admit. The social worker seemed extremely competent. Easy to communicate with, experienced. She'd had no reason to doubt.

"I don't know." Grace sighed. "It still doesn't make sense to me. Amey never wavered in her decision to adopt. Even after she had Hope, there's nothing in her notes to indicate she was having second thoughts. In fact, I found a text message between her and her social worker three days later that said, 'So glad that's over. I feel like myself again. I can't wait to get back to my life.' There were no questions or expressions of conflicting emotions."

"Maybe she was embarrassed."

Grace shrugged and emptied cream into her coffee cup. "Maybe. But typically in situations like this you'll see a slew of questions. About the baby, about procedure, about timing of a first visit if the adoption is open."

"We were more than willing to have it be open, by the way."

Grace nodded. "Oh, I know. You'd think that would've been her first question since she declined that option earlier."

Jenna's eyes dropped. "I wish I understood any of this. It was the best day of our lives when we found out Hope was coming to us. Now—" Her voice broke.

Grace reached out a hand and wrapped it over hers. She wanted to promise her it would be okay. That she'd fix this and guarantee they would never have to give Hope up. But if practicing law had taught her anything, it was the necessity for precise language. "I'll do everything I can. But Jenna, if you and Country feel like it would be best to find—"

"We're not getting a different lawyer." Jenna gave her a searching look. "Do you think we want a different lawyer?"

"No, but I would understand if you did. I didn't exactly knock this one out of the park."

Jenna grabbed her hand with both of hers. "I need you to stop saying things like that, okay? This isn't your fault, and even if it was, people make mistakes. Who's to say another lawyer would've done better? I know for damn sure no other lawyer would do better now. I trust you. We both do."

Grace didn't cry often, and especially not in public, but the corners of her eyes started to sting. She pulled her hand back and reached for her coffee. "Well, I'll keep searching and pushing—gently—for mediation before we go to a public hearing."

Jenna leaned back in the booth. "Maybe André will get something from his sister. I doubt she'll say anything useful, but you never know."

Grace blinked, then slowly set her coffee cup down on the table. "André's sister?"

Jenna nodded. "Yeah. The therapist. He and Country were talking at poker night. Somehow he found out that she's Amey's therapist. I have no idea how with HIPPA and all that, and honestly, I didn't think the two of them were close after—"

"André's sister is Amey's therapist? Elodie Shaw?"

Jenna nodded again. "Did you not know that?"

No, she sure as hell did not know that. Her head dropped into a tailspin. Elodie Shaw. André's sister.

Heat flashed through her, and a cold sweat broke out on her brow. She told him she'd been trying to meet with the therapist, hadn't she? Maybe not. Now she was second-guessing herself.

He knew? How could André have known this and not said something? Elodie had phoned her while André was at her house with the damn tacos.

Jenna kept talking—something about André being pissed that his sister was involved, how Country had talked him down because it was her job, not a personal vendetta. How she was surprised that Grace wasn't aware since André had talked with her the other night, which, by the way, Country had nearly decked him for. Apparently, when he gave André Grace's address, André was under strict orders not to go over there under any circumstances and—

"It's fine, sorry, I need to go to the washroom. Hold that thought?" Grace stood with a shaky smile, then stood and beelined for the WC. She needed a second—just a damn second to get her head around this. She wanted to storm out the door and hunt André down, but unlike him, she hadn't sleuthed out his address ahead of time.

She burst through the door and found an empty stall, then closed her eyes and forced herself to breathe. *Asshole.* He'd seen how stressed she was. And yes, she'd definitely told him she was trying to get in touch with the therapist. That was one of the first things she said to him before he went all taco-dominant on her. Ugh, it was so hot, but now it felt like a slap in the face. He had a potential key to solving one of her problems, and instead he'd chosen tacos?

Grace walked back out to the sinks and washed her hands. She was going to go back out there, plaster on a smile, and enjoy her smashed avocado with spring greens and pickled onions on seeded sourdough.

Then she was going to get André's effing address.

ANDRÉ

ANDRÉ DROPPED onto the bench and rapped his stick on the boards. Three minutes left and they were up three to one on Pucks Deep.

"Sent one buzzing past the tower, eh?" Sean clapped him on the shoulders as their water boy for the night, Sean's fourteen-year-old nephew, held out his bottle and gave him a squirt.

"You see Bowen nail Wheatfill?"

Sean laughed. "Hell, yes. Mashed potatoes. He's going to be pissed." The glee on his face was contagious. This wasn't the tourney for the cup, but it was one of three leading up to it. This one was the only one on the Snowball's home ice, and they wanted it. Hard. The free month of Timmies and bonus checks for the winners didn't hurt either.

Country launched himself over the boards, and Sean exploded onto the ice. Two minutes left. The puck snapped up from Wheatfill's stick, and Sean slapped it to the ice with his glove, then sprinted down the boards. He dropped the puck back to Mike who sent it to Brett at centre.

This was a possession game now, and Pucks Deep knew it. Chubbs came flying, and Brett offloaded to Darcy. He sent it left to Tyler, and Wheatfill lowered his shoulder, stabbing for a touch. He got it.

Jordan exploded past centre, wrapping the puck behind the net to Chubbs, then took up residence at Boyd's four o'clock. Before André could shout at Mike to guard the back door, he was moving, but not fast enough. The biscuit flew, but before it hit tape, Mike kicked out a skate fast enough to slice a watermelon. The puck ricocheted past the blue line where Brett picked it up, hustling his ass through the neutral zone.

The bench and the Snowball's fans in the crowd roared their approval. Because Brett and Tyler were badass, they didn't play soft. Brett flipped momentum, catching his outside edge like frigging Kerrigan and stretched to send the puck wide. Bowen flicked it topshelf. It nicked Matty's shoulder pad and rolled to the ice next to the post, but before Matty could smother it, Sean swooped in, threading the defenders like dental floss and snapping the puck home. He flew forward, sending the net skidding, but the siren was already blaring.

"HOLY SHIT, Thompson!" André yelled as he, Country, and the others poured out over the boards, slamming into their guys in front of the penalty box.

Sean couldn't keep the shit-eating grin off his face as his head wobbled with helmet rubs. They skated back to the bench, still laughing and chirping as Sean snapped them back into focus. "Just over a minute left. Get after it."

They held Pucks Deep and won the game four to one, undefeated in the tourney. Alex Beaty brought out the handheld mic and presented the teams with first and second place medals along with their certificates. Checks would come later since the Elite League would never waste paper printing two sets of checks beforehand.

The energy was palpable as they made their way through the tunnel to the locker room. Beer was already being passed around by the time André removed his helmet. He grabbed one, popped it open and chugged, then crushed the can and finished stripping. He couldn't hear himself think with all the echoing voices, but that was just how he liked it.

André pulled out his bluetooth speaker and started "Shake That Ass," a team favourite. Damn it, he wanted a cigarette, but Nora in administration had ripped him a new one when she got a whiff after the game two weeks ago. Plus . . . there was a part of him that hesitated. Grace didn't like kissing smokers.

Not that it mattered. She didn't seem too interested in kissing him at all, but something about leaving the option open made his ribs tighten.

André grabbed his towel and feigned grinding with Country on his way to the showers. He closed his eyes and let the warm water course over him, washing away the sweat and blood from the game. Somehow he must've split his eyebrow, based on the blood streaked on the inside of his helmet. He pressed his fingers to the area. Didn't seem to be bleeding anymore at the moment.

André washed his hair and rinsed, then frowned as the music stopped abruptly. "Mike, did you sit on my phone again?" he shouted. No response. The locker room had gone silent. He turned off the water.

"Uh, André, you should—"

"I can't hear you!" He burst out of the shower stall, grabbing his towel as he stalked forward, his feet slapping on the tile. He froze as he rounded the corner.

Grace. She stood in the middle of the locker room, staring at him standing in front of her. Bare ass naked.

Country swallowed hard, his towel clutched over his crotch. "I was saying you should dry off and cover up."

André didn't drop his eyes. Grace's expression was cold, but she couldn't hide the blush rising to her cheeks. What the hell was this all about? She was annoyed, he wasn't stupid enough to miss that, but if her plan was to come into his inner sanctum and chap his ass, he wasn't going to make any special accommodations.

"Evening, Grace." André lifted the towel and rubbed it over his hair, then started drying off his neck and shoulders, thinking of anything other than the fact that Grace's hair was pulled up into a tight ponytail and that she wore another silk blouse under her blazer. The guys would never let him live down a hard-on under these circumstances, even just a semi.

"I've been trying to find you," she snapped. "Do you ever go home?"

André worked to hide his surprise. *She knew where he lived? Did her blouse have those tiny straps?* "Not on tournament weekends."

Grace pursed her lips. "Well, that would've been good to know."

Half the guys hurried into the showers and the other half migrated behind the middle set of lockers, changing like they were about to miss the cut off for half-priced beers at One Place.

André lazily dried his torso, trying not to laugh as Grace did her damndest to keep her eyes north of the border. He took a step closer before wrapping the towel around his waist. The breath Grace released was visible.

He walked past her to his locker at the other end of the bench. "I might be a minute if you want—"

"No. I'll wait."

A chorus of disembodied "Ooooohhh shit" rippled through the room. André rolled his eyes.

Sean, who had been unwrapping the tape from his shin pads, stood up and clapped André on the back. "Good luck, bud." At least he had pants on.

André shrugged him off, glancing to the side to find Country, but the bench was empty. He must've disappeared behind the wall with the others. A nervous flutter hit the back of his ribs. He hadn't done anything wrong, but he also hadn't exactly told

Country he'd gone over to Grace's unannounced. He may have led his friend to believe he was invited, which, if Grace's unannounced appearance had anything to do with that night, wouldn't go well for him.

Thankfully, she didn't say anything. André dropped his towel, giving her full view of his backside as he reached for his boxer briefs. "Did you see the game?"

Grace scoffed. "That's not why I'm here."

"That's not an answer." André pulled on his boxers and turned.

Her eyes flashed. "I saw part of it."

"You didn't want to storm down to the bench? We could've had whatever conversation you want to have there."

She crossed her arms over her chest, looking unimpressed. "Why the hell didn't you tell me?"

André frowned and pulled his T-shirt over his head. "Tell you what?"

Grace glanced around. The other guys were still filtering through. She gave him a look that said, *If you don't know the answer to that, I'm not telling you until we're alone.*

André shrugged, ignoring the slam of his heart against the back of his ribs. What could he have possibly kept from Grace that she'd be this pissed about? He wracked his brain, but the lack of obvious answers rankled. They'd just won the Tom Hart tourney, and now he had to sit here and listen to this while everyone else walked to the pub? What about his cigarette in the parking lot?

One by one, the guys grabbed their stuff and filed out. André finished dressing and packed up his gear. The smell of sweat and cedar soap clung to the air, mingling with the faintest trace of Gatorade and damp hockey tape. Laughter and shouts sounded faintly from the tunnel.

When he turned, the room was empty. Just him and Grace.

"You knew." Her voice was low.

His stomach dropped, but his mouth quipped, "You're going to have to narrow that down for me."

She didn't smile. Didn't flinch. "You came to my house, and I told you I was trying to contact the therapist on this case, and it was *your sister?* Really?" Grace threw out her hands, and her blazer split, revealing her slightly untucked blouse and the line of her pants along her hips.

Focus. His sister? That's what this was about? André cleared his throat. "Ah, no. I did not know." He stepped toward her. "I found out when I saw her name flicking across your phone screen. Maybe I should be pissed that you didn't tell me."

Grace's jaw dropped. "How the hell was I supposed to know that Elodie Shaw was your sister?"

"I told you my sister was a therapist."

She laughed out loud. "I couldn't tell what was true in that conversation! And even if I had believed you, am I supposed to assume any therapist I talk to is related to you?" She screwed up her face. "You know what? It doesn't even matter when you found out because you've known all week and you didn't say a damn word!"

"You want to drop mitts? Fine, let's drop mitts." André took a step toward her.

"Yes. Please. Let's talk in terms your jock brain will understand."

André gave a sardonic laugh. "I didn't know why she was calling you. For all I knew, you two were bosom buddies."

"I don't have bosom buddies."

"Gee, I wonder why!"

"Mm. Nice." Grace glared at him and stalked forward, planting her hands on her hips and staring up at him. "Why didn't you tell me when you found out she was working with Amey?"

He wet his lips, remembering the phone call he'd had with Elodie in his driveway that night. "Because she was pissed I was asking her about a patient."

"Well, yeah."

"So now you're mad that I was trying to get information?"

"It's not really your place—"

"Not my place? Country's one of my best friends, and he's about to lose his little girl. I find out my sister is working with the birth mother, and it's *not my place* to ask her about it?"

Grace snapped her mouth closed. She thought for a minute and lowered her voice. "It would've been more helpful if you told me since there are legal pathways—"

"As previously mentioned, you told me those weren't working. Elodie can be a stubborn shit."

"Must run in the family."

André dragged a hand through his still-damp hair. "You know what? Throw your little tantrum. I wasn't going to blindside you when there was nothing to tell."

Grace's jaw clenched. "It would be nice to *not* find out information you should know as the *lawyer* working on this case at brunch. From the woman you're supposed to be advocating for."

He nodded once. "Hm. So that's what this is about? You're pissed because you looked like an idiot in front of Jenna?"

Grace growled in frustration. "I thought—" She balled her hands into fists. "I trusted you!"

The words landed like a puck to the chest. André blinked, waiting for his lungs to inflate. "You think I'm messing with you?"

"Oh, I don't know, André. Between the half-naked flirting and the taco bribery, it's a little hard to tell what your motivations are."

That got his blood pumping. "First of all, I gave you an out in my truck, and I've been completely honest with you, in case you've forgotten. But the tacos weren't about me trying to sleep with you. I'm just as worried about Jenna, Country, and Hope as you are, and—for the record—I was worried about you, too. You walk around wound so tight, I'm waiting for you to snap, and if you don't think I'm capable of losing sleep over this, then—"

"Don't twist my words."

"You should be used to it, no?" André breathed like he'd just finished a shift on the ice.

Grace's eyes hardened. "Wow. You know what, André? You're exactly who I thought you were." She spun on her heel.

"And you're scared shitless," he snapped. She froze and turned back. "You're scared. And you don't know what to do, so you came here to take it out on me because it's easier to blame someone than admit you have zero control in this situation—"

She threw up a hand and started to turn away from him again, but André grabbed her elbow. Grace whirled and shoved him. Hard. He stumbled, his hand tightening over her arm, dragging her with him.

André hit the lockers with a metallic crash, his knees nearly buckling as the bench slammed into the tops of his calves. Grace landed against his chest with a gasp, and then—

He didn't know who moved first, but suddenly her mouth was on his, her hands moving over his chest, his neck. André wrapped her ponytail around his hand, tugging so he didn't have to reach so far.

This kiss wasn't gentle. It wasn't sweet. It was teeth and tongue, fury and frustration, rough hands, and, damn, if it wasn't perfect.

André groaned, dragging her hard against him, her curves molding to the planes of his body as her fingers tangled in his hair. He spun her, backing her into the lockers with a thud, her breath punching out in a gasp.

She tasted like toothpaste and lip gloss. Her skin was warm under his hands, her blouse as silky as it looked, her thighs pressing into his as she angled against him.

Grace moaned into his mouth and clawed at his shoulders. Her lips broke away just enough for her to pant, "This doesn't change anything."

He kissed her jaw, the pulsing line of her throat, and murmured against her skin, "Keep telling yourself that."

She yanked his head back by the hair and glared at him, breathless. "André—"

He kissed her again, wild and wrecked, like she was the only thing that had ever shut him up, shut him down, shut him off.

Grace's hands fisted the collar of his shirt, dragging him down to her mouth like she had no control left, no carefully measured words, no accusations. Just heat and breath and fury.

"You don't taste like nicotine," she murmured. "I thought you would."

"You thought about this?"

She pushed against his chest, but he only pressed her harder into the lockers, reaching under her thighs and hoisting her up to rest on his hips. She curled her legs around his waist. "Maybe." Her nails scraped the back of his neck, and he nearly lost it.

He fought with the hem of her blouse, his fingers trembling as he finally met warm skin. She was softer than whatever silky fabric she wore. He bit down lightly on her lower lip, and she sucked in a breath, her body bucking against him. He wondered if Nora from admin would have a problem with him taking Grace right there on the benches.

Grace's hands fumbled with the tie on his joggers, then froze at the sound of a door slamming open.

"Hey, have you seen my—oh damn."

Grace dropped her legs, pushing away from him and skittering to the side. André turned to find Brett standing in his coat and toque at the end of the row of lockers.

André tried to catch his breath. "Seen what, bud?" His heart thundered in his chest, blood roaring in his ears, and he was two seconds away from launching Brett into the wall.

Brett's throat bobbed. He motioned to the bench, then stalked forward and picked up his roll of hockey tape. He started to retreat, his eyes wide, but Grace peeled away from the lockers like she'd been burned. She didn't meet André's eyes as she straightened her blazer and strode toward the door. "I have to go."

"Grace—"

"No." She shook her head, already rounding the locker bank.

And then she was gone. There was a bang of the door and the echo of her boots as her footsteps faded down the hall.

André stood there, chest heaving, lips tingling, hands still shaking.

Brett's nostrils flared as André turned a murderous glare on his friend. "How the hell was I supposed to know you were still here?"

"Because I hadn't walked up the damn stairs," André growled. Brett looked between him and the door, the corner of his mouth twitching. "Don't laugh, bud. You're going to make it up to me." André grabbed his hockey bag off the bench.

"Yeah?"

He punched Brett in the shoulder a little harder than necessary. "You're going to help me quit smoking."

CHAPTER
Fifteen

TEXT CONVERSATION BETWEEN ANDRÉ AND GRACE.

SUNDAY, MARCH 2ND, 8:39 AM

ANDRÉ

> Good morning

GRACE

Now you know how to text?

> Something must've jogged my memory

If you're still pissed, that's cool. I was going to apologize

I'll allow it

Thank you, your honour

I haven't talked to my sister in two years. When I phoned her Monday and led with 'Why the hell are you calling Grace Fairbanks?' it didn't score me points

Don't know why you're complaining. Seems like you're scoring plenty of other points

So you did watch the game

It didn't occur to me that you'd need to know right away. I wanted to smooth things over. Plus, I didn't know Jenna knew. Turns out Country and Jenna have a healthy relationship and communicate. My bad

What would that be like?

Exactly

Was that supposed to be an apology? Sounded more like a defence.

I'm sorry

Also, you're just as much of a stubborn ass as I am

Don't deflect

My pride is fragile

I'm sorry things haven't been good with your sister

Mostly her fault

Obviously

I want more tacos

I want more of my hands up your shirt. So . . . we don't always get what we want

Tacos will cost you less

How about waffles?

I'm listening

Brunch Tuesday. Me, you, and Elodie

Are you serious?

Comes at a price

I know I look it, but I'm not a sex worker

Work the charity game. A couple hours of paperwork max

Done

Shit. That was easier than I thought. I should've asked for at least another bra viewing

Yeah, missed opportunity

Prepare for awkward family conversation. And don't listen to a word Elodie says about me

Does she know who I am and that I'll be there?

I figured it could be a surprise. Holding back information seems to be working well for me

I hope I get to watch her stab you with a wooden fork

Paper straw would be more her style

I like her already

CHAPTER
Sixteen

EMAIL CONVERSATION between Grace Fairbanks and Neel
Patel

From: Grace Fairbanks g.fairbanks@fairbankslaw.ca

To: Neel Patel n.patel@patellawgrp.com

Subject: Re: Petition to Revoke Consent – Amey W.

Date: Monday, March 03, 10:14 a.m.

Dear Mr. Patel,

I've received the formal petition. I've had the opportunity to thoroughly review the submitted documentation as well as the agency's records. I'd like to note that throughout the adoption process, there is no indication—written or verbal—that Ms. W was misled or pressured in any way.

Given this, I'm reaching out informally before our next filing deadline to ask: has your client expressed what specifically led to this reversal? From a procedural standpoint, we followed the process to the letter. If something changed for Ms. W after the fact, I'd like the opportunity to understand that before this becomes unnecessarily adversarial.

Best,

Grace Fairbanks
Partner, Fairbanks & Associates
g.fairbanks@fairbankslaw.ca

———

From: Neel Patel n.patel@patellawgrp.com

To: Grace Fairbanks g.fairbanks@fairbankslaw.ca

Date: Monday, March 03, 10:45 a.m.

Dear Ms. Fairbanks,

Thank you for your message. You'll note that within those documents, there is also no written indication that she received information explaining the ten day revocation window.

While I appreciate your desire to understand my client's position, I'm sure you also understand that I am not at liberty to discuss Ms. W's state of mind beyond what has been included in the petition.

If you're confident your clients followed procedure correctly, then the court will no doubt come to that conclusion.

Sincerely,

Neel Patel
Patel Law Group
n.patel@patellawgrp.com

———

From: Grace Fairbanks g.fairbanks@fairbankslaw.ca

To: Neel Patel n.patel@patellawgrp.com

Date: Wednesday, March 03, 11:09 a.m.

Mr. Patel,

I'll be candid: my preference is to avoid escalating this unnecessarily. A contested hearing will be difficult on all parties—your client included. If this is about unresolved feelings or new circumstances, I'm willing to explore alternative solutions. But I can't do that if I'm kept entirely in the dark.

This isn't a tactic. It's a genuine attempt to understand what changed. Your client signed the necessary paperwork, was provided with counseling options, and never expressed concerns during the process. Something shifted. I'd like to know what.

Would you be willing to ask Ms. W to authorize a limited disclosure? A conversation with her caseworker or support team, in confidence, could clarify whether this is a legal concern—or something better resolved through support and discussion.

Best,

Grace Fairbanks
Partner, Fairbanks & Associates
g.fairbanks@fairbankslaw.ca

———

From: Neel Patel n.patel@patellawgrp.com

To: Grace Fairbanks g.fairbanks@fairbankslaw.ca

Date: Monday, March 03, 12:17 p.m.

Ms. Fairbanks,

I understand your concerns, and I respect your desire to resolve
this amicably. That said, I must reiterate: my client is not
currently prepared to authorize disclosure of any personal
communications or counseling records.
She has asserted, in writing, that she felt undue pressure and
was not adequately informed of the implications of her consent.
If you believe that claim lacks merit, then I'm sure your clients
will be confident moving forward in court.
I will advise my client of your request, but at this time, she has
expressed no desire to engage further outside of formal
proceedings.

Best regards,

Neel Patel
Patel Law Group
n.patel@patellawgrp.com

CHAPTER
Seventeen

GRACE HADN'T EVEN STEPPED out of her car and already regretted her outfit.

The silk blouse felt like overkill. The tailored slacks, too tight? Her boots had a heel, for heaven's sake. She was going to scare Elodie off or at the very least, make her clam up.

But there was a reason she hadn't worn jeans and a T-shirt, wasn't there? Because every time André saw her like this, his eyes communicated exactly what he was thinking. She flushed thinking about him standing nude in the locker room.

She didn't think he noticed her looking. She'd fought against a magnetic pull so strong, it yanked her insides through her feet, but had definitely slipped a few glances. If she thought André leaning over her counter was seared in her memory . . .

Grace popped down the sun visor and flicked open the mirror, straightening her hair. She'd been tempted to wear it in a ponytail, but thought that would have been far too obvious. The feel of him tugging her head back—his teeth scraping her lip—

She threw the door open and closed the mirror. Her breath clouded in the frosty morning air as she stepped out of her car into the parking lot, hitting the lock button and pushing the door closed behind her.

And there he was. Leaning against his truck like he'd been sculpted into it, arms crossed over his chest, wearing a black hoodie that should've looked plain but on him was anything but.

His jeans were faded and had that worn ripple in the crotch that made her fingertips tingle. His hair was still damp from a shower, curling slightly at the ends. That felt purposeful, considering. He hadn't shaved, and her stomach absolutely did not flip at the sight of his stubble.

"Morning," he called, that crooked grin already on full display.

"If you're checking for wardrobe malfunctions, I counted all my buttons before I left the house."

He pushed off the truck with a lazy shrug. "Damn shame. I've gotten used to being flashed before coffee."

Grace lifted her chin. "So entitled."

He chuckled, slow and rich. "You're feisty this morning. Not quite as riled up as—"

"Okay, thank you." She fought the blush rising to her cheeks, hoping it looked like it was from the wind chill. "That isn't going to happen again, by the way." She said it as much to reassure herself as to set a boundary.

André sauntered forward, one hand in his pocket. He paused beside her and leaned in. "Seventy-thirty."

"What?"

"My odds of sleeping with you. They've increased."

Grace made a sound in her throat. "Your statistics are skewed."

André continued on toward the restaurant with a near hop in his step. "Where's my coat, Grace?"

She spun and jogged to catch up. "Okay, that's not fair. I keep forgetting—"

"You're not a forgetful person."

"You could've grabbed it when you left the other night! It was hanging by the door."

He reached for the cafe door and flashed a smug smile. "I noticed."

Grace rolled her eyes and stood in front of the hostess stand. The space was warm, bright with hanging plants, vintage mugs, and playlists that made you feel like you were in an indie movie. The clink of cutlery and soft morning chatter buzzed beneath the hum of the espresso machine. "I think I'm too old for this place."

André laughed. "I'd believe that if every man didn't just turn his head when you walked in." Grace gave him a look, but he only shrugged. "Don't make me take another poll." He stepped up beside her. "Elodie's a few minutes away. I told her we'd get a table."

We. The word sent a shiver down Grace's spine. Just as she was berating herself for being flattered by André even for a split second, the hostess appeared. She gathered three menus, then led them from the entryway to a booth next to the window, per Andre's request.

Grace's spine curled like a flower opening to the sun as André's hand landed on her lower back. "When you show up with your outfit all shiny and pressed, all I can think about is messing it up."

She stumbled a step. André moved past her and slid into the booth, making small talk with the hostess like he hadn't just sent her heart into a cartwheel. He was dangerous. A straight shot of adrenaline into her veins.

She sat, forcing herself to look at anything but his mouth. Or his jeans. Or his hands— *Ugh.* Grace buried her face in her menu.

"Forget your glasses?"

"Is that an old lady joke?"

He laughed. André knew precisely what he was doing to her, and if she couldn't figure out how to stop giving him the exact reaction he wanted, he wasn't going to stop. *Did she want him to stop?*

Grace blew out a breath, then ran her fingers over the smooth, laminated menu and inhaled the scent of maple syrup, toasted bread, and espresso.

André whistled, and her head shot up. She followed his gaze to see a woman with dark curls and round spectacles standing just inside the door. Her coat was buttoned to her chin.

"Did you just whistle at your sister like she's a dog?"

André grinned. "We've done it since we were kids." He stood and waved her over, but just like at the hockey game, Grace picked up on his false bravado. He was all smiles, but his fingers fidgeted, first with the hem of his sweatshirt, then with the pocket of his jeans.

Elodie wove through the tables, her mouth pinched. "André."

"El," André crooned in a "fancy-seeing-you-here" kind of way, as if they were running into each other by coincidence. He pulled her into an embrace and kissed both her cheeks.

Elodie gave him a tight smile, then glanced at Grace. "What did you do to get him to show up on time?"

André raised an eyebrow, and Grace looked away. Do not say *"accidentally showed him my bra the other day and got his hopes up."* He grinned. "Promised a man bacon."

Elodie's mouth twitched in a small smile. "You're not Kosher anymore?"

Grace's eyes widened, and André laughed out loud. "She's kidding. El, this is Grace Fairbanks. I think you've already spoken on the phone."

Elodie nodded as they shook hands. She sat beside André and unbuttoned her coat. "How do you two know each other?"

"Hockey," Grace replied just as André said, "We're dating."

Grace's eyes nearly bugged out of her head. "We are *not* dating."

"I mean, we're—"

"Not dating," she repeated.

Now Elodie was grinning. "I see you haven't changed much."

"She's a hard sell."

Elodie pulled off her coat, and as she turned her head, Grace noticed the resemblance between them. It was in their jawline, posture, and the cadence of their voices.

"Get whatever you want," André said to both women. "My treat. And before you argue—" he pointed a finger at Grace then Elodie, "it's necessary."

"So you can make good on your prior statement?" Elodie scanned the daily specials.

André grinned. "If I'm paying, it's a date."

Grace scoffed. "With your sister."

"I don't think she's opposed to threesomes."

Elodie smacked André's chest, and Grace couldn't help but like her instantly. Elodie hadn't been short or unkind with her on the phone. She just hadn't given her what she wanted. She couldn't hold that against her.

Their server approached, and Elodie promised she'd decide fast if he started with Grace. She ordered something simple— eggs, sausage, sourdough toast, and coffee with almond milk. Elodie went for a chia pot with berries and peppermint tea. André, predictably, ordered the greasiest breakfast on the menu and added a cinnamon bun on impulse.

Grace and Elodie shared a look that said *How can men get away with crap like this and look like that?* Although, if she was working out on the ice four times a week, maybe she could do bacon, sausage, and corned beef smothered in green chili, too.

That only made her think of the locker room. Which wasn't helpful.

Grace crossed her legs. "I want to be clear, I'm not here to pressure you or your patient, or question your ethics. I'm only trying to figure out what made Amey change her mind. I'm convinced the adoption followed all required procedures, even though the ten-day window wasn't officially noted, which is problematic. The social worker's notes are thorough, and there's no documented coercion or miscommunication."

Elodie exhaled. "Listen, I get it. I do. But there's not much I can do to help. You'll have to see if Amey will talk."

Grace nodded. "I've tried. Through her lawyer. Through follow-ups. I've been stonewalled at every turn. And I'm telling you, it doesn't add up. If something new triggered her decision, I want to understand it. Not to undermine her—just to be sure this is necessary." She leaned back against the padded booth. "I don't know, something feels off. Maybe I'm making it up, but I don't think I am."

Something about Elodie sitting across from her made her open up more than she'd planned. Maybe it was the thought that a therapist could see through any attempts to talk around the issues? To pretend she was seeking something she wasn't?

André's leg bounced as he leaned over the table. "I've known Country for years and Jenna since she moved back to town. They're incredible people. They've given that baby more love in the past couple of months than most people get in a lifetime." Elodie glanced up. They shared a look before she dropped her eyes back to her plate. "Amey's a single mom—"

"That doesn't mean she's going to be a bad one," Elodie interjected.

André nodded. "No, I know. You're right. I should probably shut the hell up. You two are the professionals here."

Grace stilled as he leaned back and scrubbed a hand over his jaw. Troy would never have done that. Turned a conversation over to anyone when he had a talking point. He was convinced he was the expert even when he knew nothing about the topic.

André threw an arm up over the top of the booth. Like it was the easiest thing in the world to admit he didn't know anything. His jaw was tense, though. His hand clenched.

"You didn't seem to think I was the professional the other day." Elodie's words had a bite to them.

André wet his lips, pausing before he responded. "I don't think that conversation was about Country and Jenna. And I'm sorry I waited this long to have it."

Elodie's posture tightened. She nodded once, then leaned back as their server brought water for the table and their drinks.

Prepare for awkward family conversation, and don't listen to a thing Elodie says about me. Grace couldn't help it. She was more than intrigued.

She didn't know anything about André besides the fact that he played Elite League hockey, was a smoker, and welded for a living.

That wasn't true. She knew he cared about his friends. That he apologized when he was wrong. That he lit up a room when he walked into it. That he kissed hard. And that he had excellent taste in tacos . . .

Something swooped low in her belly, leaving her fingers tingling. She reached for her coffee and the thimbles of cream.

Elodie cleared her throat. "You know I never would've—"

"I know." André dropped his arm. "I was angry. At Luc, at Dad. Since I couldn't take anything out on them, I took it out on you."

Grace took a sip of her coffee, and Elodie looked up. "Sorry, this is rude. I suggested André and I get together on our own, but he insisted—"

"This is the first time you're getting together?" Grace turned to André, her eyes flying wide.

"I told you we hadn't talked in a long time."

Grace set her cup on the saucer. "Right, but I thought you meant that was true *before* you talked. Since you absolutely would've done that before all three of us got together. If I would've known—"

"I wanted you to come."

Grace motioned to Elodie. "Well, I don't think she did."

Elodie waved her off. "No, it's fine. I just think I need to explain so we're not talking over your head. I'm assuming you know about Luc?"

Grace had another moment like the one with Jenna. Was she supposed to know about Luc?

"She doesn't know." André took a drink of water, his brow furrowed.

Elodie raised an eyebrow. "I assumed since she was working on the charity game you'd told her the whole thing—" Elodie stopped herself and turned. "Sorry, I'm talking about you like you aren't sitting across from me." She blew out a breath. "So. Luc and André were both playing Juniors—" Grace pretended to know what that was— "and Luc took a hit. His helmet flew off, his skull hit the ice." Grace winced. "He suffered a traumatic brain injury, and he's never been the same. That's why André runs these games."

Grace gave him a questioning look. She'd been under the impression that this was a one-night-only kind of thing.

André read her thoughts. "This is the first time we've done something at this scale. In the past it was basically shinny with a couple of beer leagues."

Elodie looked skeptical. "You've raised over a quarter of a million dollars in the past three years."

André shrugged. "It's not enough." He didn't say it like he was looking for validation. He was simply stating a fact.

Grace pursed her lips. "Where does Luc live now?"

"Out East." Her eyes flicked to André's. "He's in an assisted living facility."

Grace's breath left in a whoosh. It was bad, then. He couldn't live on his own. Her heart panged at the thought of watching a family member—a sibling—suffer like that.

André shifted on the bench. "He's happy as all get out. A little volatile at times. I just wish we could bring him closer."

"You know Dad would never let that happen."

"Oh." Grace lit up. "Your parents are still there?"

André's expression darkened. "Unfortunately."

Elodie was about to say something when their server arrived carrying three plates. He passed out their food then left the table. Grace stared at her eggs. She didn't have a clue what she was supposed to say.

"I'm so sorry," was the best she could come up with.

Elodie gave a small smile. "I was going to say, André's dead-set on supporting research."

André lowered his voice. "Don't say that like it's a pipe dream." Grace had the urge to reach out and hold his hand. She might've done it if he hadn't reached for his fork.

Elodie shook her head. "No, I didn't mean it like that. There's a chance with some of these new innovations that his brain could heal. I attended a CE event last fall that reviewed promising stem cell research."

André took a bite of his hash, chewed and swallowed. "My parents think we should accept that Luc's not getting better."

Elodie set her spoon down. "Well, after what happened—"

"I know. I get it." The furrow in André's brow deepened. "We tried Neurofeedback. It made his migraines so bad, he couldn't function for months."

Grace nodded. "When was this?"

"Two years ago."

Ah. The pieces snapped into place. Two years since he and Elodie had spoken. Two years since the therapy went wrong.

"The whole family hated me." André took another bite.

"Hey, that's not fair, at least not where I'm concerned." Elodie scooped up chia pudding and dropped a few berries on top. "I was never mad at you for pushing for Neurofeedback."

"Then why were you mad?" André looked up from his plate.

"Is that a real question?" André waited for her response. Elodie tried to mask her surprise. "Ah, well, I was pissed that you wouldn't get any help. You were drowning, and you treated all of my suggestions like I was hocking crystals and voodoo."

"I mean—"

"Don't." She held up a hand, and André's mouth quirked.

"You carried everything and then acted surprised when it crushed you."

André scooped more eggs onto his fork. "Or maybe I wanted it to."

The table fell silent a moment, the only sound the scrape of their cutlery against ceramic. Finally, André cleared his throat. "Hey, El?" Elodie looked up. "I'm sorry. For snapping. For everything with Luc. I didn't know how to handle it, and I definitely didn't handle it well."

Grace froze with her fork halfway to her mouth.

Elodie blinked, visibly surprised. Then she exhaled slowly and gave him a small, tight nod. "Thank you. And I'm sorry I tried to get you to howl at the moon."

André almost spit out his food.

Grace tried not to stare. André had just offered a real apology. Calm. Sincere. No smirk. No dodge. This entire conversation was messing with her head more than she wanted to admit. It took her a moment to remember why she'd come to brunch in the first place because it was weirdly starting to feel like she was . . . on a date with André .

She set down her fork with a clatter and straightened. "Thank you for sharing all of that. I just noticed the time, and I only have a few minutes left before I need to run. So. I want to be honest about this whole petition thing. I know there are limitations. I respect the boundaries of your client relationship. I'm not asking for you to break confidentiality, but if there's a way to request a release—a way to help Amey understand that you and I talking isn't a plot to keep her from her daughter?"

Elodie blew out a slow breath. "I'll talk with her. No promises. But I'll ask."

Grace nodded, relief rushing through her. Talking and asking were the best-case scenario for this morning. André's eyes met hers, and Grace looked back to her plate. She couldn't handle holding eye contact right now because André smiled like they had a secret.

She finished her breakfast, then stood to excuse herself. Elodie stood and they hovered in the dance between handshake and hug before Elodie made the decision and pulled her in, kissing the air in front of both her cheeks.

Grace stepped back to find André beside the booth, his thumb looped in his pocket. Damn it. Was she going to have to—

André reeled her in, crushing her to his chest. He leaned down and kissed both her cheeks, slower than he had with Elodie. Not just catching air.

"Um, okay." Grace stumbled back. "Thanks for breakfast. This was a wonderful . . . networking event."

"Date." André raised an eyebrow in challenge.

"Well—" Grace closed her mouth, glancing between the two of them. "I'll see you both soon." She turned on her heel and walked toward the entrance.

Outside, she dragged in a lungful of cold air, revelling at the relief against her flushed skin. She walked to her car and pulled out her phone when it dinged in her purse. It was Jenna. And Country. A group chat?

She swiped up as she hit the button on the door handle and pulled it open.

Hey friends! We know this is last minute, but we'd love for you all to join us for an important meeting tonight at Curtis's place. Bonfire, free beer and mocktails (you're welcome). Don't kill yourselves to be there, but it would mean a lot to us. XO J and C

Grace frowned, rereading the first line when a text from Jenna came in privately with the address of Curtis's house.

"Hey, Grace?" She whirled. André jogged toward her from the restaurant. He held up his phone. "Did you see this?"

Grace nodded. "Do you know what it is?"

He shook his head. "First I've heard of it." He slowed at the curb in front of her. "I didn't know if you had Curtis's address—"

"Oh, Jenna sent it."

He shoved his phone back in his pocket. "Right. Okay. I was going to offer to pick you up. If you want."

Heat flashed down the inside of Grace's thighs. She wasn't one for premonitions, and maybe it was all the talk of woo-woo therapies, but an image of her and André in the backseat of his truck hit her like a freight train.

Was she going to keep doing this? After what happened in the locker room, she obviously couldn't be trusted when her emotions were high, and that was nearly a hundred percent of the time at the moment.

She couldn't make the excuse that André was exactly like Troy, not after what she'd seen over the past few days. But that almost made her want to sprint faster. Whatever André was doing, whoever he was . . . all of it was foreign. It made no sense. It felt inconsistent and volatile. Everything she didn't need in her life right now.

Her throat tightened. "I have a meeting tonight," she lied. "I'll have to drive over after."

"Oh. Got it." He nodded, scuffing his shoe against the concrete. The motion was so boyish, her ribcage nearly caved. "Well, I'll see you there."

"Mmhmm."

"Good luck with your meeting."

"Yep." Grace dropped into the driver's seat, pretending to be busy with something so she didn't have to look up and see the expression on his face through the windshield.

CHAPTER
Eighteen

ANDRÉ

CURTIS'S BACKYARD looked like a winter Pinterest board threw up all over it. Not in a bad way. André would never admit that he knew what Pinterest was, but that was the best way to describe it.

Café bulbs glowed overhead, strung through a charming pergola. Adirondack chairs circled a blazing firepit, smoke curling up into the crisp night air. Empty planters lined the far fence, and there were still drifts of snow that hadn't melted over the past week with the Chinook. André grinned at the half-melted snowman family huddled beside the shed, looking like they'd survived chemical warfare. Barely.

André nursed a beer and let the warmth of the fire sink into his shoulders as Suraj handed him a pulled-pork sandwich stacked so high it needed engineering support. Curtis had gone full hospitality mode and ordered from Smoke Barrel BBQ, and the food was killer—brisket, mac and cheese, ribs, slaw, and cake masquerading as cornbread.

Brett was mid-rant about goalie pads when the air shifted.

André's head snapped up, and there she was. His stomach dropped through the seat.

Grace's blond hair was pulled into a loose knot, and she wore a thick knit scarf wrapped high over a navy wool coat. Her cheeks were pink from the cold.

His chest tightened, and it was difficult to draw a full breath. Somehow, in the past few weeks, his gravity had shifted. He was no longer pulled to the ice. To home. To the bar or his friends. It was as if those wires had been snipped, leaving him free floating to be pulled fully into her orbit. He was spinning faster and faster, and if he didn't do something to stop it, sooner or later, he would collide with her head-on.

Jenna popped out of nowhere, cheerful as hell, and greeted Grace with a hug, dragging her into the social vortex. Grace smiled politely and let herself be guided to the food table, where she made herself a plate as if she wasn't singlehandedly screwing with every wire in his brain.

It was then that he saw what she held folded over her arms.

His coat.

His stomach sank. No. Correction—his entire mood sank. The beer turned to ash in his mouth, his shoulders stiffened. Which was not what he needed, considering his entire body felt like it was on fire, begging for a smoke.

He felt like absolute shit. Brett told him that was a good thing, but since he'd almost bit off Mike's head for reaching around him at the cooler, he didn't trust himself coming near this whole coat situation.

What the hell game was she playing? Had their kiss in the locker room scared her that much?

To be fair, it wasn't just a kiss. It was the hottest five minutes of making out he'd ever experienced, and he hadn't been able to get it out of his head. He hadn't checked, but if he had to guess, his balls were most likely a deep shade of purple.

Grace sat down beside Kelty and Sean, and André's pulse thumped in his ears. He couldn't look away. She was all sharp angles and smooth curves, looking far too elegant for this back-yard barbecue. All of it made his mouth go dry. That coat. That scarf. Those boots. He wanted to strip her out of every carefully chosen layer until she lay under him breathless, promising him she'd only brought his coat to piss him off.

"You going to eat that sandwich or just use it to hone your grip strength?" Country asked, sliding onto the chair beside him.

André ground his teeth. Grace laughed at something Kelty said, and he tore his eyes away. "It was hot."

Country raised an eyebrow. "The meat? Bud, it's like, negative fifteen out here. I'm guessing it took about six seconds for that protein pile to approach tepid."

André grunted and took a bite. Yeah. It was cold. He looked back across the fire. Grace took a sip of hot cider. She was so dainty, taking small bites and setting her fork down while she chewed.

"Oh, sorry. Misunderstood," Country said through a mouthful of pulled pork.

"What?" André snapped.

Country swallowed. "The whole 'hot' thing. I thought you were talking about the sandwich." He nodded in Grace's direction. "Might as well knit her a sweater and call it love, eh?"

"Shut the hell up," André muttered, reaching for his beer.

Country chuckled, but André barely heard it. His coat was draped over the back of Grace's chair like it didn't mean a damn thing. The back of his neck prickled. Was she not going to look at him? Not even once? Was she engaged in that conversation or putting on a show to put him off balance?

If it was the latter, she was succeeding with flying colours. That kiss had knocked something loose in his damn chest. Sitting at the same table as her at brunch had taken every ounce of self-restraint. He'd wanted to touch her so bad, his fingers ached. That brief brush of his lips against her cheeks had only been oxygen on coals.

He clenched his jaw and took another bite of sandwich, barely tasting it. If it was the former . . .

What if she was serious? What if this wasn't a game she was playing? What if André was falling into the deep end and she'd already climbed out of the pool? Here he was with elbows up when it might not be a fight he could win.

That only made him want her more. Just as he was about to stand and try to draw in a full breath, Jenna stood and put her finger and thumb in her mouth, whistling to get their attention.

The chatter around the fire pit died down instantly, and Country crossed to stand beside his wife. "Okay," she smiled, her lip trembling a little. "We just wanted to say something to all of you. Thank you for coming on such late notice. After talking with our lawyer, it's looking more and more like we'll be going to court over Hope's adoption."

A ripple moved through the group. André's gut twisted as he glanced at Grace. Her eyes were down, focused on her plate.

Jenna didn't flinch. "We're okay. We're doing okay." She reached for Country's hand. He stepped closer, their fingers threading together like that was their natural state. "But we don't want to spend the next few weeks living in fear. We've decided —we're not focusing on the what-ifs. We want to soak up every second. Every laugh. Every cuddle. Every diaper blowout."

A few people chuckled.

Jenna continued, "You're all part of our family. You've shown up for us in ways we'll never be able to repay. And if you're able, we'd love for you to be part of this with us. However much or little you can. Just . . . be there."

André's chest felt like it was cast in cement. Country was a brother to him, and Jenna a sister. He loved these people. He'd bleed for them on and off the ice, and it cut deep to know there was nothing he could do to fix this.

Jenna reached into her coat pocket and pulled out a folded piece of paper. "We made a list. Things we want to do. Starting with the tournament this weekend in Edmonton. We want to hit West Edmonton Mall—Hope's first aquarium visit, maybe even the wave pool."

Country grinned beside her, squeezing her hand. "We'll send the whole thing to the team chat or text it to you or whatever."

A few of the guys called out support, clapping, nodding. Someone raised a drink. André's throat burned, and then his heart stuttered as Grace stood. She crossed the snow-dusted patio and wrapped her arms around Jenna, whispering something too quiet for him to hear.

And then she left.

Just like that.

Didn't look at him. Didn't say goodbye. Just left his damn coat draped on the back of the chair and rounded the side of the house.

André didn't think. He set his plate down on Country's chair beside him and stormed after her. The snow crunched under his boots, cold air biting at his face, but it did nothing to cool the fire crawling up his spine.

He barely registered the holiday lights twinkling along the edge of Curtis's garage, or the wreath on the gate. All he saw was Grace's figure disappearing down the walkway, her scarf trailing behind her.

He didn't know what he would say, and he was already berating himself for making this about anything other than Country, Jenna, and Hope, but he couldn't let her walk away. Not like this.

"Grace," he called, his voice low and sharp.

She slowed, then turned after passing through the gate. "What?"

He jogged the last few steps, exited the side yard, and stood under the golden glow of the street lamp. "You forgot something."

She frowned, glancing at her purse. "Pretty sure I didn't."

"For someone with such a strong sense of decorum, this is kind of disappointing."

Grace looked annoyed. "Look, I've got to go, so—"

"You weren't even going to hand it to me?"

She bristled, mouth tightening. "You looked busy."

He laughed. "Nope. For you to make that assumption, you would've had to at least glance my direction. Which you didn't."

Grace's eyes flicked toward the fence. "I've got a lot on my plate, André. I need to focus on work. On the lawsuit. As soon as that's finished and the building is renovated, I'm going home."

André considered this. "Home to what?"

Her eyes narrowed. "What do you mean home to what?"

"It seems like you're doing fine working remotely, so what's waiting for you there?"

She scoffed. "Friends. Family."

He shook his head. "Didn't you come out here to help Tyler's dad before he passed? Your ex?"

"Someone's been doing their research."

"Why would you do that? If you had a life you loved back home, why would you come to his rescue?"

She turned toward her car, which was parked on the curb. "I don't have to explain my relationships to you."

He followed a few steps behind. "Are you with someone right now?"

"I just told you, I need to focus on work and—"

"Then what are you going home to, Grace?"

She spun, her eyes flashing. "What are you going home to, André? Are you with someone right now?"

"I'd like to be."

"Mm. So all this—you pointing out how my life is cold and empty, how I'm uptight, a workaholic, that's your idea of flirting? Making me realize how desperate I am? Maybe this won't make sense to you until you're a bit older, but women don't typically jump into bed with you after being criticized."

He faced off with her across the hood of her car. "I'm not crit-icizing."

"Really? Then what are you doing? Are you pissed because you're not getting exactly what you want?"

André laughed. "Yes. Absolutely. You piss me off more than any other woman I've met." She started to give a curtsy, and he held up a hand. "Don't take that as a compliment. Here you are, a gorgeous woman, funny, smart, and you're so scared shitless—"

"Is that your only play? Tell me I'm scared, and I'll fall weeping into your arms?"

"No. We'd probably need tacos for that."

Grace opened her mouth, then snapped it closed and straightened, dropping her eyes as the gate behind him swung open with a creak. André shoved his hands in his pockets.

"Hey, I thought you left." Brett and Penny walked up to the curb, all smiles.

André exhaled. "Yeah, no, just talking for a second." Why the hell was Brett always showing up at the most inopportune moments?

They looked between Grace and André. Brett grabbed Penny's arm, probably seeing the rage flickering behind André's eyes. "Well, we were just heading home. Hope you both have a good night."

Brett gave him a sidelong glance which André ignored. When they were out of earshot, André rounded the hood and planted himself in front of Grace, keeping his voice low. "You can't run from everything that scares you."

She looked up, her jaw set. "And you should know? What are you going home to, André? Hmm?" When he didn't answer, she yanked on the driver's side door. "You spend your life playing hockey—working what, ten hours a week?—and holding on to teenage invincibility with every cigarette you smoke." She threw her purse in the seat. "You know, someday you're going to have to grow up, and maybe then you won't judge those of us who have."

Grace dropped onto the seat and slammed the door. André stepped back onto the curb, his blood rushing hard enough he was lightheaded. He waited until she peeled away and disappeared around the corner before storming back to the walkway, slamming his hand against the fence.

CHAPTER
Nineteen

GRACE

FRIDAY MORNING, Grace stepped outside into the crisp morning air, her boots crunching softly against the thin layer of frost that had settled overnight. The sky was pale and cloudless, the sun just starting to warm the tops of the houses, making glistening black circles on the snow-dusted roofs. Her breath curled in front of her as she pulled her coat tighter and wheeled her suitcase toward the top of the steps.

Country's truck idled in the drive. She clicked the button to drop the handle of the suitcase.

"I've got it."

Her head snapped up.

André sauntered toward her, hands in his jacket pockets, that lazy, cocky grin already curving one side of his mouth. His dark hoodie peeked out from beneath a slate-colored canvas jacket, and the wind tugged at his hair making it look deliberately tousled.

Grace froze. Her grip on the suitcase tightened. He wasn't

supposed to be here. Jenna said she and Country would pick her up.

He stopped at the base of the steps, tilting his head up to her. "You coming or planning to stand there until Hope starts kindergarten?"

Grace's heart kicked hard against her ribs. She glanced past him and realized her mistake. That truck was weathered navy, not black. "You're driving?"

André stepped forward and plucked the suitcase from her hand like it weighed nothing. "I told them you'd be thrilled." He walked toward the bed of the truck, and Grace followed, still in shock.

Inside the cab, Country sat in the back seat, a car seat between him and Jenna. Hope's fuzzy pink blanket was draped over the side, her tiny feet kicking beneath it. Jenna leaned out the window, brows lifted in apology. "Country's alternator started acting up yesterday. We didn't want to risk it on the highway. André offered to drive. Hope that's okay?"

Grace's throat went dry. It wasn't like she'd said anything to Jenna. How would they have known that spending three hours trapped in a vehicle with André sounded worse than being waterboarded?

She inhaled through her nose and forced herself to smile. "Of course. No problem."

André closed the truck bed and looked up just as she reached the passenger door. His grin was still in place, maddening and smug.

"How are you always available?" she asked.

André frowned. "What do you mean?"

"I get how Country can take time off. He has Polk and his parents at the ranch, but it doesn't feel like you ever have to work." She'd been chewing on this since brunch. Jenna said he was a welder, but she'd never seen him turn anything down for his job.

"I'm like you. I run my own business."

Grace climbed in, careful not to let her coat snag on the frame. The seat was warm from the heated cushion, and she adjusted the belt as André slid into the driver's seat. "But I can work from anywhere. Don't you have to be on location? Or in a garage or something?"

"Sometimes. But mostly in my home studio."

Studio. That sounded more artsy than she expected. Grace set her purse to her left just as André put the truck in reverse. Their fingers brushed as he lowered his arm, and she jolted, quickly folding her hands in her lap.

"I keep telling him he should open an Only Fans and he wouldn't have to work at all." Country piped up from the back.

"Right." André shot her a look. "Because of my huge dick."

Grace snorted.

"Wow. Is that how this drive is going to be?" Jenna rolled her eyes in the rearview.

"I actually enjoy what I do," André added, a slow blush on his cheeks.

"Yeah, so do I, but c'mon. You already have an audience." Country picked up a rattle from the diaper bag and waved it in front of Hope's carseat.

The truck rumbled to life, easing down the block as the sun rose higher behind them. In the back seat, Jenna and Country started talking playoff predictions.

"An audience?" Grace asked.

André waved her off and launched into hockey talk. It felt purposeful, and Grace pulled out her phone. What was he trying to hide?

"I'm telling you," Country said, "if the Leafs can keep their top line healthy, they're taking the East."

Grace played it off like she was answering emails as she typed "André Leclerc hockey" into her search bar. She angled her phone low enough to stay out of Jenna's line of sight in case she peeked over the seat.

Google spat out exactly what she expected. Elite League.

Calgary Snowballs. There were rosters, stats, a few old interviews, and photos.

She clicked *Images.*

One tap and it was all action shots. Him shouting after a goal, his face lit up like a firecracker, grin wild, helmet half off, sweat on his brow. There were team images, some from an article GCBN did for Hockey Evening in Canada.

He looked good. Grace discreetly crossed her legs.

André scoffed. "That's cute. But have you seen what Boston's been doing? They've got depth in all four lines. No chance the Leafs push through."

Jenna leaned forward slightly. "You're all dreaming. If the Oilers lock in a wild-card slot, they're dangerous. You give McDavid a sniff of the Cup, and he'll run the table."

"Only if their goaltending holds up," André shot back, tapping the steering wheel. "That crease is a mess."

Jenna groaned. "Please don't use the word crease."

Grace tuned them out and continued to scroll until an image made her freeze. Her mouth went dry. *What the hell?* It was André. In black and white. All abs and thighs, shirtless and pressed up against—was that Melanie Tress? He wore Polo's, half-covered in sheets, one arm slung around her shoulder.

Her pulse kicked like it was trying to punch through her throat. She clicked on the link and started reading, digesting each sentence like she'd been starved for a week. He played in France? Lyon? The stats meant nothing to her, but the commentary did. *All-star. Most sought after bachelor.*

No shit, he had an audience.

"What about you, Grace?" Jenna leaned forward in her seat. "Did you see the Prime Minister's speech yesterday?"

Grace fumbled her phone, then stuffed it in her coat pocket so fast she nearly gave herself carpel tunnel. "Uh—what?"

Country grunted. "Yeah. Still don't buy the energy transition plan."

Grace nodded, not quite sure what she was agreeing with.

She glanced at André, then quickly turned back to the window. All-star? Lyon? How had he never brought that up before? If he was trying to make himself look good, wouldn't that be top of the list?

She drew a deep breath, trying to recover from the mental whiplash. He was not what he seemed, but she couldn't figure out what he *was*. More importantly, why was she an absolute trainwreck when she was around him? Couldn't she just be normal?

Grace circled back on her fight with him in the street. She'd been an ass. So had he, but she had no control over that. Twice she'd typed out an apology text, but never sent it. She had communication skills. She knew how to diffuse an argument, to take the higher road. But somehow with him, everything went out the window.

She sipped from her water bottle and stared out the window as fields and frost-covered fences rolled by, tuning back into the conversation.

André shrugged. "Alberta always ends up eating it."

"Carbon tax is killing ranchers." Country shifted in his seat, holding up another toy for Hope to swipe at.

Grace perked up. "There's a constitutional challenge underway. If it succeeds, the tax authority reverts to the provinces. But they'll still have to come up with their own climate policies."

André glanced at her, eyebrow arched. Grace turned back to the window, hoping he couldn't see her blush. Jenna and Country were chatty, and their conversation filled the truck with warm, easy energy. It carried them all the way to Red Deer, until Hope started fussing in the backseat, her cries rising like a slow crescendo.

"She hates being strapped in too long," Jenna murmured, trying to soothe her with a stuffed giraffe.

Country leaned over awkwardly to reach her. "Maybe we need to change her?"

Jenna nodded. "Maybe. I'll try a bottle first."

The truck rolled on, engine humming, the heat just high enough to fog the corners of the windshield. The bottle bought them a little time, but when they reached the outskirts of the city, Hope's fussing had turned into a high-pitched, breathy cry that wouldn't settle.

"Let's pull off." Jenna's voice was tight. "Sorry."

André nodded and took the exit, merging into city traffic before pulling into a Tim Hortons off Gaetz Avenue. They all got out, Jenna carrying Hope and heading for the bathroom to use the change table.

Grace, André, and Country found a table in the corner near the window. André grabbed them each a coffee, and Country told her not to bother when she tried to pay. "He loves taking care of people."

Grace put her wallet back into her purse as André finished up at the counter. "Doesn't seem especially wise."

Country gave her a quizzical look. "What do you mean?"

She motioned between the two of them. "We're the ones with steady income. If anything, we should be paying for him."

Country's brow pinched, but before he could say anything, Jenna approached the table. "She feels warm. Like, really warm. I know we've been in the truck, but I think she might have a fever."

Country leaned in, pressing the back of his hand to Hope's forehead. "What do you want to do?"

"We should get her checked. We're going to be in Edmonton all weekend, and if it's more than a cold . . . "

André stepped up next to her, setting their coffees on the table. "She's not feeling well?"

Jenna nodded. "Might be an ear infection or something? She's been rubbing the side of her face."

They finished their food quickly, then drove to the nearby Red Deer Regional Hospital Centre's urgent care. There were only five people in the waiting room but after twenty minutes with no movement, it wasn't looking promising.

Jenna worried her lower lip. "Maybe we should just go? See if we can find something in Edmonton?"

André shook his head. "Stay. We can just go wait in the truck."

Grace swallowed hard. This wasn't about her. Jenna was obviously stressed, and it would only make the situation worse for them to be sitting there looking bored.

They walked outside and Grace settled into the passenger seat again, clutching her coffee. He turned the truck on, and the heater hummed softly as snowflakes drifted lazily down, blurring the windshield.

The quiet between them stretched, thick like taffy. Finally, André shifted in his seat, glancing sideways at her. "You mind if I crash for a bit?"

Grace shrugged, a little too quickly. "Do whatever you want."

He grinned faintly, reclined his seat slightly, and pulled his toque lower over his eyes. Within minutes, his breathing evened out.

Grace dug through her tote bag and pulled out her book. She cracked it open, the familiar scent of library pages calming her nerves. The silence in the cab now felt warmer, softer.

"What are you reading?" he murmured, not as asleep as she'd thought.

She held up the cover. It was Tessa Bailey's newest release.

He peeked out from under his hat. "Romance?"

Grace nodded once and settled back in the seat, trying to ignore his eyes still on her.

"Hmm."

She wet her lips, not able to focus on the words in front of her. After a few seconds, she lowered the book. "'Hmm', what?"

André shrugged. "I didn't say anything."

"No, you just sighed with judgement."

He turned his head. "I guess I just find it interesting. You like to read about love but not experience it?"

She barked a laugh. "Are you seriously going to comment on my love life?"

"I'm just saying." He crossed his arms over his chest and closed his eyes.

Grace fumed but couldn't think of anything to say that wasn't reminiscent of a high-school rant with her parents. She was glad she hadn't texted him an apology. *Asshole.* Yes, he had his moments, and yes, he was a damn good kisser, but she was soooo glad she hadn't fallen for any of it.

Maybe she was learning. She mentally patted herself on the back and started chapter three.

———

Hours later Grace jolted awake, blinking as she tried to orient herself. There was a tap on the window, and she turned.

Jenna. Right. They'd been at the urgent care. Grace fumbled for the window control, but André beat her to it. He lowered the glass. *What time was it?*

Jenna looked exhausted. "We're good. They gave us something to keep the fever down and to use if the diarrhea gets worse. Should be fine."

Diarrhea? Grace straightened her clothes and checked her hair. Everything seemed to be intact. She turned to find André watching her.

"What?"

He shrugged. "You're cute when you sleep."

Something pinched behind her ribs. Thankfully, Jenna and Country provided a distraction by opening the back doors and piling in, locking Hope's car seat into place. André took off his toque and ran his hand through his mussed hair.

Grace kept her eyes trained out the windshield.

. . .

———

They didn't reach Edmonton until nearly seven. André parked close to the Fantasyland Hotel's side entrance. The mall was lit up with evening lights, its giant marquee glowing over the snow-covered lot. They stepped out into the cold, hauling bags from the bed of the truck. André didn't even pretend to let her get her own bag.

Inside, the hotel lobby was hopping. Music from the late nineties pumped through the speakers and laughter echoed from the open restaurant. André and Country went to the front desk.

Grace followed, and once they'd checked in, she stepped up to the counter. "Checking in, Grace Fairbanks."

The attendant typed. Paused. Typed again. "How do you spell that?" She gave him the letters of her last name, but a moment later, he was frowning. "I'm not seeing anything."

"I booked last week." Grace opened her phone and navigated to her email. She typed in the hotel name and frowned. She tried "reservation" and "Edmonton" but got nothing. No confirmation email. "Sorry, just taking a second."

She swiped to her browser and searched through the open tabs. Maybe she'd saved the confirmation there? Forgot to have it emailed?

Spotting the Fantasyland Hotel logo, she tapped on the screen, relieved until she saw the words "Your session has timed out. Please refresh to begin a new reservation."

Her cheeks heated. Had she seriously gone through every page and not clicked book?

"Ma'am?"

Grace exhaled. "I don't think it went through." She dropped

her phone. "It's fine. I'm happy to book whatever you have now."

The attendant's fingers flew over the keys. He winced as he looked at the screen. "Unfortunately . . . it looks like we're completely full. There's a hockey tournament, the Oilers game, and an oil and gas conference this weekend." He gave an apologetic smile.

Grace's fingers stilled on the countertop. Full. Okay. That was fine. Maybe she could find another hotel close by.

Jenna was already pulling out her own phone. "There has to be something."

Grace stepped back, arms crossing tight over her chest. The lobby bustled with families and players, suitcases and duffel bags dragging behind them.

Jenna's face twisted, and she turned her screen toward Grace. "Closest thing I found is twenty minutes away. And it's only three stars."

"That's fine," Grace said quickly. "I've survived worse."

"No," Jenna said firmly, already shaking her head. "That's not acceptable. You are not going to be the only one off-site in a crappy hotel. We're supposed to be doing stuff together all weekend."

Country stepped up, resting a hand lightly on Jenna's back. "We've only got the king bed."

"Okay." Jenna started thinking aloud. "What about—Keltie and Sean? Do they have two queens?"

Country shook his head. "Even if they did, it's Sean. Do you not remember the tent debacle?"

Jenna snorted. "I heard about it." The wheels turned in her head, and Grace went down her own mental list. Tyler and Emma. Suraj and Rashi. Aelin and Ryan. *Why the hell were there so many couples?*

Jenna grabbed Country's wrist. "What about Rhonda? Didn't she say Anne wasn't able to come?"

Country scrolled on his phone. "No, she ended up coming. They texted last night."

"You guys, it's really fine. I can leave early and get over here—"

Jenna turned, her eyes glistening. "There's got to be something. I just—you know it's not going to be the same. You'll have to leave early, you won't be able to get drinks after the games. It just sucks, and—" Jenna froze, her eyes turning on André. He stood off to the side, arms crossed, waiting with her bag.

Grace's pulse fluttered under her skin. "No."

Jenna winced. "I mean . . . you *could*."

"I absolutely could not."

"It's just for two nights," Jenna said softly, her tone switching to diplomatic now. "It's not ideal, but . . . "

Not ideal was an understatement. *Not survivable* was closer. She'd barely gotten through the drive with him, and now Jenna wanted her to sleep in the same room? She couldn't even look at him without wanting to throttle him. Or . . . something.

She turned to Jenna, but all her words died on her tongue.

"Okay." Jenna's lips were tight. "No, you're right. I get it." She blinked fast, the stress, the exhaustion, the sheer hope that this weekend would be exactly right when everything else was so wrong, all evident with the tears welling in her eyes.

Grace's chest caved in. She swallowed the lump rising in her throat. "André, what kind of room did you book?"

André glanced up, doing a good job playing oblivious if he had been listening. "Two queens. Why?"

Jenna's shoulders slumped in relief. "Are you sure? I wouldn't ask—"

"It's fine," Grace repeated. "It's not a big deal." She walked toward André. "There isn't another room available right now and the closest hotel with vacancy is across town. Would it be alright if I crashed on your extra bed?"

André's lips twitched. "Sixty-forty."

Grace huffed and grabbed her bag, heading for the elevators.

CHAPTER
Twenty

Andre

HOLY SHIT. *Holy shit. Holy shit.*

André couldn't turn off the fire hose streaming those two words on repeat as he walked ahead of Grace down the lush corridor of the Fantasyland Hotel, rolling her suitcase beside his. He'd been shocked when she opted to stay in his room instead of finding another hotel.

But this was best case scenario. This wasn't his fault—she'd forgotten to make the reservation—and he didn't suggest she join him. He looked like the knight in shining armour in this situation. Unless he did something to screw it up. Which was quite likely considering he was on day three of no cigarettes and wanted to rip off the first ten layers of his skin. Or have sex. A lot of sex. Which would make him want a cigarette, so. Winning.

He tried to keep his hands from shaking as he reached out and hit the elevator button. He had to look cool. Chill. Like he wasn't thinking about the fact that she'd be brushing her teeth three feet from him while wearing something that was definitely not a pantsuit. Or that she might leave her shampoo in the shower.

What did she sleep in? He swallowed hard.

"What floor are we on?" Grace stepped into the elevator and looked at the bank of buttons.

"Three." André cleared his throat. His voice cracked like a fourteen-year-old boy.

Grace hit the button, and the doors closed. The golden lighting reflected off the overly ornate mirrors on all sides. She filled his field of view entirely, and that wasn't helping the "oh shit" situation.

Grace stood on the other side of the elevator, her arms crossed tightly. Her ponytail was slightly mussed from the long ride, her coat slung over her arm, and her lips pursed like she regretted every life choice that led her to this moment.

André shifted his weight. He was not going to stare. He was not going to—

"I can see you, you know." She caught his eyes in the mirror.

He grinned. "Wasn't hiding it."

She huffed, turning her head to hide her blush when the elevator doors opened. They entered the hall to the chemical scent of some kind of tropical air freshener.

"I can carry my bag." Grace put out a hand.

"Wow. Nice of you to offer now that we're a few metres from the door."

Her lips twitched. André turned left, following the gold-plated sign, and Grace followed him down the hall.

"I'm sorry," she murmured as they slowed in front of room 317. "I'm mad at myself, not at you."

"Very self-aware." He grinned, then tapped the key to the black box above the handle.

"You don't have to rub my face in it."

"Well—" André stopped mid-sentence. He stared at something in front of him, moving to the side as Grace crowded in next to him.

"What the . . . " Grace made a sound in her throat.

A round bed sat in the centre, framed by velvet drapes that screamed Caesar's brothel, and there was a heart-shaped jacuzzi tucked beneath faux marble columns. Cherubs adorned the wall. Real ones. Carved. Edged in gold.

André blinked. "I swear to you, I booked a standard room."

Grace held back a grin. "Sure you did."

He gave her a sidelong glance, but she pushed past him, taking in the full scope of the Roman decor. "You didn't have plans to bring someone back here?"

André rolled his eyes. "I'm here for a hockey tournament."

"Yeah, and nobody at tournaments brings puck bunnies back to their rooms?"

"First, I'm impressed you know the term puck bunny. Second, how dare you insinuate that I'm a man of such loose moral values."

Grace snorted. "Mmkay." She spun in a slow circle.

André set their bags against the wall and walked over to the jacuzzi. "If I didn't think I'd get Hep C, I might use this after our games."

"That or a yeast infection."

He grimaced. "That was over the line."

"We're roommates now. Get used to it."

Something fluttered in his chest, and his eyes narrowed. Grace stood with her arms still crossed over her chest and her jaw set. *That's* what she was doing. Setting boundaries. Making this feel as unromantic as possible. Controlling the narrative.

To hell with that.

André dragged his suitcase over to the end of the bed and opened it on the moon-shaped bench. Then he pulled his shirt over his head.

"What are you doing?" Grace snapped.

André looked over his shoulder. "We're roommates now. Get used to it."

Her nostrils flared. "There's a separate bathroom. You can change in there."

He turned toward her, running a hand over the back of his neck so his stomach crunched a bit. Just enough to show off some definition in his abs. "I've already seen you topless. I figured it was only fair."

Grace's lips drew into a tight line. She looked like she was in a self-proclaimed staring contest, right down to the eye twitch.

"You can look. I'll give you a minute." André grinned.

"Shut up." She rolled her eyes and walked to her suitcase. "I'm not going to have sex with you, so you can stop trying so hard."

"You haven't seen me try hard. Not by a long shot."

Grace ignored him, dragging her bag to the other side of the bed and opening it on the floor. She rifled through her things, grabbed two clothing items, then pulled out a toiletry bag and stalked into the bathroom.

André stared at the closed door. Now what? She hadn't said anything about the bed. He turned back, appraising it. The mattress looked large enough, but with the shape, he wasn't sure he'd be able to sleep straight without his feet hanging off the end of the bed. But if he slept diagonal, there was a chance he'd be touching her. And he hadn't brought any pajamas.

He pulled out one of his T-shirts. Grace would be pissed if he pulled the "Oh, sorry, I sleep in my underwear" excuse, even if it was true. And for the first time in a long time, he found himself caring what a woman thought. He wanted to push but not that hard.

Settling on a pair of shorts that he'd thankfully thrown in his bag last minute in case the guys went for a warm-up lifting sesh in the gym, he got dressed and dropped onto the bed. He grabbed the TV remote from the nightstand and . . . that's when he noticed the mirror.

Mounted above the bed. Same size as the mattress, actually. It covered the entire circular inset in the ceiling.

"Are you going to shower at the arena or back here in the room?" Grace exited the bathroom and padded back to her suitcase.

"I'm just wondering because the shower is glass, so I want to make sure that I take care of everything I need in there so you can have it to yourself."

"I'll probably shower at the arena."

"Okay. That makes things easy."

She laid the neatly folded clothes she'd been wearing earlier on one half of her suitcase clamshell, then straightened and put her hands on her hips. "See? You can change privately."

She wore a tight tank top and yoga pants. Her bra strap was visible, and he barely caught himself from asking whether she would sleep in that or not. Grace's all-business expression flickered as she looked at André relaxing on the bed.

André smirked. "Did you just realize that it's eight thirty? And there's no way in hell you're going to sleep right now but that means it's just me and you in this room for the next four waking hours?"

Grace scoffed. "I don't go to bed past ten thirty."

"Perfect. I love watching you sleep."

Grace's eyes widened. "Not creepy at all."

André laughed. "I'm kidding."

"Not sure you are." She walked toward the bed.

"I have to be at the rink at six thirty for practice."

"Did Sean choose that time?"

"He had to if we were going to be able to make it back for ten o'clock breakfast and shenanigans."

Grace nodded. They'd all received an itinerary from Jenna the day before. First, it was a buffet breakfast at the restaurant downstairs, then the water park, then lunch—some place he couldn't remember—followed by the seal show and aquarium.

Despite living in Alberta for a huge chunk of his adult life, André had never done any of those things. He couldn't remember the last time he'd been to a water park, and he'd be lying if he pretended that the first thought entering his head wasn't, "I'll go anywhere if I get to see Grace in a bathing suit."

"Are you coming to all of that?" he asked, turning his attention to his phone.

"Of course, I am. Why else would I be here?"

"You're such a big hockey fan, I assumed—"

"Don't be an ass."

He looked up and grinned, adjusting the pillows behind him. "Are you hungry?"

"We already had dinner."

"That's not what I asked."

Grace breathed in and held it a moment. "No."

"I saw that."

"You saw what?"

"You hesitated."

André leaned over and picked up the room service card from the nightstand.

"No. Don't—" Grace leaned across the bed and tried to snatch it from his hands, but he held it out of her reach. "I just had to think about it for a second."

"Yeah. I know what that means."

She gave up. "Right, because you know me so well."

"Yeah. I do. It's about decisions, isn't it?"

Grace blinked. "What are you talking about?"

André didn't answer, just scanned the QR code and waited for the menu to load. When the items populated, he scrolled down the list. Showing up with tacos that night had been a stroke of inspiration, because now he had the cheat code. That look on her face? It was the same one she'd had when he stood on her doorstep. And because she'd been on the verge of a mental breakdown, she hadn't been able to hide what it meant.

"I'm going to get the loaded nachos, the marinated olives and spiced nuts, and the sliders." He looked up.

Grace stood with her hands at her side. "That's a lot of food."

"Yeah. Some would say it's enough for two." He held her gaze a moment, then finished checking out. When he had the confirmation, he set his phone on the bed beside him. "Should be here in about thirty minutes."

She dropped to the bed, as far from him as humanly possible.

André lifted the remote and clicked on the TV. He flipped through the streaming options, completely tongue-tied. It wasn't often that he was speechless, but with her moving softly on the bed and his heart galloping like a racehorse, he could barely read the titles on the app icons.

"I can sign into my Netflix," Grace offered.

He clicked on the red square and it went directly to the menu with the profile "AmeliasEx" listed at the top of the screen.

"I have so many questions," Grace murmured.

André clicked on the recently watched section. The Human Centipede, Trailer Park Boys, MILF Manor, and PAW Patrol: The Movie. "Pretty sure I don't want the answers."

"Who doesn't log out of their account on a hotel TV?"

André blew out a dramatic breath. "Okay, not all of us have project management software running in our brains at all times. Some of us are just trying to remember which episode of MILF Manor we're on." The corner of her mouth turned up, and he took that as a win.

André clicked on the icon, and Grace made a noise. He grinned. "For science, Fairbanks."

She groaned and threw herself back against the pillows. "Don't pretend you haven't already watched this episode."

His grin widened. "Oh definitely. But now I want to watch you watch it." The opening credits began: dramatic music, slow-mo close-ups of middle-aged women in bikinis strutting down a tropical beach, intercut with young men oiled up and flexing.

Grace stared at the screen. "This exists? People watch this?"

"Look at the lighting. This is art." He shifted to face her.

"Someone's mom just said she wants a man with stamina. These women are advocating for themselves."

Grace gave him a sidelong glance. "Well. We don't always get what we want."

André's blood rushed south. He'd said that to her. Was it a random comment or did she remember?"

Grace adjusted the pillows and crossed her legs under her. "They overdid the slow-motion hairflips."

"How many is the right number of hair flips? In your professional opinion."

"Three. Everything's better in threes."

He grinned. "I agree."

Grace rolled her eyes as the host appeared, disturbingly enthusiastic, saying something about age being a number and explaining the potential of your son being your roommate. "Gross."

André's jaw tightened. "Please. Hammer home your disgust with younger men a little harder."

"What is that supposed to mean?"

He shrugged. "You just seem to bring it up a lot."

"No, I don't."

"Is it something with your upbringing? Daddy issues?"

Grace turned her head. "I never said I didn't like younger men, only immature ones."

André wet his lips. "Right. Sorry, I misunderstood."

"Are you really making MILF Manor about you right now?" She swivelled on the bed and leaned forward.

Elbows up. "Hey, I've never made your age a thing. That's all you."

"André, our age difference is the last reason you and I would never work."

"What's the first?"

"Uh, try the fact that we can't even sit and watch an episode of the stupidest reality show ever without getting into a fight."

"This isn't a fight. It's an inquiry."

"I don't usually interrogate my boyfriends."

André lowered the volume and turned to look at her. "What do you do with them, then?"

A knock sounded at the door. "Room service," came the muffled voice.

André stood, stretching, knowing full well his shirt lifted above his waistline. Grace's eyes snapped back to the TV. André opened the door and brought in the tray. He walked to the bed and set it down between them, then sat back in his spot. The scent of melted cheese, seasoned beef, and herbs filled the room as he lifted the first plastic lid.

André dug in. He was starving and had a morning practice plus a doubleheader tomorrow evening. He needed to eat at least six thousand calories by noon.

He watched Grace out of the corner of his eye. She didn't reach for anything, and for a moment, he wondered if he'd misjudged. He *could* finish everything on the plates in front of them himself, but he didn't especially want to. Not while she sat there and watched.

He grabbed a slider, painfully aware of every second she didn't move. But then, finally, she reached for a marinated olive and popped it into her mouth. He didn't grin. Not outwardly. But a small amount of satisfaction settled deep in his chest. Grace was like a cat—skittish, proud, and far too good at pretending not to be interested until you stopped trying.

She chewed, her back straight as a board, ankles crossed, posture all defence. Buttoned-up to the point of implosion. It made him want to rattle her. Especially when she licked her bottom lip after finally taking a bite of the nachos.

What would she look like experiencing pleasure? Would she let herself go then? Would she turn to putty? Would she talk to him or make small noises to lead him on?

"What are you looking at?" Grace asked, and André blinked.

"Uh. I thought there was a nick out of that drawer."

"Hmm. Where?"

"It was just the light from this angle, I think."

Grace nodded, picking up a slider. They watched the rest of the episode in companionable silence. Then another. And another. Eventually, André pushed off the bed, his eyes bleary. "If I don't brush my teeth, I'm going to fall asleep with jalapeño breath and wake up wondering why my mouth tastes like ass."

Grace laughed and followed him into the bathroom. The counter was long enough for them both. They stood side by side, brushing quietly, trading looks in the mirror.

André spit, took a drink straight from the tap, then moved so she could use the sink. Grace frowned and looked for a cup. When she couldn't find it, she walked out to the bedroom and returned with a glass.

André watched with amusement. When she stood, he pointed. "You have toothpaste on your lip."

"Maybe I like it that way."

"Doubtful."

Grace swiped at it with her finger, then rinsed it off, and dried her hand and face on a towel. "Who volunteers for a show like that? Those guys are so young."

"Here we go again."

She scoffed. "No, not like that. I mean, they have plenty of options. Why would they volunteer to basically be a cabana boy?"

André waited. When she stood there blinking at him, he grinned. "I think every twenty-year-old man has a secret cabana boy fantasy."

"They do not."

"And you're the expert on twenty-year-old men? Considering how gross you think they are—"

"Okay, just get out so I can pee please."

André moved past her, purposefully brushing her shoulder. She shivered, and he grinned to himself. She wanted him. She was trying so damn hard to convince herself she didn't, and he had yet to break down all the reasons for that, but her hands had been desperate in that locker room.

But what was this for him? Was he only locking in because she wouldn't give him what he wanted?

The bathroom door clicked shut, and André set their tray of empty plates out in the hall. He turned off the overhead light and flicked on the bedside lamp. Grace exited a few moments later.

She walked to her side of the bed and pulled back the sheets, then froze when she slipped in and looked up. "Oh, damn."

"Just noticed that?" André leaned back, watching her in the mirror.

"It's . . . comprehensive."

"Yeah."

Grace wet her lips. "Maybe shut off the light?"

"I sleep with the light on."

Grace looked at him like he was a serial killer.

André laughed. "Kidding." He reached out and flicked it off. They lay there in silence for a moment, the image of her lying beside him, her hair splayed on the pillow, imprinted in his mind's eye. He wasn't going to be able to sleep anytime soon, and he had to do something with the *I-need-my-hands-on-your-body* energy, or he was going to burst at the seams.

He shifted on the mattress. "Why did you go to law school?"

She was quiet for a beat, maybe longer. Then, softly, she answered, "I wanted to help people."

André turned his head toward her voice, trying to piece together her silhouette in the dark. He was tempted to make a joke but refrained. He was sure that was a real answer. The last thing he wanted to do was make her feel mocked for it. "Have you always done commercial and property law?"

She moved, her body brushing against the sheets. "No, I started in family."

"Didn't like it?"

"Too close to home."

What did that mean? "Are your parents divorced?" Every short answer felt like a hook snapping into his skin. He wanted more. Needed to know more.

She gave a small laugh. "No, they're happily married."

André waited, and when she didn't say more, he grunted. "You going to make me dig for every detail?"

"I didn't know you wanted every detail."

He swallowed hard, his heart swelling until he could barely breathe. Potential smart-ass comments filled his head, but something about lying in the pitch-black made it easier to be brave. "Maybe I do."

Her breath caught, then she said, "I was adopted. Not the kind of story you make into a Lifetime movie. My parents were amazing. Stable. Kind. But I always wondered what would've happened if I hadn't ended up with them. What if I'd gone into foster care? What if nobody had wanted me? So I thought I could make a difference there. And maybe I did, a little. But it gutted me. Every day. So I shifted focus."

André lay still, blinking up at the darkness. She swallowed at the end of her words. Her breathing came quicker.

"That's why you're doing this for Jenna and Country."

"It was supposed to be simple."

"Yeah."

Another moment of silence.

"I can't fix what's happening," she murmured. "But I can fight for them."

He visualized her face, imagined the way her brows pulled together when she got serious, the tight line of her mouth when she was trying not to show any emotion. "Well. That sucks."

"What?"

He exhaled. "Turns out you were right."

"About what?" she asked, and he heard the grin in her voice.

"That's the real reason you and I would never work."

"Oh yeah?"

"Mmhmm. You're altruistic and I'm an asshole."

She laughed. "Self-aware, at least. That's something."

He smiled, turning onto his back. He could almost convince himself he could see her move in the mirror.

"When did you start smoking?"

He scoffed. "Wow. Doubling down." She could've asked him about a hundred different things. His career for one, which he'd love an opportunity to talk about since women were always impressed. She'd never been curious about it. Slightly emasculating.

She exhaled. "No, not judging, just—"

"You can't say 'not judging' when you told me exactly how you feel about smokers."

"I said that before I knew—"

"That I didn't taste like Nicotine?" He turned back to his side, propping his head on his pillow.

"No. Before I knew . . . you."

His lungs tightened. "Hm. And that changes things?"

"Not . . . things. I—" She blew out a breath. "I answered your question."

He was so giddy and nervous that his hands were trembling. "Fair." André breathed, trying to keep his voice steady. "I started because of my brother."

"As kids?"

André nodded against his pillow. "Teenagers. Our dad smoked, so it wasn't hard to get cigarettes. Had to be careful, though. Couldn't take more than one at a time."

"Did he ever catch you?"

André's hands tensed. He thought of the scar above Luc's left eye. How he told everyone it was from dropping gloves with McGillick at provincials. "Yeah."

That old anger simmered in his gut. His father didn't give a shit that Luc had three concussions by the time he was fifteen. If he'd done something about it, that hit wouldn't have caused the damage it did.

"Daddy issues?"

André let out a sharp laugh. "You could say that."

Grace moved her legs under the sheets. André held perfectly still, wondering if any part of her would brush his skin. "So *that's* why you haven't quit."

He frowned. "Uh, not following."

"You're still smoking because it's like an eff you to your old man. He didn't like that you took his Marlboros, so now you do it whenever the hell you want."

André adjusted his arm under his pillow. "Love that you've become a therapist in the past ten minutes, but no. I don't think so." He didn't bother telling her that he hadn't smoked all week. That would only incite more questions, and the night hadn't made him quite that bold. Admitting you wanted to sleep with someone was one thing. Admitting you were making lifestyle changes? Too deep when the only date you'd been on was self-proclaimed and with your sister in attendance.

"What is it then?" Grace asked.

"I thought you'd already figured that out. I'm immature, remember? I think I'm invincible?"

She made a soft sound in her throat. "Right." She didn't sound as convinced as she had on the street in front of Curtis's house.

"You changing your mind about me, Fairbanks?"

She scoffed. "No, I just wondered what your explanation was."

"Interested in how deeply delusional I am?"

"Exactly. I need more fodder for my ongoing psycho-analysis."

His mouth curled. "Psychoanalysis? That's Freud, right? Wasn't he convinced that sexuality was key to understanding the human mind?"

Grace laughed. "His philosophies are very outdated."

"Well, how do we know that? How do we know you can learn anything about my deeply traumatized and twisted psyche unless you observe me sexually?"

She snorted. "Observe?"

"Experience. That's the technical term."

"Mm. I see Psych 101 is paying off for you."

"First time ever." He propped himself up on his elbow. "Wait, Freud thought all men wanted to sleep with their mothers. He had a term for it—"

"Oedipus complex."

André sighed. "I can't believe you, Grace. You've been setting this up all along. Shaming me for wanting you despite our age gap, suggesting we watch MILF Manor, and—"

She reached over and shoved his shoulder. "I did not suggest we watch that!"

He caught her wrist, pulling her closer. "I didn't force you to watch two hours of it."

Grace struggled, laughing herself breathless. "I was asking a question, you're the one who brought up Freud."

"You've been incepting me with these thoughts of being with an older woman, I can't believe—" He grunted as Grace's free hand dug into his ribs, trying to force him to let go.

Instead he dragged her against him and rolled, pinning her to the bed. She laughed so hard, she couldn't breathe. She tried to twist her wrists out of his grip, but her body betrayed her, and her arms went limp. "André, I can't—" She gasped, and he shifted onto his hip, taking the pressure off her ribcage. She hyperventilated, then finally succeeded in drawing a full lungful of air.

They lay there panting, their bodies pressed tight, his hands still binding hers. Grace's body was soft and pliant beneath him, no longer tense. He thought about adjusting his position a second time to keep her from noticing the response his body had to hers, but didn't.

Grace swallowed, the sound deafening in the silence. "I should—we should get some sleep."

"Mm. Exactly what I was thinking."

She let out a breathy laugh. When she tugged away from

him, he loosened his grip. But just before she rolled out from under him, he dragged his hand up the inside of her arm. Her breath caught as he leaned in closer. "Eighty-twenty."

Her breathing quickened. "See? Delusional."

He grinned. "Goodnight, Grace." Then let her go.

CHAPTER
Twenty-One

GRACE WOKE TO AN EMPTY BED. How she didn't hear André get up and get ready was beyond her—she'd slept like a rock. *I like to watch you sleep.*

She shivered and threw her legs over the side of the bed, the night before flooding her head like she'd just reached out and turned on the tap. Cool air hit her legs, and she looked down, her eyes widening. Hadn't she worn pants to bed? She scanned the floor—nothing—then threw back the sheets to find them wadded up near the bottom of the mattress. Had she kicked them off while she slept? Had André noticed?

Grace pressed her palms to her cheeks. She felt normal. Better than normal. Well-rested. Relaxed. That wouldn't be possible if he'd slipped something in her food, right?

She tapped her phone and blinked. *Nine thirty?* How had she slept until nine thirty? Shit. She stalked to the bathroom. She was supposed to be down at the restaurant at ten, which did not leave time for more than a quick rinse. Though, it wasn't like she was going to wash her hair before going to a water park anyway. Not that she planned to get it wet.

Rides weren't exactly her thing. She'd read enough stories of people losing limbs or being decapitated on water slides, she hadn't gone on one since she was sixteen.

The bathroom smelled like steam and citrus shampoo. Apparently André had showered before leaving for practice. Where he was only going to get sweaty. *Why would he need to do that?*

Her stomach tightened as she stripped off her underwear, tank top, and bra. She hated sleeping in her bra, but she wasn't going to free-boob it in the same bed as André. Especially not after what happened last night.

The heat of him, his breath on her neck. The way his thigh pressed between hers, the weight of him as he shifted above her.

He'd been hard. Fully.

She hadn't moved until he did. She hadn't dared to. Because his percentage estimate had been way off. Last night it had been closer to ninety-ten.

Grace hopped in the shower. None of this made any sense. She should have shut down last night. From the first moment she met André, she'd known he was trouble, but why was her body not locking up around him anymore?

She chewed on that as she rinsed. Troy made her feel like she'd been living with the lights dimmed her whole life, but his behaviour hadn't lined up with his words. He touted commitment and loyalty, but then he'd close down investments before his contract was up or find loopholes to shut down the purchase of an investment property after signing.

André's actions didn't line up with his words either, but in an opposite way. He played the part of a Troy Bowen, but then he picked his friends up and drove them to Edmonton, started charity games for his brother, and brought people tacos.

Why? For Troy the game was obvious. He wanted everyone to see him as a kind, compassionate man, hiding away his borderline narcissism. Why would André want people to make negative assumptions?

Grace finished washing, that image of André in black and white wearing Polo boxer briefs flickering through her memory with annoying regularity. Not helped by the fact that she'd kept the window open on her phone.

She towelled off, applied lotion, and tugged open her makeup bag, fingers darting on autopilot. Concealer. Brow pencil. Blush. Lip tint. Waterproof mascara. A natural look that wouldn't make her look ridiculous if she did end up getting wet at the pool.

She quickly applied her makeup, then walked into the bedroom in her towel and grabbed her swimsuit from her suitcase. Black, two-piece, high-cut, mid-rise. Flattering but safe. She'd picked it because it was simple. Comfortable. Something that said she wasn't there to impress anyone.

Lies.

She swallowed. She was thirty-six years old. Her abs weren't what they used to be. The skin on her thighs made her think of her grandmother's underarms.

She wasn't kidding herself, she knew she looked good. Especially for her age. But knowing that André would notice her made her wish she could've stood in front of him ten years ago.

Hadn't he already seen her half naked? *If you do that here, I'm not going to be able to stop myself from watching.*

She pursed her lips and slipped into the swimsuit, then pulled on her wide-leg pants and a breezy button-down. Easy enough to peel off later but nice enough to work for breakfast.

Grace rolled her bra and a pair of underwear into a towel, then shoved the fabric burrito into her purse. She brushed her teeth, grabbed her room key, and exited into the hall.

André and the other Snowballs players didn't make it right at ten, but they were close. They filed in and piled their plates high at the buffet. Everyone was there—the whole Snowballs team with their significant others, even some friends who Grace hadn't met yet. Emma brought two of her coworkers, and Jenna's friends Rhonda, Anne, and Tina brought a few extras.

André and Mike sat at their table. A brunette wearing a neon-pink bikini top under an off-the-shoulder sweater seemed to particularly appreciate whatever André was talking about. Not that Grace was paying particular attention.

It didn't take long for their group to eat, and then they were on their way to the water park. After walking what felt like ten miles, they arrived at the floor-to-ceiling glass windows.

"Please tell me Hope's going on rides," Curtis teased, slinging an arm around his wife's shoulders. Their four kids ran ahead, riding the escalator up and down while they waited for their parents to catch up.

"Baby slide only." Jenna gave Country a warning look. Hope kicked gleefully in her baby carrier, strapped snug against Jenna's chest. Her little feet were bare, her fists balled at her cheeks, and every time she made a sound—a gurgle, a squeal, a determined raspberry—the entire group swooned.

"She's smiling!" Rhonda cooed.

"No, she's about to poop," Suraj deadpanned from two steps back.

"Still adorable," Emma chimed, glancing over her shoulder. "Honestly, she could throw up on me and I'd thank her for the honour."

"She already has." Country grinned. "You're just immune to it now."

Grace laughed along with the others, her fingers tightening on the strap of her tote bag. She couldn't shake her nerves. Nobody here was looking at her with judgement, she knew that, but every time they gushed about Hope, it was another knife to her ribs. She didn't know what the outcome of this case was going to be, and no matter how many people told her this wasn't her fault, she still dragged that responsibility around like a sack of rocks. They might not blame her, but she would absolutely blame herself.

They stepped off the escalator and regrouped by the admissions desk. André, Sean, Tyler, Curtis, Country, Brett and the others stood in a loose pack near the entrance. André wore a charcoal-grey tank that clung to his chest and swim trunks that looked like they belonged in an Instagram ad. Grace wanted to latch onto that idea, but viewing André as vain or self-absorbed had been much easier two weeks ago.

He said something to Sean and they both laughed. It seemed to spur an entire conversation, but his eyes kept flicking over to her. Not overt. Just enough to make her stomach somersault. Grace pretended not to notice.

They paid, one by one, snapped their wristbands into place, then funneled through the changing room corridor. Grace stuck close to the women, losing herself in the chatter as the fluorescent lights gave way to the humid natural glow of the indoor waterpark.

The moment they stepped out of the changing rooms, a wave of warmth hit her. The buzz of the crowd, the squeals of children, the steady roar of water, and the smell of chlorine—all of it crashed around her like a sensory tidal wave.

Emma waved them toward a row of open lounge chairs near the tiki bar, just far enough from the splash zone. "Here's home base," she announced, already kicking off her sandals and unrolling her towel.

Grace slipped her bag off her shoulder and lay claim to a seat near the edge.

"Okay," Rhonda pulled off her cover-up to reveal a cherry-red bikini. "Who's doing margaritas with me?"

Kelty raised her hand without looking up from Hope, who was now kicking wildly in her little wrap, utterly delighted by the bright colors and sounds around them.

The guys didn't even hesitate long enough to choose a lounge chair. One by one, they dropped their towels, kicked off flip-flops, and sprinted toward the wave pool like a pack of unsupervised teenagers. Curtis shouted something indecipherable, dragging his kids with him into the waves, and Tyler launched in after him. Brett and André jogged in, earning a whistle from the lifeguard.

André held up a hand in apology, but didn't slow in the least. Grace caught herself smiling and clenching a hand to her chest at the same time. Was it pride she was feeling? Envy? There was a looseness to them, a weightlessness. They didn't seem to give a shit about whether their bodies looked right or whether their hair got wet. They were having fun. Playing. She didn't remember what that felt like.

Maybe she'd never truly experienced it. Even when she had the excuse to play, she'd been the kid hanging back. *Just watching.* Too worried about being slow playing tag on the playground, too worried about not knowing the rules, too aware of every inch of exposed skin. Even now, with a cut of suit she actually liked and legs that could run circles around her twenty-year-old self, that discomfort lingered in her ribs like a tight seam.

A low horn sounded, and Jenna tugged on her hand. "Come on. Let's dip in. Pretty sure Hope's going to be a wave junkie."

Grace pulled off her outer layer and followed to the zero-entry slope, the concrete warm under her feet until the first hint of water kissed her toes. They found a spot just past the edge, away from the stream of kids tearing toward the water, and sat. The rhythmic pulse of the waves brushed against their thighs as they planted themselves in the shallow water.

Jenna propped Hope up between her legs, steadying her tiny frame as the baby squealed and reached gleefully toward the shimmering surface. Her chubby legs kicked, her hands splashed, and every so often, she turned and beamed up at her mom like she had invented joy itself.

Her mom. *This was her mom.*

Grace's eyes burned, and she looked away until she could get a hold of herself. She sniffed and turned back with a smile. "She's fearless."

Jenna laughed. "She's going to scare the crap out of us. She already tries to launch herself out of her little tub at home."

Shouts lifted ahead of them. Country and Sean were double-teaming Tyler, trying to dunk him under the next incoming wave. André had joined Brett and Mike who were attempting to body surf, which mostly involved flailing limbs and juvenile howling.

"They're like big puppies," Jenna mused.

Grace nodded. "How are they not exhausted? All the time?"

Jenna laughed, then flinched as Hope sent water straight into her face. When Grace looked up again, André had peeled away from the group. He waded through the shallows toward them with water beading down his chest, his hair a little darker from the soak.

Grace stiffened. He stopped just short of them, towering above where they sat like some cocky sea god. He adjusted the waistband of his trunks knowing full well that his crotch was directly at her eye level.

"You look comfortable," he said.

"I was. Before you just did that."

He grinned. "Excellent. That's the spirit." Hope let out a delighted chirp, splashing both Grace and Jenna in the chest. André planted his hands on his hips. "Too bad. I was hoping I'd be the one to get you wet."

Jenna sent a wall of water his direction. "Dude! We talked about this!"

André laughed and dodged the wave of water. "You going on a slide?" His eyes locked on Grace's.

Grace's eyes narrowed. "You tell me, André. Do I seem like the kind of person who'd enjoy a waterslide?"

"Come on." He nudged her foot with his. "Live a little."

"I am living. It's delightful. Relaxing."

André looked up at the slides behind them. "Do they scare you?"

Grace's jaw tightened. "Don't even pull that out. It's your only play, and it's getting old."

André's grin widened. "Not my only play."

Jenna looked between the two of them, raising an eyebrow. Fantastic. Grace had successfully avoided questions about their shared-room situation at breakfast, but now an interrogation was definitely coming. Might as well nip it in the bud.

Grace waved the comment off. "MILF Manor doesn't count."

Jenna laughed out loud. "You watch that?"

André scoffed. "It was Grace's suggestion." Her mouth dropped open, but before she could give a rebuttal, he pointed at a white slide looping above their heads. "Dare you."

Grace stared up at him, the curve of his shoulder, the water dripping from his jawline, that maddening glint in his eyes. "I think I'm good."

He shrugged, kicking the top of the water with his foot. "Jenna, do you know if Megan likes slides?"

Grace stiffened. *Megan?*

Jenna looked over her shoulder at the brunette from breakfast. *Her name was Megan?* "Not sure, but probably. I think she plays water polo, actually."

André grinned and took a step past them, at which point a demon entered Grace's body and forced her to blurt, "Which slide is it?"

He slowed and turned back. "Does it matter? You said you aren't interested."

"I didn't say I wasn't interested, I just wasn't planning on doing rides right this second. But if you can't wait—"

"I can wait." He fought a smile. "How long do you need?"

She glanced down at Hope. "I don't know. A few minutes?"

He nodded. "Come get me when you're ready."

Grace turned back to the waves, her eyes wide. *She did not just commit to going down a water slide.*

"That was . . . something." Jenna gave her a sidelong glance.

"Mm. Yep. He's a character." Grace frowned, pretending to be worried about a kid who was trying to strap on a life vest.

"Did you—"

"Nothing happened between us," Grace snapped. "We

watched four episodes of MILF Manor and went to bed." Her gut twinged. *They didn't go to bed right away,* and why did it feel like something had most definitely happened? They hadn't kissed. Yet she couldn't get the thought of him pressed against her, his weight pressing her into the bed, out of her head. She was thinking more about not having sex with André than she'd thought about having sex with anyone else her entire life.

"Well, I'm sorry he's being weird. And about the room situation." Jenna readjusted Hope, who was leaning dangerously left, reaching for a piece of plastic floating on top of the water.

"No, it's fine. This isn't about me. This is about you and Country and Hope. I'm just glad to be here."

Jenna beamed at her. "I'm so glad you came."

Grace waited a few more moments, then when the waiting became theoretically more unbearable than the sliding, she hopped up and walked over to the chairs. Megan was perched at the edge of a lounge chair beside Rhonda, talking to André on the next chair over. Grace's ribs transformed into medieval torture devices, pinching her lungs.

"Ready!" she wheezed.

André looked up. He set down his drink and stood, not even waiting to hear the end of Megan's sentence. Heat swelled through Grace's chest as he walked toward her. Damn it. She wanted him to look at her like that. Like she was the only one in this whole water park. Like he wanted to press her up against the tiki pole and—

Grace jumped as André leaned over and his hand grazed her thigh. "Sorry." He straightened. "Don't think this is yours." He held up a sopping Band-Aid. Grace nearly dry-heaved, and André laughed out loud before dropping it in the bin. "C'mon."

He led her to the stairs, and by the time they reached the second platform, her calves were burning and the air felt ten degrees thinner.

"You okay back there?" André called over his shoulder, not even winded.

"I'm fantastic," she panted. "Really enjoying the ambiance. Love the scent of chlorine and urine in the morning."

He grinned over his shoulder. "That's better."

"What's better?"

"You were being all quiet earlier. You're better when you're pissy."

Grace's cheeks flushed and she made more of a concerted effort to not stare directly at his ass in case he turned around again. They turned a corner, and she could see the top of the structure now—a curved platform with a translucent tube coiled around it like a trap. She paused, her chest tightening.

No. Not just a tube. *A loop.* Like a rollercoaster except with *no* seatbelts. Just wet skin and gravity and what was clearly a lawsuit waiting to happen. She squinted at the sign posted at the top.

Cyclone Surge: This ride contains a near-vertical drop and full loop. Participants must weigh between 45-115 kgs and be free from the following conditions: high blood pressure, heart problems, pregnancy, spinal injuries, recent surgeries, vertigo, or general fear of death.

"Pretty sure three of those apply after climbing the stairway to heaven." Grace leaned on the railing, then thought about how many prepubescent hands had touched it and straightened.

André turned to face her. "Don't tell me you're chickening out."

Her brain scrambled for an exit strategy, but surrounded by twelve year olds who looked completely nonplussed, she struggled to land on something. "Not chickening out."

The line crept forward.

"Perfect." André shifted the waistband of his trunks.

"Can you—?" Grace turned toward the rail, looking out over the wave pool that was now just a normal swimming hole.

"Can I, what?"

Grace gave him a look. He waited. Finally, she pointed and lowered her voice, "Just stop messing with those?"

André looked down. "My shorts?"

"Yes. Your shorts." He frowned, and Grace moved closer so the entire queue couldn't hear her. "They're fine. You don't need to move them every two seconds."

André's mouth quirked. "Grace."

"What?"

He lowered his head. "If you can't stop looking at my shorts, that's a you problem."

"I'm not looking! I'm just right here and when your hand goes there, I can't help but—"

"When it goes where? Here?" André looped his thumb between his stomach and the waistband. He tugged, making a gap between his skin and the fabric.

Heat flashed up her neck, and she stepped back, nearly stumbling over the lip of the top step behind her. André's arm shot out, steadying her. She straightened and pulled away.

André turned and walked forward to keep their place in line, then turned back. "It's okay to be curious, you don't have to be embarrassed."

She shook her head. "I'm not."

"Curious? Or embarrassed?"

"Both. Neither."

André reached out, brushing a thumb over her cheek. "Then with that colour, you're extremely out of shape." Grace slapped his hand away, and he laughed. She was about to launch a rebuttal when she noticed there were only three people in front of them.

Panic set in. Her breathing quickened, her palms started to sweat. "I don't do things like this."

"What, I'm a 'thing' now?"

"Not joking," she squeaked, and his expression sobered. "I think I should go back—"

"It's safe. Look at all these kids going down." André pointed down to the bottom. "We weigh more than they do, so there's no chance of us getting stuck."

"You can get stuck?"

He pulled her against his chest. "No. Adults don't get stuck—"

"My sister got stuck—" a kid behind them started, but André held up a hand.

"Not helping right now, bud." He turned his gaze back to her. "We're not going to get stuck, and just because this feels scary doesn't mean it's not worth doing."

"You can say that because this is fun for you. Since when do you do anything hard?"

He gave her a look. "You think I don't do anything that's scary or hard?"

She shook her head. "Everything is so easy for you! You don't give a shit!"

"I give a shit."

"No shits. None."

André gave an apologetic look to the mom with her son on the steps behind them. "Give me something you think is hard. I'll do it when we get down."

Grace shook her head. "It can't be hard for me, it has to be hard for you."

"Got it. Uh . . . I could do a hundred push-ups."

Grace rolled her eyes. "You'd love that."

"Yeah. Fair."

"It has to be something you hate, like you need to order straight vegetables for lunch or—" Grace sucked in a breath. "Quit smoking." André blinked, and she slapped a hand against his chest. "Quit smoking. That's it. If I go down this slide, you have to quit—"

André laughed "For how long? This slide takes less than ten seconds."

"Nope, the time isn't the point. I don't want to get anywhere near this death trap, and you don't want to quit. Same, same."

"Is this how you make your arguments in court because—"

He didn't finish that sentence because a teenager with a blue shirt and whistle approached. "Sir? It's your turn."

André shook his head. "Nope. She's next." He planted his hands on Grace's shoulders and edged her forward.

She squinted at him and hissed, "What kind of sick bastard tricks a woman into a vertical drop with a loop?"

"I pointed at the slide!"

"I didn't see the *loop*! I don't trust centrifugal force this much!"

He leaned in slightly, his grin devilish. "It's called *living*, Grace. Also, there's a camera mid-loop. Not as good as the mirror, but it will have to do."

Her eyes widened.

"Miss?" The teenager exhaled, motioning to the death canister.

Her palms were sweating. "I'm going to die."

André tilted his head. "I'll make sure your things get home safe. Except that black bra. I'm keeping that."

"Can you shut the hell up?" She clenched her hands into fists, her heels digging into the grippy rubber mat. The lifeguard opened the door and gave her a politely blank expression. Grace turned back. "Do we have a deal?"

André smirked. "Absolutely."

Grace's lips parted. Absolutely? She was expecting at least a little push back. Definitely some balking. Something she could latch onto and use as an excuse to wait another couple of people and hopefully work her way back down the stairs. "You're going to quit?"

André nodded. "Yep. As soon as you make it to the bottom."

The employee gave another sigh. "Miss, if you're not going to—"

She stepped inside the tube, the trapdoor glinting beneath her feet.

No, no, no! Her mind screamed, but she couldn't force her legs to move in the opposite direction. If she didn't go on this damn slide, Megan would, and while she wasn't into comparison typically, the idea of André standing with her on the stairs and giving her a peek of his pubic bone made her want to stab someone with a fork.

"Arms crossed, ankles crossed." The employee pointed at an illustrated sign.

She got into position, her heart slamming against her ribs. What the hell was she doing? The door was shut. She was standing over a moving floor! Her head started to spin, and she searched for André through the scratched plastic.

He gave her two thumbs-up, and a robotic voice started counting.

CHAPTER
Twenty~Two

GRACE

THREE.

Grace couldn't breathe. Couldn't move. Her brain screamed that this was a mistake, that she could still bang on the walls and beg to be let out.

Two.

She looked at André one last time. He mimed smoking a cigarette, then crushed it under his heel and winked.

One.

· · ·

The floor dropped out from under her.

Her stomach followed.

She wasn't sliding—she was falling, vertical, head back, water whipping up around her as the tube screamed past her ears. The air disappeared, sucked out in the first second as gravity grabbed her by the ribs and flung her through the loop.

Her scream was swallowed whole. For a second, she thought she was upside down, then she was dropping again, and then her swimsuit was shoved so far into her butt crack, she wondered if it had been torn off.

She shot out the tube into the landing pool, water exploding up around her in a geyser. The world came back in pieces—chlorine in her nose, slick hair plastered to her face, lungs dragging in oxygen like it was dessert.

She blinked, coughing. And then a rush of adrenaline hit her so hard, she started to laugh. Wild, shocked, breathless laughter bubbling up until she was doubled over in the pool, completely soaked, completely unglued.

"Miss, please exit the pool." Another employee motioned for her to stand and walk forward. She forced herself up on shaky legs, extricated her bikini bottom, and stood on the concrete, her arms wrapped around herself.

The slide wobbled and then—*whoosh*. André came firing out of the slide like a torpedo, water spraying in every direction as he hit the landing pool. His long body arched up through the surface, every lean, soaked muscle on full display as he pushed himself up and adjusted his damn shorts.

They rode low on his hips as he reached back and raked a hand through his hair, grinning at her like a lunatic.

Grace's brain short-circuited. "I did it!"

"I know!" He jogged forward.

"Sir, no running—"

André yanked her up from the step, one hand sliding from her waist to wrap solidly around the backs of her thighs.

Grace couldn't stop laughing. "I didn't die."

"Not even a little."

"I didn't get stuck."

André spun her in a circle, then lowered her slowly to the pool. "You should probably listen to me more often."

Grace's hands slid over his slick skin, the heat from his body seeping into hers.

André blinked, heavy lidded. "Looks like I got you wet after all."

"Ah, sir, I need you both to exit the—"

"Yeah, yeah. I get it," André snapped, pulling Grace up the step with him. She stepped away from him, lifting her arms to pull out her hair tie and redo her bun. Her heart was still sprinting. Her skin tingling.

Shaky, soaked, and half-certain she left a piece of her soul back at the top of the launch tube, she caught sight of herself reflected in the mirrored edge of a smoothie stand. Hair clinging to her cheeks, eyes bright, lips pink with exertion.

She stopped, staring. Who was that person? She looked . . . hot. Exciting. Fun. *Happy.*

André grabbed her elbow and led her around the kids' play area. She reached the chair beside Jenna's and sank down onto the towel.

Jenna raised a brow. "Umm . . . you look pleased with yourself."

André struck a pose in front of the group. "I popped Grace's Cyclone cherry."

"Ew! Gross!" Emma threw a towel at him, and the guys laughed as he used it to floss between his legs. When he was finished, he tossed it at Grace and winked.

She rolled her eyes and threw it onto an empty chair.

The morning and early afternoon melted into snapshots. Laughter. Food and drinks. Sunshine filtered through the skylights.

Grace couldn't remember the last time she'd laughed so much—real, full-body, *ridiculous* laughter. Emma dared Rhonda to go on the double tube slide backwards. Brett and Curtis made a sport out of cannonballing as close to Tyler as possible without getting caught by the lifeguards. Country somehow convinced one of the teenage employees to let him and Hope go down the tiny frog slide in the toddler area—twice—while Jenna stood at the edge shouting, "Gentry, she's *barely* sitting up!" and "Her neck is still *developing*! Stop throwing her like she's a football!"

Hope squealed with glee every single time.

Grace nursed a frozen cocktail with a little umbrella in it, warm from the sun and from the people around her, trying to pretend she wasn't aware of every time André threw her a look.

Because he did.

Often.

Even when Megan drifted over to him. Laughing too hard at his jokes. Reapplying lip gloss like it was prescribed.

Grace hated that she noticed. Then again, she noticed *everything* that afternoon. It was like her near death experience had transported her to a more vibrant version of reality.

She noticed Kelty sitting stiffly at the edge of the lounger, watching Sean laugh with Tyler and Suraj but never moving to join him. Penny rubbed Brett's shoulders, whispering something that made him blush. Rhonda didn't leave her phone for more than a few minutes, grinning every time her fingers tapped over the screen. And Emma didn't seem to be drinking. Interesting.

Grace stirred the straw in her drink, letting the crushed ice melt a little before taking another sip. With only ten minutes left before they needed to pack up and go, she slid her phone from the pocket of her bag and tapped it awake.

She scrolled through her messages, stopping on one that made her heart stop. Elodie.

I'm so sorry, but it's a no go. Amey declined to sign the release. If you want more details, we can talk later—but this means you're preparing for court.

Grace didn't move. Her thumb hovered over the screen, the words burning into her like acid. She read it again. And again. The background noise of the waterpark faded into a cottony buzz.

Amey wasn't going to talk. Wasn't going to clarify what had changed. Wasn't going to give them anything that might stop this before it became a full-blown legal battle.

Court.

Her chest tightened.

"You okay?" Jenna's voice broke gently through the noise.

Grace didn't look up at first. Then she passed her phone over. Jenna scanned the message and handed it back. Her mouth tugged into something that wasn't quite a smile, but wasn't panic either.

Grace blinked. "You're not freaking out right now?"

Jenna set the phone down on the edge of her lounge chair and shrugged, her gaze drifting toward the wave pool where Country was relaxing with Hope in a yellow float shaped like a duck. "Kind of got that out of my system already."

Grace sat up straighter. "Is that something you get out of your system?"

She shrugged. "Maybe?"

"We're going to court."

Jenna sighed. "Yeah."

Grace dropped her phone into her bag. "I should've done more. Found another angle. Talked to Elodie sooner. I was so sure I could control this if I just—"

"That's the thing." Jenna turned toward her. "You can't. I

used to believe the same thing. That if I just worked hard enough, worried hard enough, ran all the scenarios—maybe I could stop bad things from happening. Maybe I could keep myself and those I loved from hurting."

Grace's throat tightened. "And?"

"And I lost ten good years trying." Jenna smiled faintly, watching Country paddle their float around in circles. "I was so scared of losing him that I never really let myself *have* him. And now?" She looked back at Grace. "I'm done living like that. I don't need to add pain to pain. I don't need to create pain out of nothing. If we lose Hope, we lose Hope. But I'm not going to miss the time I have with her now just because I'm scared."

Grace sat very still. There was that word again. "I wanted to protect you from this."

Jenna put a hand over hers. "I know. But you can't. And that's okay."

They sat there for a long moment. Then Jenna gave a gentle squeeze. "I'm going to go float with Country. Last chance."

Grace nodded and watched her friend walk barefoot toward the pool, her laughter rising as she strode toward the man she loved and the daughter they might not get to keep.

CHAPTER
Twenty-Three

ANDRÉ

THEY WERE TIED. Five-five. Third period, under a minute to go.

André's lungs burned even though he hadn't smoked for a week. His thighs were on fire, though that could've been because of the impromptu game of mini sticks they played in the hotel hallway after the water park.

He was too old for doubleheaders, they all were, but not one of them said a damn word of complaint. They'd earned a bye in the morning with their season record, then won their first game two to one in overtime. Now, the crowd inside the small Edmonton arena sounded like they'd been chugging gas station energy drinks and screaming into a blender.

Every guy on the Snowballs' bench gripped their stick like it owed them a safe word. The team from Winnipeg, Prairie Fire—which sounded more like a hot sauce than a hockey team—was fast. Chippy. Their first line had two guys fresh out of juniors, and damn if they weren't skating like the scouts were in the stands.

André wiped his glove across his face, shoving his helmet back down over his sweat-slicked hair. His jersey clung to his ribs. His mouthguard tasted like bile and Gatorade.

He loved this shit.

"C'mon boys. Play from your balls," Sean snapped.

André slapped Country's shoulder. "It's okay, I can lend you mine."

They both jumped over the boards and set up in Winnipeg's zone fast—Curtis digging into the corner, Country screening low, André circled high, hunting.

The puck bounced off a bad deflection. Winnipeg's D whiffed it. Just a split-second of chaos, a messy half-second where everyone shifted wrong, and André saw his shot.

He jumped on it. Cut inside. Dragged it left. One defender bit hard. André pulled it through his skates like Zegras, kicked it up, and flipped it backdoor. Tyler's slap was the sexiest thing he'd ever seen.

Buzzed past the tower.

Bar down.

Game.

The Snowballs's bench erupted. André didn't even hear the buzzer, only Sean's string of curses, Curtis's screaming, and Boyd howling from the crease.

Country tackled him into the glass. "That shit was pretty, Leclerc!"

André threw his gloves, tossed his helmet. The team mobbed him and Tyler in the corner. He skated the victory lap with his jersey flapping loose, adrenaline buzzing so hard it felt like his veins were plugged into the scoreboard.

Snowballs: 6

Prairie Fire: 5

Tournament Champs.

"Making me look good out there, bud." Tyler pulled him into a hug.

"Someone has to." He smacked him on the back, and they made their way to the bench. Before he sat, André looked up into the stands and found her. Scarf. Navy coat. Grace stood cheering with the others, her hands cupped around her mouth.

"Seems like she's into hockey all of a sudden." Tyler grinned. "Lock that down, Leclerc, or get the hell away from her."

———

André's legs were buckets of cement by the time he made it back to the Fantasyland Hotel. Every muscle ached. His ears were still ringing. He'd downed half a protein bar on the ride back and had a Gatorade sloshing somewhere near his spleen. The boys were heading for the hotel bar to "rehydrate," which was a generous word for whatever the hell Suraj was ordering.

They'd pushed for him to stay, but he'd begged off muttering something about indigestion. He hadn't told them the real reasons. One who was currently—hopefully—on the other side of his hotel room door. The second sitting in the pocket of his hockey bag.

He'd found the pack of cigarettes there while searching for his tape. Didn't realize he'd left one in there when he purged everything the week prior. If he stayed at the bar, he wasn't going to make it. He'd grab one and take it outside within fifteen minutes. But if he went upstairs, even saw her face, he thought he could get through. The strategy had worked twice already.

Grace hadn't been at the bar, which wasn't a surprise, considering. He doubted he'd catch her awake. The ceremony had run late, and it was nearly midnight. But some dumbass part of himself couldn't stop imagining tapping the key at the door and stepping inside to find her reading in bed, hair messy from her pillow, her lips parting as she turned her head.

But, nope.

He opened the door to total darkness. Quiet.

He turned on his phone flashlight and carefully set his bag in front of the door, locking the dead bolt. André padded toward the bed.

Grace was out cold. She lay curled on her side, blankets tangled around her legs, one arm draped over the pillow like she was holding it hostage. That soft little crease between her brows barely relaxed, even in sleep.

He swallowed hard, then tiptoed into the bathroom, took a piss, washed his hands, and brushed his teeth. He moved back into the bedroom and stripped off his joggers. Grace wasn't watching. What she didn't know wouldn't hurt her.

He clicked off his flashlight, plugged in his phone, and slid under the covers. Just as he exhaled, sinking into the mattress, she shifted.

He froze.

Grace moved again, her leg brushing against his. André went still as stone. Was she awake? Moving in her sleep?

He moved, resting his arm in a defencible position that also happened to cross the midline of the bed. Grace drew in a breath and changed position, her hand landing directly beside his.

Every hair on his body lifted. He wasn't going to do anything. He wouldn't touch her, not if she didn't say something. If she didn't—

Grace's fingers twitched against his, and then her pinky lifted. She brushed it over his knuckle, then curled it around his.

André struggled to breathe, any exhaustion he'd felt seconds before completely obliterated. He was wide awake. Buzzing. His blood pumping so hard, he couldn't hear himself think.

He traced his thumb over her palm and pressed against her wrist. Her breath caught. She uncurled her finger and slid her hand into his, palm to palm.

André rolled onto his side, and the heat from her body reached him before he touched her. His fingers trailed up her arm, grazing along the dip of her elbow, the curve of her shoulder. He swore he could feel her heartbeat in the tips of his fingers. Or maybe that was his. Hard to tell.

Grace shifted closer. Her thigh brushed his under the blankets, and his pulse jackknifed. She felt bare. Warm and soft. Her hand slipped behind the hem of his shirt, fingers spreading over his ribs and pausing, then tracing, mapping.

The silence between them buzzed. Electric. Holy. His palm found the dip of her waist, then followed the soft rise of her hip, thumb dragging beneath the elastic of her shorts. She gasped, a small sound, but he felt it all the way down to the base of his spine. She smelled like vanilla and something faintly floral. He wanted to bathe in it. To drink it.

Grace's hand moved to his chest, then trailed down his stomach, slow and deliberate. He flinched when her pinky grazed the edge of his waistband. His stomach clenched. His breath hitched. She didn't go farther, just let her hand rest there. A question.

André didn't answer. He couldn't. He didn't trust his voice. Instead, he slid his hand up to her collarbone and followed it to her throat, gently brushing her pulse point with his thumb. Her skin was silk, flushed, alive beneath his touch.

He pressed in another inch, and her lips were so close he could feel the shape of them in the dark. Her breath mingled with his, and he stilled, not sure where to go next. He knew where he wanted to go, but her hand held him like a tether.

Just like the first time, he didn't know who moved first, but the kiss was featherlight. A brush. A thousand volts right through his bloodstream.

Grace paused, then dragged her lower lip over his, her hand tensing at his waistband. He was going to split at the seams. Then she deepened the kiss, her hand dragging over his stomach, tugging at his shirt while her other hand looped around his back, tangling in his hair, nails skimming his scalp. His body damn near folded in on itself from the heat of it.

She kissed like she argued. Zero to a hundred. Intentional, relentless, and with a wild, focused control that made his head spin.

He grabbed her hips and brought her body flush against his. Warm. Nearly bare. Her chest was soft against his. *No bra.* He wrapped an arm around her waist and pulled her on top of him, groaning into her mouth as she straddled his hips.

Every slow grind made his vision blur. Her heart raced against his chest, and his hands roamed. They slid up under her shirt, over her back, memorizing every dip of her spine. Every shiver he caused. Her thighs tightened around his hips, and he was drowning, completely undone, unravelling in the dark.

André kissed her harder. Every flick of her tongue and sigh into his mouth driving him out of his *damn mind.*

His hand slowed at her waist, his breath catching. Was she fully awake? Had she gotten a drink with the girls before coming up to bed? *Was this really what she wanted?*

He pulled back, just barely, mouth brushing hers. "You with me?" he whispered, throat raw.

Grace exhaled, her forehead pressing to his. "Yes."

"You sure?" he asked, voice low and strained, every inch of him fighting his body for control. "Because I don't—"

"You were right," she whispered. "I don't know how to let go. I want to let go."

That hit like a knife between his ribs. Not what he wanted to hear. This wasn't about him. Grace wanted a release. She felt safe enough with him to try, so that was something. But was it enough for him?

He pressed a kiss to her cheek, knowing full-well he wouldn't deny her. "I can help with that."

She kissed him again, her fingers slipping under the hem of his shirt, trailing fire across his stomach, and that was it—his restraint snapped like a twig under a boot.

His hands skimmed her thighs, her hips, her ribs, until he was tugging the shirt over her head and tossing it somewhere into the dark. Her skin was soft and flushed, goosebumps blooming everywhere he touched.

Their mouths crashed together, frantic now, messy and open and starving.

She pulled his shirt off in return, her hands exploring like she was memorizing muscle and bone, fingers curling against his shoulder blades as she gasped into his mouth.

He rolled, hovering, pressing a kiss to her throat, to her collarbone, to the delicate line beneath her ear.

"André," she murmured, and his lungs struggled for air.

Their limbs tangled beneath the sheets, hot and slick. Her fingers found the waistband of his boxers, and that time, she didn't stop. He fumbled with the edge of her shorts, his mind going blissfully blank.

André sucked in a breath, closed his eyes, and tumbled with her over the edge.

CHAPTER

Twenty~Four

Grace

THE NEXT MORNING, Grace stared straight ahead, hands folded tight in her lap. The truck hummed along the highway, snow swirling in lazy gusts past the windshield, the wipers thumping in a steady rhythm. The inside smelled like Hope's baby wipes, Jenna's morning coffee, and *him*.

She couldn't get a single second from the night before out of her head. The feel of him in the dark. The sound of his voice murmuring against her ear. *You with me?*

Oh, she'd been with him.

Twice.

Then Grace woke up early and escaped to the breakfast buffet before he stirred. Not that she was embarrassed, she just didn't know what to say. Had she been thinking clearly the night before? Yes. And no.

All of it had been exactly what she wanted in the moment, but in the light of day, her mind spiralled out of control. What now? Was he going to move on now that he got what he wanted? Was he going to want to do it again? She sure as hell did, and that's what scared her the most.

Now André sat two feet away, his hand—the hand that had explored every inch of her body—resting on his thigh.

Jenna and Country chatted in the backseat, soft and easy. Hope gurgled between them in her carseat.

Grace couldn't breathe. *They'd slept together.* He hadn't pushed, not in the least. If anything, she'd been the instigator. She'd gone to bed without a bra knowing full-well what that meant. She'd reached her hand to his, touched him first.

Right that second she wanted to reach over and run her fingers down the vein in his forearm. She pressed her nails into her palm instead.

What was in his head? She'd been clear, hadn't she? André had been the one to suggest they make things *fun*. She'd only taken him up on his offer.

But that didn't explain why he hadn't looked her way once since they got in the truck. Was he pissed she'd left that morning? Had he expected them to wake up and cuddle?

The silence between them crackled while the miles ticked by. Endless highway. A straight shot south to Calgary. Country was mid-story about a player busted for vaping in the locker room at the tournament when he leaned forward and patted the back of André's seat.

"Hey, proud of you, man. What's this now? Nine days? Ten?"

André made a noise low in his throat, one corner of his mouth twitching. "Eight. But who's counting?"

Grace blinked. "Counting what?"

André didn't look at her.

"Nicotine." Country grinned. "This guy's off it. First time in years."

Grace's head whipped around so fast her hair slapped her cheek. She stared at him. "Wait. What?"

André kept his gaze on the road.

Jenna leaned forward. "You didn't mention that?"

"No. He did not." Grace folded her arms over her chest.

Jenna looked between the two of them. "Kay, I'm a bit confused. Weren't you saying how you didn't like kissing smokers?" She turned to André. "I assumed you'd text her first thing, considering."

"Considering what?" Grace looked over her shoulder, and Jenna winced.

"Brett might've told everyone about the locker room?"

Grace groaned, and Country blew out a breath. "Bud, I'm sorry. Didn't realize you were keeping that close to the chest."

"Extremely close, apparently," Grace muttered.

André shifted his hands on the wheel. "I told you I would quit."

"Yeah. You pretended you'd quit in exchange for me going on the waterslide. We made a deal."

"And I'm sticking to that deal."

Grace swivelled in her seat. "It doesn't count! You already started quitting—"

"Your argument was that I didn't do things that are hard for me. It doesn't matter when I started, this is hard. Still an equal exchange, and you loved that slide—"

"I didn't love it!"

"You looked like a completely different person at the bottom! Happy, loose—"

"So I don't look happy normally?"

André growled in frustration. Grace pushed back against the seat, turning her head to look out the window. Pressure built behind her eyes as his words sank in. *A different person?* That was why she always found herself sucked into stupid arguments with him. He knew exactly how to push her buttons.

No, it didn't matter when he started, and yes, she was happy to hear it. But it wasn't even about the damn slide. They'd lain in the dark talking that first night and she'd asked him about smoking. He told her about his brother—they'd had a real conversation. Why wouldn't he have said something about quitting? It would have been the natural thing to do, which meant he'd purposefully kept it from her. And *then* made her believe it was an equal trade.

"Maybe it was time to grow up." André's voice was low, each word clipped.

Grace's heart stuttered. That was what she'd said to him, wasn't it? Outside Curtis's house. She'd thrown it like a dart and meant it to stick, to draw blood.

Grace clenched her jaw, fingers tightening on the seat belt strap. She was such a hypocrite. She was lashing out at him for not spilling all his secrets when she'd kept all of her own. She mocked him for the way he played, for being silly, easy, light, when her world felt so heavy. But yesterday she'd watched him launch himself into the wave pool and make his teammates laugh until they cried.

She'd felt like a different person. She liked what André pulled out of her in every way.

Tears stung the corners of her eyes. She didn't want him to grow up. But she didn't know how to say any of it.

The silence in the truck wasn't uncomfortable. It was excruciating. She'd hurt him, she fully realized that now. When it started, she didn't know. At that first game? At Curtis's? Last night?

She was a terrible person. Her stomach knotted, her throat so tight, she didn't dare try to join Country and Jenna's conversation, their obvious attempt to cut the suffocating tension.

At least André got what he wanted.

That thought hit like a slap, cold and cruel. Was that all he wanted? The chase. The tension. The pull.

No. She knew it instantly. If that were the case, he'd be on cloud nine right now. Cocky and relaxed. André was anything but.

This wasn't just sex. This wasn't casual. And pretending it was would only dig those darts deeper.

Jenna dozed with her head tilted toward the window, Hope sleeping soundly in her car seat between them. Country scrolled through playlists and offered up a running commentary about the Oilers' odds for a deep playoff run if McDavid's linemates could get their shit together.

André responded in monosyllables.

Grace said nothing. She sat still, legs crossed at the ankle. When they pulled onto her street, her chest tightened with every passing house.

André turned onto her drive with mechanical precision, braked with calm indifference, and didn't even glance her way as he threw it into park.

"I'll grab your bag." His voice was still low and clipped.

She hesitated. "Thanks."

The back door opened. Country murmured something she didn't catch. Jenna gave her a small smile, but none of them had the words to address this.

André didn't meet her eyes as he dropped the suitcase on the step. No cheek kiss. No hug. No smart-ass comment. No offer to carry it inside.

He turned back to the truck, and Grace's heart crunched like a Christmas ornament under a boot.

"See you," he said under his breath.

"Yeah," she murmured. "See you."

The taillights flared red as he backed out. She stood motionless as the truck rolled down the street, turned the corner, and disappeared.

Grace dragged her suitcase up the last step. Fumbled with her keys. The lock turned with a click, and the door opened into the familiar hush of her temporary Calgary life.

She stepped inside.

It smelled like lemon cleaner and wood polish. The heating

had kicked on sometime before they arrived. The radiator ticked quietly beneath the window.

She dropped her bag. Kicked off her shoes. The door shut behind her, and she leaned her back against it. For a long moment, she just breathed as one voice echoed in her head.

What are you going home to?

CHAPTER
Twenty-Five

ANDRÉ

ANDRÉ WELDED THE FINAL CORNER, sparks spitting like fireworks against the sheet metal floor, the acrid tang of burning steel clinging to his tongue. He didn't flinch anymore. Not from the heat. Not from the sound.

But today he was distracted. His bead line wobbled slightly, just enough to piss him off. He stopped, leaned back, and yanked his welding helmet up, blinking through the sweat slicking his temples.

The gate was a beast. Seven feet wide. Arching across the top in a precise curve that took two full hours of coaxing out of the raw stock, not to mention the forged embellishments—a scrollwork of vines and thistles that his client wanted to match the crest on their summer property. He'd already spent sixteen hours on the damned thing. Should've taken ten.

He should've been proud of it. It was clean work. Elegant. A little gaudy, if he was being honest. But he couldn't feel any sense of accomplishment.

His body was finally starting to regulate, not feeling quite so desperate from nicotine withdrawals, but Grace was in his head like a fever. He didn't know which was worse.

Because after all his fantasizing, now he knew what she tasted like. What she sounded like when he pulled her out of her head. What she looked like beneath him, around him, on top of him.

It had been two days since they drove home Sunday morning. It felt like six months.

He reached for the shop towel slung over the edge of the bench and wiped the sweat from the back of his neck, glancing toward the office door where his laptop sat open. A new commission had come in that morning. A big one. A hand-forged balcony railing for a restored heritage house in Banff. The kind of project he used to dream about.

He felt nothing.

Pathetic.

He tossed the rag onto the bench and went back to the gate, running a gloved hand over the metal scrolls, checking for snags. The detail work was tight. He'd used a new radius bender for the curves, set the vines to wrap through the vertical bars in a perfectly asymmetrical pattern.

It was beautiful. So why did he feel like throwing a wrench through the wall?

There wasn't a damn thing he could do about any of it, so he went back to work, blasting Counting Crows high enough, he hoped a neighbor showed up to complain.

André locked up the workshop as the last swipe of orange glowed on the horizon. The tools were wiped down, clamps stacked, workbench swept. The gate leaned against the far wall, perfect and gleaming under the fluorescents, but even that little rush of satisfaction didn't stick.

He showered fast, scrubbing off the day with scalding water and charcoal soap, then threw on jeans and a Henley, grabbed a six-pack from the fridge, and hit the road for Country's place. The farmhouse looked like a Norman Rockwell painting. The wraparound porch was lit with strings of warm bulbs, and laughter already rolled out beneath the front door. Inside, the place smelled like pizza and beer and something sugary Jenna likely whipped up.

André barely got his boots off before Suraj called out, "Nobody told me I had to look pretty."

"Don't be jealous I shower, Raj," André shot back, breezing into the kitchen where the crew had already staked their usual places.

Curtis was at the head of the table, dealing cards like he moonlighted in Vegas. Tyler and Vargo were arguing about whether or not Jack Harrison was overrated while Jack sat right there with his feet up, giving zero shits since he was the only one there with a contract.

Fly—former captain, current hockey dad—sipped a soda and muttered to Brett about the blueline pressure in the last Habs game, while Sean sat with his half-empty beer looking like someone had stolen his damn lunch.

André slapped the six-pack on the counter. "Alright. Who's ready to get humiliated?"

Brett barely looked up as he shuffled chips. "By the guy who bluffed with a limp pair of threes for half the damn night last week? Yeah, I'm shaking."

"You folded to that limp pair, Brett. Let's not rewrite history."

Jenna breezed over from behind the island. "Drinks? We've got beer, margaritas, and my own creation: a blueberry bourbon smash. The cookies will be cool in a sec."

"I always love a good smash." André sat in the chair between Country and Suraj.

"Hmm." Jenna gave him a look as she handed over a glass that looked like it could strip varnish off a truck bumper.

"So. You and Grace." Tyler leaned back in his chair.

André forced a grin to his face. "You know something I don't know?"

Tyler nodded to Jenna. "Heard you two had to share a room in E-town."

"Did Jenna tell you I was a perfect gentleman?" He called over his shoulder. He could play this game all day.

Sean slammed a stack of chips down. "Can we play, or what?"

Curtis took a drink of his dirty soda. "Someone's happy tonight."

"Kelty still with her parents?" Suraj asked, and André frowned. Wasn't Kelty in Edmonton? Had he seen her Sunday morning?

Sean's eyes darkened. "Can. We. Play?"

André didn't push it, but he clocked the twitch in Sean's jaw and felt a twinge of guilt. He'd noticed Sean was quiet at the waterpark, but he'd been so caught up in his own shit, he hadn't stopped to question it.

They played for two hours straight. André lost three rounds in a row and made up for it by emptying half the jar of pickled jalapeños Jenna left out for snacks. "You clowns are cheating."

"You can't bluff for shit." Vargo grinned. "What's her name?"

André flipped him off and took another chip.

Curtis won, as usual. He always did. Something about having four kids made the man impossible to read.

"Alright, boys," Jenna called from the kitchen, holding a cookie sheet piled high with peanut butter bars. André took one, thanked her, then brushed past to step out onto the porch.

Simply existing was so much damn work. The cold air bit at his lungs, sharp and grounding, just the way he needed. He dragged a hand down his face and leaned against the railing, his fingers curling around the rough wood.

The sky stretched wide overhead, dark and velvet blue, pricked with stars. Everything felt too tight in his chest. He was doing everything right. Everything good. And he was so damn tired.

The door creaked behind him. Boots scuffed the porch.

"Didn't peg you for the dramatic storm-out-onto-the-porch type." Country stepped up beside him.

"Shut the hell up. You know I'm dramatic."

Country laughed. He offered up a beer without looking. André took it. For a while, they stood in silence.

Then Country said, "You love her?" André snorted, but Country gave him a sideways glance. "I'm serious."

André took a long pull from the beer. "She drives me batshit crazy, bud."

Country didn't even blink, and André turned his head, not able to keep eye contact.

After a few moments, Country cleared his throat. "I don't know what I'm going to do if we lose her." André sucked in a breath and held it. Country's voice caught as he continued, "If she goes back to Amey . . . I don't know if Jenna'll come back from that. I don't know if I will."

André turned to look at him. Country. The man who was all-in on and off the ice. Who played for broke. Who gave every shit and didn't apologize for it.

He stood there with his eyes glassy.

André's throat tightened. "Maybe all of this isn't worth it."

Country breathed a laugh. "Mm. No, I've lived that life. The one where I couldn't hurt because I didn't have anything to lose." He leaned sideways on the railing. "I'd take this any day of the week."

Country straightened, stretching one arm over his head, then switching his beer so he could stretch the other. "I heard Grace's permits came through. Last week, apparently. They're moving full speed ahead."

"Hmm." André's eyes narrowed.

"Should be finished in a week or two, I guess." Country let

out a slow breath, then turned toward the house. "Once the charity game is over on the twenty-second, seems like all her strings will be cut loose."

André stared out at the frosted barn, taking another swig of beer and swishing it in his mouth. The porch door creaked open and swung shut.

Twenty-Six

GRACE

THE AIR inside the Children's Museum smelled like apple juice and hand sanitizer, and Grace was almost positive she'd contracted sensory processing disorder upon entering. Or had been slipped a tab of acid. The lights, colors, and cacophony were equal to an out-of-body experience.

A blur of small humans darted from exhibit to exhibit like tiny meteorites in light-up sneakers. The space was bright and sprawling—painted murals of clouds and planes stretched across high ceilings while clusters of interactive stations buzzed with activity. There was a play grocery store stocked with plastic kale and tiny shopping carts, a sensory bin filled with kinetic sand and buried dinosaurs, and an art studio where children in oversized smocks splattered paint with more passion than precision.

In the middle of everything was Hope, secured snugly in Sharla Thompson's arms, her face tilted up with open-mouthed wonder at the waterworks installation that sent ping-pong balls swirling through tubes. Rob hovered nearby with a grin so wide it practically split his face. The man had barely let go of the baby since Jenna passed her off.

Sharla and Rob were all of their adopted parents. They loved without condition and fed the entire Snowballs team as many times a week as Sean and Emma would let them. Grace's heart squeezed seeing their pure joy whenever they were around Hope.

And in April they were going to court.

Grace tugged her cardigan tighter around herself. She was glad she came. She needed the distraction. Not from work or the renovations. She needed this break because she was *miserable*.

It had been a full week since Edmonton. Seven long days of silence from André—aside from a few very professional emails about the charity game logistics. They were curt. Polite. Painfully impersonal.

Each one felt like a paper cut to the wrist. She hated how much it bothered her that he wasn't following her into the parking lot or showing up in her driveway.

She tried to shake off her sour mood as she followed the group through the echoing halls, past the dino dig, and into the toddler zone where Kelty sat cross-legged on the floor with Curtis and Sasha's youngest, helping her build a block tower. Suraj's wife, Rashi, sat nearby chatting with Emma, while Penny wrangled one of their twins, convincing him not to lick the plexiglass.

Grace slipped onto a padded bench near the play mats and tried to focus on the moment—on the people around her, on the cheerful chaos, on the happy screech of a little boy who just launched himself down a foam slide.

It was a good day.

She was surrounded by good people.

But that didn't stop her stomach from knotting every time she saw André's name in her inbox with nothing but details about auction forms and business sponsor logos. She hated how petty she felt. She was a grown woman. She had a law degree, a property portfolio, and a five-year plan. And yet all she could think about was that night in Edmonton.

"Grace!" Sharla stepped over with Hope on her hip. "She's so alert, isn't she?"

Grace smiled despite herself. "She's a genius. We all know it."

Sharla rocked gently side to side. "I told Jenna we'd get a membership and come here every week. I don't even care if I pull a hip chasing her around here. Rob's already planning to build a baby gym in our basement."

Grace glanced toward the older man, who was crouched down beside the play grocery store, grinning as a two-year-old handed him a toy potato.

He was adorable. They both were. She had to find a way to keep this family together.

Jenna wandered over, trying to catch Hope's attention, but she was laser focused on a ribbon hanging from the ceiling.

Jenna gave a tight smile. "She loves it here."

Sharla nodded her agreement. Jenna wrapped her arms around herself, her eyes glued to Hope. She was soaking in every second like she could stitch them into her skin.

Sharla saw it, too. She passed Hope back to Jenna with a knowing smile, then slid a hand around Jenna's shoulders and murmured something low and warm into her ear.

Whatever it was, it made Jenna blink hard and nod.

Rob, who'd been supervising one of the twins trying to grocery-scan a plastic cucumber, came over and plucked Hope out of Jenna's arms again. "Alright, have you told her?"

Sharla beamed at him. "I was waiting for you."

Emma joined the group. "I feel like this is an official meeting."

Rob puffed out his chest. "Yep. Premeditated. We're stealing Hope Saturday evening."

Jenna started to protest, but Rob waved a hand. "You need a break, kiddo. You and your girlfriends need to get out and relax. Dance, drink. Whatever you need. Don't come home early. The door will be locked."

Sharla grinned. "We're doing all the things we used to do with our kids. Kitchen dance party, bubble bath in the sink, and I promise we'll get her to bed on time."

Emma shook her head. "This isn't good. The more they see of her, the more they're going to—"

"When are you and Tyler giving us grandkids?" Sharla planted a hand on her hip.

"Don't," Emma warned, pointing at her mother. "Don't do the thing."

"Oh, I'm doing the thing."

"She's definitely doing the thing," Kelty jumped up, brushing off her jeans. "I've got to run."

Grace glanced over. Something was off there. Kelty usually lit up rooms, but since Edmonton, she'd seemed dimmer. Like someone had turned the volume down on her brightness.

Emma seemed to notice, too. She gave Kelty a searching glance, but Kelty shoved her hands in her back pockets and looked away.

"Girls night? Saturday?" Jenna asked.

Kelty nodded once. "I'll check my schedule, but I should be good." She gave a small wave, then bolted for the stairs.

"You in, Grace?" Jenna gave her a hopeful look.

She pulled out her phone and scrolled through the week's calendar, pretending she didn't have Saturday's schedule burned into her brain. Ten o'clock, the final logistics run-through for the charity game, hosted at the Heads Up Alberta offices with NHL players present. It was supposed to be casual, but she felt like she was walking into a performance review she hadn't studied for. André would be there.

She needed to talk with him, she knew that. But what would she say? She couldn't wrap her own head around what she was feeling. None of it made sense. How could she want someone and at the same time feel desperate to run the other direction? It felt as if her body was being torn in two, and she just needed it to stop.

Grace lowered her phone. "Looks like I'm free."

CHAPTER
Twenty~Seven

ANDRÉ

ANDRÉ LEANED his shoulder against the wall of the conference room, chewing absently on the cap of a pen that had long since stopped working. This oral fixation needed to stop. He looked like a douche, but he couldn't help himself. Chewing gum, mints—anything to keep his tongue busy. He could think of plenty of options for that where Grace was concerned, but those fantasies didn't help the current situation.

He'd almost driven to her house three times that week, but he couldn't do it. He'd been the one showing up for weeks. The one telling her exactly how he felt, the one chasing her down. His ego couldn't take much more, and that was saying something. This wasn't a game to him anymore, and he wasn't going to keep bidding if she couldn't meet him halfway.

He worked to tune back into the meeting, already in full swing. The long rectangular table was packed—Sean, Tyler, Ryan, Brett. Jack Harrison sat near the end with his girlfriend Delia

Melise. André had met her before, but he still felt a little starstruck every time they came around. Just last week their over-the-boards kiss after the Blizzard's win over Vegas went viral. He couldn't stop seeing Jack shoving his tongue down her throat if he'd tried.

Again, tongues. Not helping.

A couple other NHL guys were scattered along the table. On the far end sat Dev Singh, the shutdown defenceman from Toronto. That guy moved like a steamroller on skates and made his living ending dreams in the neutral zone. beside him was Leo Tremblay, the Canadiens' chirpiest winger and power-play sniper who once scored four goals in a single game while mic'd up. André had watched that clip at least eight times. Probably twelve.

Across from them was Weston Price, the baby-faced goalie from Vancouver, already a fan favourite at twenty-three because he played like he'd sold his soul for glove saves and had a habit of chirping from the crease like he was hosting a stand-up set. Since Fleury was winding down, they needed more goalie shenanigans, and he seemed primed to try and fill his skates. André had never seen someone bait a shooter and rob him blind so smoothly.

They were casual, calm, dressed like they were at a Cactus Club happy hour. There was no ego in the room, no bullshit. Just guys here to do some good, and that he respected more than game stats.

Jenna and Country sat closest to the door with Hope in the stroller. Sean sat at the far end, and Grace was beside him, her hair pulled up into a low twist, scribbling notes on a yellow legal pad.

Business as usual.

"Alright." Micheal from Heads Up Alberta gestured to the checklist on the whiteboard. "Security's been confirmed, merch orders are in, and the final player list is being updated with the late additions. Thank you again to those of you who took time to be here in person. It means a lot to have those last minute promo photos."

Jack gave an easy smile. "We're excited. This is a hell of a cause."

Delia nodded, crossing one leg over the other. "We'll hit the CJAY92 interview this afternoon. If there's anything else we can do before we fly out, let us know."

Grace straightened in her chair. Her cheeks flushed pink as Delia smiled at her, and André grinned. Grace Fairbanks. If she had a tell, that was it. Hell it was cute to watch her pretending she wasn't fangirling.

They wrapped the final logistics. André was helping with most things, and Brett would be at the Saddledome early to help coordinate with the staff. Tyler and Ryan would coordinate the player entrance. Country, Jenna, Jack, Delia, and the PR team would run media coordination. Sean would help coordinate post-game tear down.

When the meeting adjourned, everyone filtered out toward the brunch spread laid out near the windows. Muffins. Coffee. The fruit salad that always seemed like a filler but somehow disappeared first.

André poured himself a coffee and turned just in time to see Grace standing at the table, eyeing a cranberry-orange muffin.

He stepped beside her. "You want chocolate. Life's too short for citrus in baked goods."

She gave him a side-eye, then grabbed a chocolate muffin and pulled on the wrapper. Heat flashed through him, his throat thickening.

He didn't let himself say more. Didn't press. Didn't flirt the way he wanted to. Didn't reach for her hand even though it was right there beside his. He couldn't keep doing this if she didn't want *him*. Not just a release or a way to let go, as she put it.

Do you love her?

He'd laughed at Country's question. But he wasn't laughing anymore.

"Okay. Um. Is that a *ring*?" Jenna's voice rose through the room. She leaned across the table, blinking dramatically at Delia's left hand.

Delia paused mid-sip of her latte. "Uh—"

"She's pregnant!" Jack blurted, grinning like he'd been holding it in for hours.

Delia groaned and shoved him lightly in the shoulder. "*Jack!* I told you I wanted to—"

"You were taking too long," he said, utterly unrepentant. "The full spread with *People* comes out next week. Might as well give our friends the scoop first."

Delia turned to the room, sighing. "Okay, fine. Yes. We eloped. And yes, I'm pregnant. Nine weeks, so keep it quiet for a bit, will you?"

Jenna gasped, hand going to her chest, and immediately burst into delighted squealing. "Delia!"

She nearly climbed over the table to hug her, and in seconds Grace was at her side, asking questions and offering congratulations with a wide, dazzling smile that made André's heart flip in his chest.

Because while the others buzzed with excitement, his gaze slid to the corner of the room where Country stood with one arm around Jenna's empty chair, the other hand on Hope's buggy.

Country smiled. A real, full smile. André felt like someone had taken a crowbar to his ribs. How? How did Jenna and Country keep doing this? How did they keep smiling when they didn't know what was going to happen in two weeks? When everything they loved could be yanked away with a court ruling?

He looked at Hope, tiny and perfect in her sleepy snuggle. They were superhuman, that was the only explanation. Because the idea of Grace walking away right now made his ribs tighten until his chest ached, and he didn't even have her yet.

"Yes! Come! It's tonight at Dusty Rose!" Jenna clasped Delia's hands in hers. André frowned. What was at Dusty Rose?

Delia laughed. "Can I do girl's night incognito?"

Jenna's eyes sparkled. "I'm thinking a wig and glasses. You'll be the mysterious cousin from Vancouver. I'll make a backstory and everything. No one will suspect a thing."

Delia gave a mock bow. "I'm honoured."

André glanced over, and right on cue, Country met his eye across the table. And there it was—a glint in his eye, a flick of his brow.

He grinned to himself. Yeah. The girls were going out tonight. But they weren't going alone.

GRACE

THE BAR WAS HUMMING when they walked in. Musicians warmed up in the corner, and the air was thick with the scent of wood shavings and whiskey. She'd only been to The Dusty Rose a few times since landing in Calgary. It was a dive, but the place had major heart.

Grace pulled her coat tighter as they slipped past the host, heading for the long high-top their group had reserved near the stage. Country music played at a low pulse, but it was early still. The real chaos would start when the house band kicked off.

She gaped when she saw Delia. Her disguise was shockingly good. A dark auburn wig—soft bangs, layered waves. Oversized rose-tinted sunglasses. A denim jacket pulled over a vintage Johnny Cash tee, tucked into slouchy black trousers and paired with boots, she looked like someone who drank mezcal and wrote moody lyrics in leatherbound journals.

Grace leaned over to Jenna. "How the hell did you pull this off?"

Jenna laughed. "This is all her."

Delia leaned in and whispered, "I'm regretting the wig. It itches."

The waitress dropped off a pitcher of beer and glasses. Grace didn't anticipate drinking tonight, so she asked for a pitcher of water as well. The last thing she needed was a migraine in the morning.

She slung her coat over the chair and adjusted her halter top. She'd gone through ten outfits before landing on this one, then figured what the hell? She was out with the girls, so why not be a little slutty?

If she was being honest, a small part of that decision was catalyzed by dropping through the tube of death on that water-slide. That moment had unlocked something within her. It was as if she hadn't understood all the possibilities before that robotic voice counted down.

She could break the rules and do something reckless, and the world wouldn't end because of it. Grace had put butter and jam on her English muffin that morning. She'd left the dishes in the sink, not loading them as she typically would. And now she wore a halter top with high-waisted jeans like she was twenty-eight instead of in her mid-thirties.

And the world kept on spinning.

"Damn, girl! You look—" Jenna froze, her brow pinching as she looked past her shoulder. "Oh, I am going to kill him."

Grace turned toward the entrance. The Snowballs filed in one after the other, not even trying to be subtle. Brett first, already waving. Then Tyler, Sean, Ryan, and—

Her hands tensed.

André.

He wore a heather-grey T-shirt that clung to his chest and a backward ball cap. Casual. Effortless. Unfair.

He clocked her instantly. His eyes took a long, low sweep of her, causing a record-breaking temperature increase beneath her skin. Grace felt a strange surge of power then.

Let him look. Let him want. Because she sure as hell still did.

André nodded toward the bar, then peeled off from the group to grab drinks. He didn't come straight over. Didn't make a beeline for her like he used to. No casual graze of her waist. No whisper in her ear.

Grace pasted on a smile and turned back to the table, but the sound of her pulse thrumming in her ears combined with the music made it impossible to hear the conversation. She leaned in, feigning complete and total interest in Delia and Penny's intense discussion on favourite lubes. Aelin, Ryan's fiancée jumped in with her take—one brand for the shower, one for the nightstand—and Grace was glad to ride the wave of conversation.

After an hour, she took a quick break to hit the bathroom. When she returned the house band was starting their second set. André was two stools away from Sean, shoulder to shoulder with Brett, tossing back a shot and shaking his head with a grimace. His grin flashed quick and wide.

He looked happy. Relaxed. Like he'd up and gotten over everything that happened between them in Edmonton.

Grace stood abruptly.

"Where are you going?" Rhonda asked.

Grace pointed to the flashing lights on their right and mouthed, "Dance floor."

She didn't wait for a response. She just headed to the centre of the floor, shouldering past a group of girls in denim skirts and cowboy boots until she hit the open space.

Her shoulders curled inward as she realized the situation. She stood alone. And yet if she didn't move, she was going to split at the seams.

The music was loud—twangy guitar over a driving bass—but it didn't matter. Her body remembered the basics of how to do this. She'd taken a dozen dance classes as a kid, everything from jazz to contemporary to Latin ballroom. Back then, she'd danced because she didn't want to play soccer, and her parents required her to participate in a sport.

Now?

Her hips caught the beat, and her arms lifted instinctively. She let herself forget about the legal briefs waiting in her inbox. About the court date and therapists and what-if scenarios and the panic clawing at her throat anytime she thought of Jenna handing over Hope.

And then—

Hands.

Strong. Familiar. Settling low on her hips.

She didn't have to look to know who it was.

Grace exhaled, allowing André to press in behind her, waiting for him to match her movements. His chest grazed her back, his thighs brushing hers. The rhythm between them shifted and synced.

He leaned in, breath hot against her ear. "You're trying to kill me."

Heat flooded her middle. "Is dancing a crime?"

He laughed, low and rough. "The way you do it, it is."

They moved together, his hand sliding over her thigh, shameless and slow. Grace felt him hard against her, his hand sliding to her waist, guiding her hips as the tempo climbed.

"You're drunk," she murmured, leaning back against his chest.

"Just a little buzzed."

"I don't think you'd be standing here if you were just a little buzzed."

"Why is that?" he drawled.

Grace swallowed. "You've been avoiding me."

His hand tensed on her hip. "Self-preservation."

She closed her eyes, the beat humming through her. "André, my permits came through. I'm leaving in a couple of weeks—"

"Then why haven't we been spending time together?"

Grace laughed. André sounded so sappy, it was comical. "You haven't texted."

"Neither have you." His voice wasn't playful anymore. "Don't think that night doesn't run through my head every damn second."

Grace's ribs cinched. André tugged at her waist, turning her around to face him. He slid his hands into the hollow of her back and leaned in, exhaling near her temple. "I'm trying, Grace. To be what you want."

She pulled back to look at him, but he kept her pinned to his chest. "I don't want you to be something different—"

"Bullshit. You want me to be everything different. You want me to be like you." Grace opened her mouth, then closed it. André wasn't finished. "Country found out he was a dad overnight. One minute, the most important thing in his life was hockey and his ranch, the next minute a baby lay in a bassinet with his name on her paperwork."

She blinked, her throat thick as something clicked in her chest, and everything else in the room fell away. A name. A detail. A line from a case file she hadn't thought about in days.

He found out he was a dad overnight.

Holy shit. Amey never told the birth father.

Grace's eyes widened. There'd been a note from the adoption agency. A letter that was sent. But no follow-up. And a text from Amey weeks later—something vague about her husband being overseas. It had been nothing then, but hadn't there been a date?

"He grew up fast," André concluded. "Maybe that's all it takes. Someone in your life that makes you want to be something more. And then you're not just looking for fun anymore."

What if he hadn't seen the letter? What if he got back and—

Grace gasped, reaching for André's arm like she needed it to stay upright. "I have to go," she whispered.

He pulled back, his expression annoyed. "What?"

She turned, her fingers gripping his shirt. "I'm so sorry, I have to go. Now."

And then she was gone—racing toward her bag, digging out her phone, fingers flying as her brain tore through timelines and conversations.

She had a call to make. And if she was right? Everything in this case could change.

CHAPTER
Twenty-Nine

André

ANDRÉ SHOVED open the back door of The Dusty Rose with more force than necessary. The hinges groaned in protest, but he didn't stop. He just needed air. Space.

The gravel crunched under his boots as he stomped toward his truck, the cold night air snapping against his neck. Alberta spring was elusive as always. Still snowbanks in the ditches, still a bite in the wind.

Grace.

She'd looked like sin in that halter, all legs and long lines. He'd taken a leap by dancing with her, by saying what he had, and then she bailed. No explanation. No goodbye. Just disappeared like she hadn't heard a damn word he said.

Hadn't Country suggested he make a move? Tell her the truth? Well, he did, and look where it got him.

He was still fuming when his phone buzzed in his pocket. He swiped it out, already halfway to hitting ignore, when the name on the screen stopped him cold. It was Luc.

His chest tightened. He hit accept and held the phone to his ear. "Hey."

There was a pause. Then Luc's voice came through, soft and shaky. "Can't sleep."

André's jaw clenched. "It's one in the morning."

"I know what time it is." A pause. A shuddering breath. "It's all loud again. My head's loud."

Shit.

André closed his eyes and leaned back against the seat. "You take your meds today?"

Luc didn't respond.

"Luc."

Another beat of silence.

"Yeah," Luc answered finally. "Didn't help. Not tonight."

André rested his forehead against the steering wheel. He could picture it—Luc pacing his apartment, barefoot, still in whatever threadbare sweats he wore too often. Lights on too bright. Music too loud.

"I thought about cutting," Luc whispered, like he was confessing a sin in church. "Didn't do it. But I thought about it."

André's stomach dropped. He didn't answer right away, couldn't. His voice was a ragged thing when it finally came out. "You've got nothing sharp near you now?"

"No."

He didn't sound convincing.

André ground his palm into his eye socket, trying to block out the memory—Luc two years ago, arm wrapped in a dish towel, eyes wide and terrified, saying it was an accident. It was always an accident.

"Where are you right now?" André asked.

"In the kitchen. On the floor."

André swallowed. Hard. "Open the drawer." He heard the creak. The shuffle. "Put the knife back." Another pause. Then the heavy, final click of a drawer sliding shut. He sagged with relief.

"You called me, Luc. You remembered the number. That's everything."

Luc didn't say anything for a long time, but he didn't hang up. He never hung up when it was this bad. Eventually, his breathing leveled. He muttered something about putting on his headphones.

André stayed on the line until Luc said he was okay. Until he promised to text when he got up again. Then he ended the call and sat there in the dark, the hum of The Dusty Rose sign overhead buzzing like a wasp in his ears.

André glanced at his hockey bag in the backseat. He could almost feel the cigarette between his fingers. The flick of the lighter. The first drag.

He shoved open the truck door and stood, breath misting in the frigid air. The craving hit so hard it made him dizzy. And then he was back in that hotel room with Grace, talking in the dark.

Why did he start smoking?

André sucked in a breath. It was Luc. It was always Luc.

Luc shouldn't have been playing as aggressively as he was with a history of concussions, and his parents knew it. After that hit, Luc's life slowed to a standstill.

No more hockey, no more education. They were told he'd be lucky to ever live independently again, and at least they'd gotten to that point. He had a caregiver that stopped in once a day, and the doctors were mind-blown that was all he required. That he'd become so self-reliant.

Here André was living the life he'd always dreamed. He went on to play pro hockey, lived all over the world, found pretty girls and good food, and built a business from the ground up. He had everything his brother didn't. He'd moved on, eclipsed him.

André reached into the back, pulling the pack of Marlboro's from the pocket. He tapped the box, pulling out a cigarette. This was all they had left. The only thing they both still did after all these years.

Tears slipped onto André's cheeks. He slipped the cigarette back into the box. He didn't want to smoke anymore, hadn't wanted to for years, but didn't realize until that moment why he'd never considered giving it up.

"I don't want to leave you behind again," he whispered, dropping the box against his thigh. He sniffed, wiping his nose with the back of his hand, and laughing at himself. What the hell had been in that shot he'd taken with Sean?

André opened the door and walked to the edge of the building. He reached out and dropped his last pack of cigarettes in the trash bin, then stalked back to his truck.

What he wouldn't have given for ice right then. He needed to skate until his thighs burned, until his lungs gave out.

Before he could start searching for Nora's number at the Ice Centre to drunkenly beg for a way to open the rink, his phone buzzed in his hand.

His stomach dropped as he swiped up, looking for the message from Luc.

But it wasn't him. Grace's name popped up at the top of his messages.

Are you free tomorrow morning?

His brows shot up. He started to type.

What are you thinking?

He waited, staring at the screen until her reply popped up.

I need your help with something. Moral
support.

Andre's heart picked up speed.

Sure. What are we doing? Do I need a shovel or
a suit?

Three blinking dots appeared. Then stopped. Then started again.

Just bring yourself. Wear something
intimidating?

He frowned. That narrowed it down precisely zero percent. But
something in his chest shifted. Just slightly. Like one of the bricks
he'd been carrying all morning eased off his spine.

He texted back.

When and where?

CHAPTER
Thirty

Grace

GRACE STARED at the text from André the night before. What did it mean that she'd texted him first? Last night she'd justified it by convincing herself it was the only reasonable option. She couldn't text Country or Jenna since she had no idea whether this visit would amount to anything. She couldn't text Tyler or one of the other guys because they were close with Country . . . and that's where the argument lost steam.

André was close with Country. Wouldn't texting him hold the same amount of risk that he'd mention something? And yet, sending that message had been automatic.

As soon as Grace got home after her hasty exit from Dusty Rose, she jumped onto her laptop. Finding the letter to Hope's birth dad didn't take long. She'd been through the records so many times, she knew exactly where to look. Brady McGinnis. The letter was rerouted through the Department of National Defence forwarding, and by the time it reached him, he'd been out of service six weeks. He'd moved. No follow-up. No certified mail. Just a single attempt, and it died in the system.

She could get in touch with Veterans Affairs, but since it was a weekend, she opted for internet sleuthing and searching public records. She found him. Brady McGinnis had moved back to Calgary and his address was updated two months ago when he registered for provincial healthcare. After searching a few socials, she found a dating profile with pictures of him in his military gear. Same guy. It had to be.

"Grace?"

She blinked. Looked up. Her contractor, Matthew, stood a few feet away, arms crossed. "Sorry." She slipped her phone into her back pocket. "Yes?"

He pointed toward the far wall, now lined with new baseboard trim and a fresh coat of eggshell paint. "Colour okay?"

Grace nodded. At this point, she didn't have any colour opinions. It wasn't abrasive, and this project was almost finished. It would've taken a sewer-green to make her even consider repainting.

Matthew nodded. "The last cabinet doors are being installed Friday. The new electrical passed inspection this morning. Fire code stuff's done. Plumber came and signed off on the hot water system. After that it's just touch-ups and a deep clean."

She turned slowly, taking in the space—the wide hallway, the updated lights, the muted scent of fresh paint still clinging to the air. It wasn't flashy, but it was beautiful. Clean. Functional. Safe.

"It looks . . . " She exhaled. "It looks *really good*, Matthew."

He grunted. "Not perfect. But up to code and then some. You'll make your money back three times over."

Grace smiled and nodded, clearing her throat to fight the emotion building there. She exited into the main foyer, then out the front steps. Outside, the late March sun blazed through the large east-facing windows, glinting off the remaining patches of crusted snow.

She turned and looked at her reflection in the windows. This was hers. A sense of pride and gratitude washed over her. This gift didn't erase the hurt Troy caused when their marriage ended, but enough time had passed that she could accept it for what it was. Troy cared as much as he was capable of caring.

The thought sent a drop through her belly, and she clutched her scarf to her chest. Was she any better? Sure, she wasn't chasing after her next potential partner, but she was putting up her own brand of emotional walls.

André scared her. The idea of opening up to anyone again was terrifying, but what she was feeling for him made the fear ten times worse. Troy had signed divorce papers and jumped from woman to woman to avoid getting vulnerable. She took the even easier route of going radio silent.

Grace swallowed hard and pulled out her phone. She made a note to contact Troy's real estate agent, Gina, to see if she could bring in a photographer early next week. Hopefully they could get it listed as early as the first few days in April.

She walked to her car and slipped into the driver's seat. Just as she hit the start button, her phone buzzed on the passenger seat.

Grace glanced over and saw her mom's name scrolling across the screen. She hit Answer.

"Hi, Mom."

"Well, hi, sweetheart!" Her mom sounded bright for that early in the morning. "Just checking in to make sure you're still planning to be here by Easter?"

Grace nodded automatically. "Yep, that's the plan." One week. The building would be listed. The charity game would be over that weekend. And depending on what she found out at her next meeting with Brady McGinnis, she'd at least have something to bring to their court date. But that was something she could work remotely. There would be no reason for her to stay in Calgary after that point.

She flicked on the defrost and stared out the windshield,

watching condensation melt into rivulets that traced the curve of the glass.

"Perfect. I booked your haircut for the Saturday before. Nadia had a cancellation. You know how far she books out."

Grace blinked. Right. The throwback to home was almost jarring.

She was going home. The realization should have made her relieved, and a part of her was. The part that was tired. The part that wanted to crawl back into her old life even though she saw clearly now how much it was lacking.

It was Toronto. Her apartment, her practice, her espresso machine and overpriced ergonomic desk chair and whole-wheat morning muffins from the bakery on Queen Street that always got her order wrong but somehow remembered her name.

It was home. *Wasn't it?*

So why did her stomach feel like it was lurching sideways? Why was she thinking about girls' nights at Dusty Rose and nachos at hockey games and Sunday Suppers and bonfires in Curtis's backyard?

Grace cleared her throat. "Sounds great."

"You okay, honey?"

Grace loosened her scarf and made her voice lighter. "Just tired. The reno's been a lot. And we've got the charity game this weekend."

Her mom hummed thoughtfully. "That's a lot. I'm sure it will be such a relief to be back to your old routines."

Yes. That sounded like her. Safe. Predictable.

But the truth pressed hot and heavy under her ribs. She'd been checking flights without booking. She hadn't answered her assistant's email about which clients she wanted to schedule first.

Her mom sighed. "Well, we'll have champagne ready when you land. And maybe something from that little bakery you like. The one with the raspberry almond tart?"

Grace swallowed. "Perfect."

. . .

———

Grace turned the corner, and there was André leaning against his truck. Ball cap pulled low, black hoodie stretched across his chest, faded jeans, and slip-ons. Her breath stalled.

"Wanted exercise this morning?" he called.

Grace gave him a look. "It seems someone took the last good parking spot.

He pushed off his truck and gave her a crooked smile. "You snooze, you lose."

"I was coming from another meeting. Ran a bit late."

"Yeah?" André fell into step beside her.

"For the renovation. Just an update."

"I hear it's almost finished."

She nodded. "Yep. Should be able to get it listed next week, hopefully."

André didn't respond to that, which meant they walked up the front steps in silence. The house was a modest split-level tucked on a quiet street. Not falling apart, but not thriving either. The siding needed a power wash. The shrubs out front didn't look like they'd be making a recovery from their winter hibernation.

"You going to tell me what this is about?" André asked.

Grace froze in front of the door. Right. She'd asked him to come but hadn't given him any details. "This is Hope's birth father. He was supposed to receive a letter about the adoption, but it didn't ever get to him. Now he's back in Calgary."

"His information was in the file?"

Grace pursed her lips. "Nope. I Google stalked him."

André grunted. "He knows we're coming?"

"Umm, yes."

"He knows about Hope?"

"He does." She swallowed her nerves as André observed her, nodding slowly.

"Did you tell him?"

Grace scoffed. "No, I would never do that. The last thing we need is another parent petitioning."

"So we're here because . . . "

"Because I think he's the reason Amey is going after Hope." Grace raised her hand and knocked twice, not sure if André was regretting his decision. Finding Brady had been easy enough, but figuring out whether he knew about Hope? That was another story.

She would take the profile she made on Hinge and her personal chat with Mr. McGinnis to her grave.

Seconds passed, then a minute. Grace shifted her weight on the step. After what felt like a year, she knocked again. That time, there were sounds inside the home. Footsteps approached, and the door creaked open.

"Uh, hey." A man stood in the gap, his hand on the door frame. Early thirties, thick build, dark hair buzzed short, sleeves rolled to the elbows.

"Hi, are you Brady?"

He pulled the door open another inch. "Grace?"

She nodded. "Grace Fairbanks. This is André Leclerc. He's a . . . friend."

He shook both their hands. His grip was tight, not rude. Just tense. Wary.

He stepped back so they could enter the house, and Grace's skin prickled as André put a hand on her lower back. Her nerves immediately calmed. Yes, it may have been stupid to waltz into a stranger's home like this, but somehow with André there, she felt completely safe.

The air smelled like reheated coffee and burnt toast. The furniture was sparse, functional, but clean. No pictures on the walls. No clutter. The blinds were drawn halfway.

He led them to a small kitchen table. There was a cane leaning against the fridge.

"Man, I thought you wanted to hook up when you DM'd me." He ran a hand over his head and sat down.

André gave her a look, and Grace straightened her shoulders before taking a seat across from him. André sat beside her, moving his chair so their thighs were nearly flush. "Sorry. I didn't want to say anything until I was sure you knew the situation."

Brady nodded. "I didn't even know she existed until six weeks ago." He rubbed the back of his neck. "Letter got sent to the wrong address. I'd moved bases twice. Finally made it here after my release."

André exhaled. "You were overseas?"

"Four years. Two in Latvia, one in Poland, and a shit rotation back home. Didn't even know Amey kept the pregnancy. She said she was getting rid of it." Brady leaned back in his chair. "Didn't believe the letter at first. Thought it was some scam. Then I texted her. Asked if it was real."

Grace leaned in. "What did she say?"

He shrugged. "Said she took care of it like we planned, but I don't know. It felt different. Knowing a baby existed. A little girl. I was pissed."

"I would be," André muttered.

Grace wanted to kick him under the table, but Brady's expression brightened. "Right? I didn't mean to blow up her life, but I was crashing out."

André glanced at her. Perfect. So they both didn't know what that meant.

Grace folded her hands on the table. "What did you say to her?"

Brady glanced away, rubbing his jaw. "I told her she had no right to give my daughter away without my permission. I was going to get a lawyer and sue."

The pieces clicked together. Amey's financial situation was unstable at best, nonexistent at worst. Grace had wondered often how she was paying Patel to oversee this petition in the first place. A lawsuit? That would be astronomical. "Were you serious?"

He blew out a breath. "I don't know. Maybe. But that weekend Amey told me she could get her back. Said it wasn't final."

Grace worked to keep her breathing even. "Are the two of you planning to raise her together?"

"Together? Nah. Amey and I aren't a good fit. We were never really together."

Grace blinked. "So . . . you're going to raise her? Alone?" Panic rose in her chest. She wasn't here to judge whether Brady was fit to be a father, but looking around the room . . . she was sure as hell judging his fitness.

André dropped a hand on her knee. "Bud, you working?"

Brady nodded. "Yep. Gordon's. Construction."

"Nice. That's a good gig. How much are you making?"

Brady's mouth twitched. "Sixty. Hoping to go up to seventy-five by the end of summer."

André's hand tightened on Grace's leg, and she dropped a hand from the table, covering his with hers.

He flipped his palm and laced their fingers, then gave a soft squeeze. "I get it, bud. This has to be heavy. But she's with a family she's been with them since birth. Do you want to tear that apart?"

Brady's jaw clenched. "I haven't even seen her."

"Because Amey closed the adoption," Grace explained. "The family—Jenna and Gentry—they're good people. Loving. Stable. They were never pushing for it to be closed."

"What if I want to be part of her life? I didn't get a choice." Brady blinked fast, trying to hide his emotion.

Grace counted to three as she inhaled. "No one's saying you can't be. We could explore open adoption—visits, letters, a relationship. But you and Amey aren't in a place to co-parent. You'd be introducing a custody battle where none existed."

He stared at the wall. Silent for a long beat. "Custody?"

Grace nodded. "Listen, I know I'm biased in this situation. I believe your daughter is in a beautiful home, and I believe in the process that was followed. I know Amey doesn't believe she was given all the information—"

"What?" Brady frowned. "Wasn't given what information?"

Grace's jaw tightened. The petition wasn't public record, which meant she couldn't give him specifics. Her heart sped in her chest. She was already on shaky legal ground, but this was Country and Jenna. Maybe there was a way to work around it. She had to find something that could stop this petition in its tracks. "She's saying . . . certain steps in the process weren't fully explained to her. That she didn't understand all of her rights before signing."

Brady made a low sound in his throat. "That doesn't track. She was pissed at me when I reached out. Said I'd already missed the window."

Grace's heart ticked faster. "What window?"

He shrugged. "I don't know. She said I'd already bailed on her, which isn't true." He pulled out his phone. "I can show you if you want. She told me she signed, that it was done. That's when I went a little crazy."

Grace could barely breathe as he scrolled. His thumb flicked over the screen, then he paused, squinting. "Here. Found it." He turned the screen to her.

Amey

> I already signed the papers. The ten day window is up. The social worker sent you a letter and you never responded. You had your chance to be involved.

. . .

The timestamp was perfect. It was before the petition. Weeks before. And *she knew*. Grace's stomach bottomed out. "Can you forward that to me?".

Brady nodded. "On Hinge?"

Grace's cheeks heated. "No, no, just—here." She focused hard on her screen, pretending André's eyes weren't boring into her soul, and opened her contacts. She handed Brady the phone and had him type in his number.

When he was finished, she texted him, then waited for a buzz in response. When it came through, she held her breath. The message sat there, damning and undeniable. A loaded gun for court. Grace opened her case app and archived the screenshot immediately.

Holy shit. This was it. This was the hole in Amey's case.

She exhaled slowly, her whole body vibrating. She only had to keep Neel Patel from finding out she'd given Brady sensitive information. *But had she?* She hadn't exactly told him what Amey's petition was, and Amey had technically already exposed everything by saying the adoption was under scrutiny hadn't she? "Thank you, Brady. I know this is a lot."

He ran a hand over his buzzed hair. "I just want to be part of my kid's life. I didn't get to choose anything."

Brady walked them to the door. André shoved his hands in his pockets, and Grace pulled her coat tighter around herself. They exited the house and walked in silence past his truck. He didn't stop, instead following her to the corner. As soon as they were out of eyesight and earshot, Grace stopped and whirled toward him.

"They're going to get to keep Hope!" she hissed, shaking with relief. "Can you believe that? She knew about the ten day window. I knew she knew it. Her social worker checked all the boxes, and now I have proof." Grace turned in a circle, tipping her head to the sky. "This is exactly what I needed." When she lowered her eyes, André wasn't smiling. "What?"

He wet his lips, his brow furrowed. "I don't know."

"You don't know what?"

André blew out a breath, hunching over and pushing his hands deeper into his pockets. "This doesn't feel right."

She gaped at him. "Doesn't feel right?"

André met her eyes, setting his jaw the way he always did before he said something she was going to hate. "Amey filed a petition with false information, and that was wrong. I get that. I hate that it's putting Jenna and Country through the ringer. But this dude? He didn't know he had a kid. She kept that from him, and now he's in the shit about it and we're going to slam this home? Cut him off?"

"I never said he'd be cut off. I said we'd discuss options—"

"Yeah, the lawyers will decide for him. Meanwhile he's never met his damn daughter."

Grace snapped her mouth closed. She drew a deep breath and exhaled. "If he decided he wanted Hope, he would have a case to fight the adoption, André. I'm trying to save Jenna and Country."

He took a step back and dragged a hand over his jaw. "I don't think this is something you can control, Grace. What if he changes his mind in a year? Two? How is that going to impact Hope?"

"How is it going to impact our friends?"

He winced, pain flickering through his features. "If it had been your dad. If he didn't know—"

"That's not fair. Don't you dare use that against me—"

André stormed forward and pulled her into his arms so fast, she forgot to breathe. She stiffened, but as his hand rubbed up and down over her back, she couldn't help but sink into him. Tears pooled in her eyes as his heart beat against her cheek.

"I told you that first night that there's always a reason for a fight." His voice rumbled through her. "But you—Grace, you're out here dropping gloves with every damn thing that breathes."

"This is something worth fighting for." She pushed against his chest, but he held tight.

"Not the point. You're trying to kill every penalty yourself and refusing to pass the puck."

"Don't give me that hockey shit." She wrestled her arms between them so she could look up into his face. "You can't say a damn thing. Not when you're busting your ass for Heads Up—"

"I've got a team." His hand cupped the back of her neck, thumb brushing the edge of her jaw. "And you do too, if you would stop being a stubborn ass and use us."

"I texted you! I asked you to come—"

"And now you're going to let everyone else in, too. You're going to stop questioning whether you're making the perfect choice because there isn't one. You're not going to jeopardize your career because you don't want to make a mistake." He drew a deep breath, and his arms relaxed an inch. "I've done this before. When everything happened with Luc. I've learned this the hard way, and I don't want you to burn out like I did."

Grace's mouth went dry. "But the stakes are too high and—"

"To hell they are. The only way we lose is by cutting each other out, do you hear me?" His jaw flexed. "You're trying to win the game with a five-man forecheck and no goalie."

Her lips parted, but the words didn't come.

"You don't have to take every shift, Grace. You don't have to carry the whole ice. Sometimes . . . " He leaned in, forehead pressing to hers. "Sometimes, you have to trust your teammates to take the drop."

Her breath hitched, the ache in her chest threatening to bury her. "What if I can't?"

"You can't or you won't?"

She shook her head, throat too tight to answer. He pulled back enough to see her face, eyes burning into hers, and she was suddenly standing inside that plastic tube, waiting for the floor to drop out from under her. "I don't think I'm built for letting go."

He smiled. "Yeah, you are. You just haven't seen what it feels like when someone's got your six."

Thirty-One

André

ANDRÉ BALANCED HOPE on one knee, making ridiculous horse sounds as she grabbed two chubby fists full of his hair.

"Easy, cowgirl," he muttered, ducking his head just as she squealed with delight and drooled down his shirt collar. "Hope, please, I just did laundry."

"She's already calling your bluffs." Polk sprawled across the floor with one of Hope's stuffed foxes over his face. "You haven't done your laundry in weeks. Otherwise you'd be wearing that old-ass T-shirt."

"The dusty-blue one!" Country laughed from the couch.

André flipped him off and earned a delighted cackle from the baby.

"Language," Jenna hissed from the kitchen without even turning around. Her hair was a frizzed halo around her face, her sleeves half-soaked from rinsing fruit, and the oven timer was beeping like a car alarm. "André, hand me that platter."

"You own a platter?" he asked, hoisting Hope under his arms and standing with a groan. "What's this, a royal banquet?"

Jenna whirled around with a spatula in one hand and a twitching eye. "I have to impress these people. Shut the hell up and put it on the counter."

Country laughed. "I love it when you come over. Takes all the pressure off."

André grinned and pulled the white ceramic plate down from the cupboard over the fridge. Grace stood stiffly beside the counter, arms wrapped tightly around her midsection, staring down at her phone.

She looked good. Even tense and pale and biting at the inside of her cheek. Probably because of it. The idea that he could be the one to unravel her made his jeans tight. Every single time.

André swallowed. They made a plan. Together. For once, she hadn't tried to do it all herself and brought him along for moral support. He wasn't sure which part of that made his chest ache more. The fact that she'd trusted him, or the fact that it clearly scared the hell out of her.

He crossed the room, gently handed Hope to Polk, and then made his way over to Grace. "You okay?"

She looked up at him with eyes too bright, too sharp, and too damn wide. "Mm. Yep. Great."

"Cool. Yeah. Seems like it." Grace shot him a look. He didn't budge. "Grace. You're vibrating like a fridge light. I think the only reason you're still upright is because you forgot how to sit down."

She opened her mouth, but before she could throw something sharp back at him, the doorbell rang. All the air snapped out of the room.

Jenna went rigid by the oven. Country shot up from the couch. "Uh, I'll get it." He swung the door wide, and they all held their collective breath.

Brady stood on the porch in jeans, a worn fleece jacket, and scuffed boots. "Hey."

Country put out a hand, and Brady shook it. "Gentry Maddox. Come on in."

Brady stepped inside like he wasn't sure he was allowed to touch the floor. His eyes swept the farmhouse slowly, taking in the mismatched picture frames on the wall, the baby swing by the fireplace, and finally, to where Hope sat in Polk's lap, blinking up at him with those wild, curious eyes.

The guy stopped dead. Like the sight of her punched the air from his lungs. Brady stared at Hope, then cleared his throat and dropped to a crouch. Not close. Not reaching. Just lowering himself to her level, his hands dangling helplessly between his knees.

"Hi," he said softly. "I'm . . . my name's Brady."

Hope blinked. Then gave a delighted squeal and reached toward the crinkle of his jacket. Brady's face cracked like a dam.

Polk shifted slowly and handed her over. To his credit, Brady didn't bolt. Didn't burst into tears. Just picked her up like he'd done it a thousand times and had only forgotten the rhythm. His hands were solid. Gentle. Hesitant at first—but then, she tucked her little fist into the collar of his coat, and the tension sighed out of him.

"She looks like me," he whispered. Something ruptured in André's chest. Brady looked up, eyes glassy. "I didn't know."

Jenna stepped forward, her voice steady but soft. "It wasn't your fault."

He glanced at her, nodded once, then dropped his head to look at Hope. They stood through a long silence, then jumped at a knock on the door.

Jenna frowned and strode forward, flinging it open.

André's eyes widened. Elodie stood there, hair half-pulled back, her expression calm, but he knew her well enough to see her feet kicking under the surface. Beside her, that had to be Amey. She was small, pale, with quiet eyes ringed with sleeplessness.

Grace's whole body snapped tight beside him. She stepped forward instinctively.

"Elodie," she said tightly. "What is this?"

Jenna turned back and smiled. "It's alright. I let Elodie know we'd be here."

Elodie and Amey walked in. "Sorry we didn't confirm. It was a last-minute decision."

André cut a glance at his sister, surprised and a little proud. What therapist came with her client to see her baby daddy for the first time in years?

Amey paused when she saw Hope in Brady's arms. Her mouth opened. No sound came out.

Brady stood, Hope still tucked against his chest, and turned to face Amey. "Why didn't you tell me?"

Amey swayed like the words knocked her off balance. "You said you didn't want kids."

"I said not *now*," he choked out. "You didn't even give me the chance."

Amey blinked, tears finally spilling. "I didn't know how."

André wanted to disappear. Wanted to throw Grace over his shoulder and get the hell out of there.

Amey looked at Jenna, eyes wet. "I'm sorry. I lied about the ten days—" Her eyes widened when she saw Grace standing behind her.

Grace put up a hand. "This is off the record. You're okay."

Amey nodded, her lip trembling.

Grace picked up the pen and legal pad sitting on the counter beside her. André moved a bit closer. He didn't touch her, didn't say anything—just crossed his arms over his chest and waited.

She flicked her gaze up for only a second, but it was enough.

He gave her a nod. *I've got you.*

Her shoulders lowered by a fraction, and then she turned her attention back to the room. "This conversation is informal. Nothing you say here will be used in court. We're not here to strategize or talk legalities. We're here to talk about Hope."

Brady's jaw flexed as he looked down at the baby against his chest. "That's all I want."

"Same." Jenna dropped onto the couch. Country sat beside her and motioned for everyone else to find a seat.

Amey and Elodie sat on the loveseat, and Polk gave Brady the rocking chair. Amey swallowed hard, her knuckles white around the tissue in her hand.

"I'm twenty-two," Amey started. "I don't even know who I am. I barely have a place to live. My parents stopped talking to me after I chose adoption. Then when I found out Brady had come home and he didn't know—everything you said, it scared me. I thought if I fought for her, I could fix it. If there was a problem in the case, I wouldn't have to pay for my own lawyer—" Her voice broke, and she clapped a hand over her mouth.

Brady cleared his throat. "You could've told me that."

"You could've not yelled at me over the phone."

They stared at each other, past and pain written into the lines of their faces.

André nodded to Polk, who was still leaning against the back wall. Polk gave him a knowing look and moved to Brady's side, clasping a hand on the man's shoulder.

"Here's the thing. You two made a beautiful little girl, and we all love her, which means we love you. So. You have people now. You might not have chosen this family, but you've got it."

Amey blinked like a bird that hit the window.

Brady looked stunned. He looked back at Hope in his arms. "I've been thinking a lot. Since I found out about her. I don't have my shit together, you know? But the idea of not being in her life—" His voice cracked.

Jenna stepped forward. "That's not even a question. You want to be in her life, you're in it."

Grace scribbled notes on her pad. "An open adoption isn't a legal requirement. It's a mutual agreement between the adoptive parents and the birth parents—one that's built on trust, not enforceable by the courts. But it *can* be formalized through something called an openness agreement."

She looked to Amey. "That means you can choose to be part of Hope's life—letters, photos, visits—whatever's agreed upon. But it has to be what's best for her, not what's easiest or most comfortable for us."

Brady shifted Hope in his arms as her eyelids began to droop.

Grace continued. "These agreements can be flexible. They evolve as the child gets older. Maybe it starts with a few updates a year. Maybe someday, it's birthdays and school concerts. But the foundation is respect. For the adoptive parents and for each other."

She turned to Amey, gently. "You'd still have a place. Not as a co-parent, but as someone who loves her. Someone who matters. If that's something you want."

They sat in silence for a moment, and André prayed for some sign of resolution. They all knew this plan wasn't foolproof. It wasn't result oriented. Looping Brady in was the right thing to do, but it also could mean Hope leaving Country and Jenna forever.

Country cleared his throat. He hadn't said a thing about Hope or the adoption since they'd arrived earlier. But now, with everyone looking at him—Hope curled in her father's arms—he spoke up.

"I spent a good chunk of my life not fighting for what mattered most. Not because I didn't care, but because I was afraid of hurting more than I already did." Jenna blinked up at him, eyes wide. "But that's not how life works. It's not how family works."

He let the words hang for a beat, then looked at Amey and Brady directly. "You two made a decision that brought a little girl into this world. A real one. With cheeks like marshmallows and eyes that have sucked up my entire world. And maybe you weren't ready then. Maybe you aren't ready now. But me and Jenna? We are." His voice cracked, but he didn't back down.

"And I'll tell you this: I didn't just wake up one day and decide to love her. It wasn't a choice. It happened somewhere between the midnight feedings and the first laugh and the moment she reached for me with her whole heart like I was the only thing keeping her world from spinning apart."

A tear slid down Jenna's cheek. Amey pressed her tissue to her nose.

Country continued, "I'll fight for that little girl 'til my last breath. Whether she calls me Dad or not. Whether she lives under my roof or I only get to see her on birthdays and back porches. I'll fight with everything I've got. Because that's what she deserves. Not fear. Not fighting. Just love." He let out a shaky breath. "I should've learned that a long time ago. But I know it now. And I'm not letting go."

The room was silent. Jenna reached over and took Country's hand, and Grace gripped her legal pad like it was the only thing keeping her upright.

After a few moments, Country sniffed and stepped back like he hadn't just dropped an emotional bomb worse than Gretsky at his 1988 press conference. "We made dinner. So unless anyone wants to cry into cold lasagna, I suggest we eat."

Jenna huffed a breath that was halfway between a sob and a laugh, wiping her eyes as she stood. "It's not lasagna. It's chicken parm, and I made a salad. Don't forget the damn salad."

The spell broke, just like that.

People stood, plates were passed, and the scent of garlic and cheese melted over crispy breading filled the warm kitchen. Jenna helped Brady lay Hope in her swing, and they all sat around the table together.

Elodie took a sip of wine and cut a narrow glance at André. "You always make such a mess when you eat pasta."

André raised a brow. "At least I eat it. Still pretending you're gluten-free?"

Elodie rolled her eyes. Polk pointed between the two of them. "You're related, eh?"

"She's adopted," André deadpanned, earning a sharp kick under the table.

Elodie gaped at him. "Seriously?"

"What, too soon?" André grinned, and Country threw a roll at his head.

Grace sat half-smiling beside André. For a second he wondered if she was pissed by his joke, but she didn't seem tense—just tired. Deep-in-her-bones tired. He wanted to touch her, slide his knee against hers, remind her they'd made it through the hard part.

Something held him back. The room buzzed with warmth and clatter. Even Amey cracked a smile when Jenna handed her a mountain of garlic bread. Polk made an obscene joke about meatballs that got a gasp from Elodie and a groan from everyone else. He looked a little too pleased with himself.

It was a good night. Against all odds, it was a damn good night. Yet something tugged at him, a thread attached to his centre. He glanced around the table—Jenna curled into Country's side, Brady still staring at Hope in her swing with eyes full of shattered awe, Elodie making fun of Polk's farmer tan.

André had spent years avoiding the heavy stuff. Making the joke. Walking it off. Keeping his gloves up until no one could get close enough to land a real hit.

But Country's words ran through his head like ticker tape. He hadn't said he'd fight until he got what he wanted. It hadn't been about him at all.

He just said he'd fight. That's it. Because Hope was worth it. And André, shoveling food he could barely taste, started to wonder if he'd ever fought for anything like that in his entire life.

No deals. No conditions. No crowd. Just dropping the gloves and going all in.

Grace caught his eye just then, and André stood so fast his chair screeched across the tile, rattling against the wainscot behind him. The scrape of it silenced the table. Even Polk paused mid-forkful.

The air in his chest felt thick, hot—like trying to breathe in a steam room. Everything was suddenly too warm, the smell of garlic and red wine too rich on his tongue. His pulse hammered in his throat as the edge of the table dug into his hip.

André's voice came out rough. "Can you come out to the porch?"

Grace blinked up at him from her seat across the table, her brow pulling slightly. "Now?"

He nodded once and set his napkin beside his plate. "Now."

GRACE

THE DECK WAS SOAKED in gold from the porch light. It glinted off the railing and blanched the bare branches overhead. The Chinook swept in earlier that afternoon, softening the edges of winter. Now the air was strangely warm for March.

Grace still shivered as she stepped out and pulled the door closed behind her. She'd barely made it two steps before André turned.

He looked wrecked. His dark hair was messy, his jaw locked like it might snap. His black thermal shirt clung to his shoulders, sleeves shoved up his forearms, veins taut beneath his skin.

"I can't do this," he said.

Grace blinked. "Okay. Do what?"

"This in-between." He stepped closer, voice low and rough. "I'm walking around like a guy who got clipped mid-shift and doesn't know which way is up." Her breath caught. "You don't owe me anything. Not sex. Not staying in Calgary. But I need to know if I'm the only one who felt like last weekend meant something."

The wind shifted. Warm and gentle, sliding across the porch and lifting a lock of her hair. She didn't move. Of course he wasn't the only one. Every moment of the weekend was branded into her. She was different because of it—changed.

André was like a whisk thrust into her perfectly graduated life, mixing everything up until it was unrecognizable.

"You told me you needed to let go," he continued. "I get that. I get needing an out. But what I feel with you . . . " He broke off, dragged a hand through his hair. "That wasn't an escape, not for me. That was a damn lifeline."

Grace's throat tightened. "André—"

"I'm not done." He stepped closer again. Inches separating them now. His body heat permeated her sweater. Grace's heartbeat roared in her ears. "I want you. And not just in my bed. I want to hear your voice in the morning. I want to argue with you about stupid reality TV shows and takeout and apparently shit-near everything because that's what we do. I want to fight with you about whether we should paint the bedroom or buy another bookshelf. I want you to tell me that I'm young and stupid. I want to win and I want to lose, and hell if I don't want to make up after every damn argument."

Despite herself, she let out a half laugh, half broken sob.

André looped a finger in her jeans and tugged. "I want all of it. You in my life. You with your silky blouses and legal pads and your over-prepared suitcase and your mouth—" He hissed a breath and dragged a hand over his face. "That mouth."

Her skin flushed like fire.

"But this isn't a decision I can make for you, Grace. I can't tell you to stand at the kitchen counter and eat. I can't make a deal with you to get you onto the waterslide."

"That wasn't a deal."

"It was a deal because I quit so you wouldn't taste smoke on me—"

"I didn't taste it. In the locker room."

He laughed and tucked her hair behind her ear. "Are you arguing with me right now? I'm telling you I quit smoking for you and you're telling me I didn't have to?"

Grace pursed her lips. "Sorry. Continue."

André chewed his lower lip. The silence stretched. "Tell me what you want, Grace."

What did she want? That question was so foreign, she didn't know how to begin to tackle it. What did she want? It had never been about that. She'd done what she was supposed to do, wanted the things everyone would want—a good job, great income, and a husband. She'd done everything right, and that house of cards had collapsed around her.

What did she want? She wanted to be safe. She wanted not to hurt. It sounded trite, but it was the honest-to-goodness truth. The idea of allowing herself to want more than that . . .

A tear slipped onto her cheek. "If I let myself want—" She sucked in a breath. She couldn't finish the sentence. *It would hurt too much not to get it.*

André's words cracked her heart open just enough to envision it, but admitting it? Asking for it?

Her life was predictable. It was safe. She'd built a situation that gave her exactly what she wanted theoretically.

What are you going home to?

Grace turned and looked through the window at Country taking Hope from Jenna, kissing her cheek as she and Elodie washed the dishes.

Spending time with the Snowballs was like unwrapping a present layer by layer. She saw it now. They were a family. A team. But all her life she'd felt like that gift had never been for her. Not that her parents hadn't tried, they were wonderful. But she'd always known—always accepted—that she wasn't quite a part of it.

How did one step into a family? How did you simply believe the gift was for you?

"How do you do it?" she whispered. "How do you play on a team? Trust they won't let you fall?"

His eyes wandered over her face as he considered. Finally he said, "I don't."

Grace blinked.

"I don't trust they won't let me fall," he clarified. "That's not how it works." He pulled her closer, slipping his hand around her waist. "I trust that if I fall, someone's going to be there to throw a glove. That they'll drop whatever they're doing and haul ass across the ice. And if they can't?" He shrugged. "They always have a damn good excuse."

Grace stared at him, heart thudding.

"You know what makes a great teammate?" He leaned closer, his stubble rubbing against her cheek. "They're the ones who don't skate away when the play gets messy. When things go sideways, they dig in. They don't have to score the goals, but they're always in the right spot when it counts." He slipped his hand up the inside of her shirt, and she gasped when his cold fingers met bare skin.

"I thought you said this was my decision."

"Doesn't mean I'm not going to fight dirty," he whispered, his fingertips pressing against her spine. "A good teammate calls you on your shit. They don't care about our ego, they only want you to get better."

Grace swallowed, the air sticking in her lungs. "Is that all?"

He dipped his head, brushing his lips over her neck. "They look amazing naked."

"Hey, we were in the dark. You haven't seen me naked."

"I was talking about Tyler."

Grace laughed out loud, sucking in a breath as he nipped at her collarbone. He straightened, his mouth brushing her temple, then her cheek, then lower—hovering just beside her lips. "Tell me to kiss you," he murmured, "or tell me to walk away."

She trembled. *Tell me what you want, Grace.*

That crack he'd started split wide open. She wanted him. Not just in the aching, breathless way that kept her up at night—but in the slow, terrifying, life-altering way that made her bones shake. She wanted his energy and excitement. His grin and his grit. She wanted Sunday mornings with coffee, weekends at the rink, and tacos in the kitchen. She wanted something bigger than safety. Bigger than predictability. She wanted to drop through the floor and have André scoop her into his arms at the bottom.

Maybe she couldn't expect him to always catch her when she fell. But she'd seen him haul ass across the ice more than once. And every time he missed, he had a damn good excuse.

It's called living, Grace.

She wrapped her hands around his neck. "Kiss me."

André was excellent at doing what he was told.

Grace's breath caught in her throat as her back hit the porch railing. Her fingers curled into his shirt, and André moved like he'd already mapped this moment in his head a thousand times. Like he knew exactly what he wanted to touch. To taste.

He was everywhere. His right hand slid up her arm, rough knuckles grazing over the soft inside of her wrist before he cupped her cheek. His other hand gripped her waist, firm, anchoring her in place like he wasn't sure if she'd bolt.

She whimpered, and as soon as the sound escaped her, he growled low in his throat, pressing her harder into the railing. His palm slid into her hair, fingers tangling in the strands, tilting her head so he could have access to more of her.

Then they were moving, André's hand wrapped around her wrist. She blinked, dazed, as he tugged her down the stairs. "And where exactly are we—"

"Silo."

"What?"

"I need you naked. In bed. Now."

He scooped her up in his arms, carrying her across the yard, through the spring-wet grass.

"André," she hissed. "Isn't that someone's rental?"

"Not tonight." He set her down in front of the door and pulled out his phone, thumbing a quick text.

She laughed. "You can't just break into a—"

"I'm not breaking in." He crouched, flipped a paver stone, and plucked the spare key from beneath it. "I'm letting us in. Huge difference."

Grace crossed her arms, still catching her breath. "And if someone's booked it?"

He held out his screen.

André

> Please tell me silo #1's empty
>
> I'll pay a cleaning fee

Country 🤠

> Don't break anything or this conversation never happened

André flashed her a devil's grin. "Permission granted."

Grace's heart fluttered at her throat. "I didn't bring anything, I wasn't—"

"I'm fully prepared." André unlocked the door and shoved it open, his breath coming in quick bursts.

She raised an eyebrow. "Yeah?"

"Don't act like you're surprised."

Grace scanned the room. The silo was cozy—wood-paneled walls, a round bed with a ridiculous number of pillows and one of those fake fur throws. "Are we those people? We only do themed rooms now?"

André chuckled, and the second the door shut behind them, he was on her. "Do you want to be in control tonight, Grace?"

Her pulse thudded in her ears, a wild, staccato rhythm. "No," she whispered before she could stop herself.

"Good." His hands slid around her waist, gripping tight, and she gasped. His mouth brushed her jaw, her ear, down the side of her throat, and her knees buckled. "Let me take care of it," he murmured. "Let me take care of you."

Grace didn't realize she was shaking until he pressed her back against the wall and cupped her cheek, thumb dragging slowly across her bottom lip.

André pulled back for the briefest second, gaze locked on hers like he needed the green light. Her lips parted. Her heart screamed. "One hundred percent," she murmured, then reached for his shirt and yanked.

That was all he needed. His mouth crashed into hers, and she was consumed by the heat of him. His weight, his scent. He kissed her like he'd earned it. Like she was the only thing that had ever made sense.

Her clothes disappeared—she didn't know how, didn't care. Every time she tried to think, his hands dragged over her skin and wiped her mind clean. She let him lift her, carry her, lay her across the bed like she was fragile glass and then immediately prove she wasn't.

"You always try to stay so quiet," he whispered against her collarbone. "Let's see how long that lasts."

CHAPTER
Thirty-Three

André

ON SATURDAY NIGHT, the Saddledome buzzed like an angry hive, the stands jammed past the club level with screaming fans, kids waving signs, and enough flash photography to give a man a seizure. André tightened the chin strap on his helmet and grinned as he skated past the blizzard-blue centreline. This wasn't just a game—it was a damn show.

"Bowen, you mic'd up?" Jack Harrison circled like a smug bastard in his Blizzard jersey. André would've chirped, but tonight Jack was *his* smug bastard, so he turned to Tyler instead.

"I know all your tricks, bud. Don't expect me to bite on those outside edges, eh?"

Tyler flipped him the bird and pointed to his helmet in response to Jack's question, then turned back to his team on the bench for the night. The Snowballs were split fifty-fifty with the pros, and André couldn't wait to get a good check on Country. Hopefully two.

It was Team Maddox versus Team Thompson. Country captained one side, Sean the other. Fly had suited up, much to everyone's delight. The man's knees looked like they'd been stitched together by a blind raccoon, but he was grinning like a kid in a candy shop.

Jenna had helped extend player invites, and she'd been right about the branding. She went for controversial picks, hot heads, and personalities. He had to give it to her. These NHL players drew a crowd.

The puck dropped, and it was pure chaos in the best way. Even though nothing was on the line, every guy out there played class A hockey. Because hockey didn't know how to be casual.

Hockey was always a show, not in the flashy plays, not in the lights, but in the way it demanded your whole heart. The boys knew that. You laced up, you taped your stick, and you gave everything. Even in a charity game. Especially in a charity game. Because it was about more than goals. It was about the fans in the stands who paid for a night of magic.

And the guys next to him? For the next few hours, they were brothers. When you sat on the bench wearing the same crest, you belonged to each other, no matter where you came from or where you were headed next.

André crushed Country against the glass, digging with his stick. "Let me take it, bud, and I'll be gentle."

Country laughed, flicking the puck between his legs. "You know I like it rough."

Every whistle, the DJ blared theme songs—AC/DC, Carly Rae Jepsen, Nickelback. During breaks, Jenna ran on-ice mini-games: kids in bubble suits racing from blue line to blue line, a "fastest shot" competition for fans with actual radar guns, and a "Guess the Face" segment where the jumbotron showed baby pictures of the players.

Country had the crowd in the palm of his hand. With a wireless mic, he hyped fans during intermissions, shouted out donors, and auctioned off a signed jersey mid-period, making jokes that had the whole arena doubled over.

"André Leclerc has volunteered to shave his legs live on stream if we hit our goal," Jenna announced over the PA.

André leaned over the boards. "Balls! I said *balls!*"

The crowd roared. Grace was somewhere in the VIP section. He needed to see her. It was the first time in his life that he was anxious to get off the ice.

Second period, he and Jack played the point together and orchestrated a filthy one-timer. Curtis chipped it from behind the net, Jack caught it mid-air and dropped it to André, who rifled it low glove side. The crowd went nuclear.

"That's what happens." Jack skated by the bench. "Now give us the sexy line change."

"I've had better passes from my wife," Country muttered, but couldn't hide his smirk.

By the third period, it was tied. Four to four.

Colin Fraser from Toronto fed André a look on a line rush—sneaky, sharp. He took the charge even though he was typically a fourth-line grinder. Their D-men were slightly out of position, giving him a chance if he bolted.

He deked once, then twice, and went top shelf while falling to his knees. Absolute highlight reel shit. The goal horn blared, and André fist-pumped to the crowd, lungs burning, legs on fire. He hoped to hell Grace was watching.

They'd spent the night together at Country's but couldn't ditch their responsibilities leading up to the game. He'd seen her twice over the week, and neither visit had been long enough. There was still a part of him that wondered if she'd close up and get scared, but every time that thought entered his head, he remembered Country.

He knew his reasons. And it was worth fighting for whether or not he won. Just like every single time he got on the ice.

Brett crowed from behind him, "Where was that in Edmonton?"

André struck a pose, then threw himself over the boards.

The final seconds of the third period ticked down, and the roar of the crowd rose as fans surged to their feet. Five to four. They only had to hold them.

For a moment, the whole event snapped into focus. They were in the Saddledome playing to a packed crowd. He had no idea what the numbers looked like, but ticket sales alone pushed them close to their goal.

André bent over his stick, lungs burning, sweat stinging his eyes. He glanced at Country on the far wing and Tyler at the point, waiting for the drop.

Face-off. Ten seconds left. The puck hit the ice, and everything blurred. Country snapped it back, and Tyler took off like he'd been shot out of a cannon. Two strides. Three. He flicked it back to Cade Bishop who tapped it on to Brett, and Boyd wasn't ready for the back door. Brett fired a wrister, and it snapped past the post.

The crowd exploded. Tied.

André shook his head, slamming his stick to the ice. Country grabbed Tyler around the neck, and their entire bench emptied, howling, pounding each other on the back.

He couldn't have asked for a better game. It was sudden-death overtime. Ten minutes. One goal.

They didn't wait long. Two minutes in, Fly sent a pass along the boards to Suraj who gave a one-touch to Jack Harrison. André leaned over the boards, screaming nonsense.

Jack lost the puck to Tyler but reached out at the last second and sent the puck around the back of the net. Fraser was set up like they'd planned it. He snagged the puck and looped it around the post.

He took off, pumping his stick over his head, and the dome went nuclear. André launched over the boards like a rocket, joining the dogpile around Jack and Colin. Gloves and helmets hit the ice, and it wasn't long before both teams were laughing and hugging at centre. They honoured their goalies, lining up and slapping sticks on the ice as they made their way to the benches.

Jenna stepped out on a mat in front of the penalty box a few minutes later, Hope strapped to her chest, a mic in her hand and a wide smile on her face. "We want to thank you," she said, her voice a little shaky. "Every single one of you here tonight helped us raise money for a cause that means the world to our family. To our team."

The Jumbotron lit up behind her, a montage rolling—footage prepared by *Heads Up Alberta*. Clips of youth hockey and players rehabilitating never failed to tug on heartstrings.

"And thanks to your support and our incredible sponsors . . . " Jenna paused for dramatic effect. "We raised $407,800!"

The dome lost its damn mind. Country skated up and pulled her and Hope into a bear hug. André got choked up, then lifted his head searching for the one person he wanted to see after a game like this.

He beelined to the locker room and showered in three minutes flat. André towel-dried his hair, yanked on his jeans and a hoodie, and grabbed his phone. He fired off three pictures to Luc of the pregame. Jenna hired a videographer for the game, so he'd send on footage later. He texted:

> Tonight was hot. Blasted past our fundraising goals. Love you, bud

André checked his reflection in the mirror, raked a hand through his wet hair, and grabbed his bag. Then he bolted for the elevators.

———

The hallway upstairs near the press room felt muted compared to what had just happened on the ice. He didn't even make it to the door before Grace bolted out. She ran to him in her heels.

"You were unbelievable out there." She threw her arms around his neck and kissed him straight on the mouth with her red lipstick. He wrapped his arms around her, drawing what felt like his first real breath of the night.

"Your *goal?*" She pulled back to look at him, eyes bright. "Is Country pissed about that hit?"

He grinned, his chest so full, he could barely speak. "I love this Grace who loves hockey." He dipped his head, nuzzling her neck.

She laughed. "Do you love her enough to help with a transaction?" He groaned, but then she put her finger under his chin. "I'll make it worth your while."

Now he was listening. He followed her into the room she'd been using as her personal office.

"I'm almost finished with this, but I've scoured every record I have from you, from Heads Up, and I cannot find a contract for this sponsorship." She flipped her phone around like she was about to throw down a royal flush.

André saw the name and relaxed. "Oh, yeah. You don't need to worry about that one."

Grace frowned. "Yes. I do need to worry about it. It doesn't matter if you have some kind of verbal agreement with this person or group or whatever, everything needs to have a paper trail or—"

"Trust me, Grace." He dragged her closer. "This one's fine."

She gave him a look like he'd just told her he used gasoline as mouthwash. "Okaaay. But how do you know it will be fine in three months, six months, or a year? Businesses can be volatile, and if something were to happen—"

"Nothing's going to happen." He shouldn't love pushing her buttons as much as he did, but she was so sexy when she got fired up. He wouldn't let it last too much longer. "This isn't from a business. It's from a holding."

Grace looked back at her screen. "Yes, but it doesn't matter. You asked me to come into this and ensure everything was above board. You didn't want Heads Up to be exposed to any unnecessary—"

"I gave you an expectation. You just want to do your job right."

Grace exhaled. "I'm doing it again, aren't I?" She squeezed her eyes shut. "I'm sorry, I don't want to end up missing something—"

"Do you have a contract there? Can you print it?"

She nodded. "I could."

"Do it. I'll get it signed for you."

Her shoulders relaxed. "Really?" He patted her hip as she walked past to open the file on her laptop. It only took her a minute to send it to the printer. The machine whirred to life. Grace grabbed the fresh double-sided document and handed it to him.

"Do you have a pen?"

Her brow furrowed. She lifted one from the desk and handed it to him. "Are they here? I didn't—"

André bent over and dated the document, then signed at the bottom. "Can you fill in the rest?"

She blinked. "André, I don't just need any signature. I need the actual sponsor."

He handed the page to her. "And you've got it."

Grace glanced down at the contract, then back up at Andre. "You donated fifty-thousand dollars to Heads Up?"

André nodded once, trying not to grin as she processed. He pulled the paper from her hands, set it on the desk, and planted himself in front of her. "Right now, you're wondering how I have that much money to give away. Because I hardly ever work, and I need to grow up?"

Grace's eyes flared. "I didn't mean that. I wasn't in a good place—"

"No, you were right. About a lot of things. I may be immature and shortsighted in many areas, but money isn't one of them."

She drew in a breath and blew it out. "Oh, damn it, is this residual from the Polo ad?"

André gaped at her. "You know about that?"

Grace nodded. "I might have it saved in my phone."

André laughed out loud, then pushed her back until he could lift her up on the desktop. "Well, I found your Hinge profile, so—"

"I deleted that!"

He pressed closer. "I still have a couple pairs of those boxer briefs."

"The blinds are open," she murmured.

"Does it look like I give a shit?" André ran his hands through her hair, watching her eyes roll back in her head.

She sighed. "I'm worried I like you more now that I know you have money."

"I'm worried I like you more now that you watch hockey."

Grace laughed. "It's probably not healthy. For you to keep telling me things that make me fall deeper in—" She stopped herself, her eyes flying open.

André raised an eyebrow. "Please. Continue."

"I didn't—I wasn't saying—"

André pulled her lips to his, kissing her until she melted into him. "I love you, too, Grace."

She made a soft sound in her throat. "It's too soon to say that."

He shook his head. "Nope. You've followed enough arbitrary rules in your life. You don't need to follow that one." She gazed up at him, her ankles wrapping around his calves. He kissed her forehead. "Love is a heavy burden to carry on your own."

Grace released a breath, arching into him and pressing her cheek against his. "I think what I know of love is so small. But all I have is yours."

He smiled, kissing her jaw. "We're a team, Grace. We'll figure out the rest of it together."

Epilogue

Grace

THE THOMPSON HOUSE was lit up like a holiday card. String lights ran along the porch railings and stretched across the backyard. The firepit crackled in the centre of the lawn, surrounded by folding chairs and blankets. Someone had turned on a speaker near the grill, and country music hummed low over the laughter and clatter of beer bottles.

It wasn't warm enough on paper to have a backyard BBQ, but in Alberta, fifteen degrees Celsius in March felt like a beach day.

Inside, the kitchen table was loaded with smoked brisket and pork ribs from a place Country swore by in Okotoks, two kinds of potato salad, because Anne and Tina refused to compromise, sweet buns from Penny's favourite bakery, and one veggie tray that Grace had brought.

Jenna stood barefoot by the island, Hope propped on her hip, cheeks pink, eyes wide.

"She looks lighter," Grace murmured.

André frowned. "I don't know. She's gained a ton of weight."

Grace smacked his shoulder. "Not talking about Hope." He smirked and picked up a rib.

Amey dropped the petition two days earlier. The court filing came in that morning, withdrawing the claim and finalizing an addendum to the adoption agreement. Elodie worked with both parties to help navigate the language, ensuring Amey and Brady could have contact in a healthy, moderated way. Hope wouldn't grow up with question marks. She'd grow up surrounded by an entire family who loved her.

"Do you wish you knew your birth parents?" André asked.

Grace pondered. "Sometimes. Of course, I'm curious." She thought about the lengths she'd been willing to go to for her friends and the decisions Amey and Brady had made. Something inside her softened. They were all just trying to do the best they could.

Jack raised his beer from the couch. "To Jenna and Country, you survived legal hell with YouTube smiles and perfect hair."

Country laughed and leaned over to clink his beer.

Fly reached over his wife, Jess, and adjusted their new baby in a wrap. "Seriously. You two showed us all what it means to go to the boards for your kid."

Country slung an arm around Jenna and kissed her temple. "You don't want to drop mitts with this one. She'll smother you with that big heart of hers."

Tyler groaned. "You're getting soft."

Emma scoffed. "Stop! I love it!"

Across the room, Suraj, already three drinks in, hollered, "All I know is that if I ever go through a custody battle, I want Grace Fairbanks in my corner."

There was a chorus of agreement. Grace held up her glass with a modest smile, cheeks flushing pink. André leaned in and murmured, "He can't have you."

She grinned, then nearly bit her cheek as he slipped a hand up the inside of her thigh under the table.

Needing a distraction, she picked up her phone and went through the last texts from her mom.

> I can't say I'm thrilled not to see you, but glad you've found good friends there.
>
> How long are you staying?
>
> Is there someone in particular you're staying for??

André snatched her phone, and Grace yelped. "Don't—I'll tell her eventually—"

He held her arm down and lifted the phone for a selfie, then handed it back with a wink. "I didn't press send. Up to you."

Grace looked at the photo of them. André's cocky smile, her reaching for him. She looked . . . happy. Relaxed. Like she was about to strip off her swim cover and jog into the waves with her friends.

She loved it.

Grace hit the blue arrow, and André squeezed her thigh. "We look good together."

The doorbell rang just as Rhonda sliced into a second tray of Nanaimo bars.

Jenna turned, but Country stepped past her, brushing his hands on a dish towel before opening the door.

"Hey!" Country boomed. "Come on in!" He flung the door wide and clapped the man at the door on the back.

Grace's eyes widened as Brady walked in. Fly stood and gave him a fist bump. Curtis steered him toward the food. André appeared at Grace's elbow, a bar in hand.

"Didn't know he was coming," she whispered.

"It was pretty obvious he needed something." André placed a hand on her back.

Grace turned to look at him. "Is he joining the team?"

He shook his head. "Brady's only twenty-seven. Can't play in the league yet. But he'll practice with us. Train. Be around the guys." André glanced across the room. "Sometimes you just need a team."

Her chest pinched. She watched Brady laugh at something Suraj said, a little uncertain but leaning in.

Grace looked back up at André, her heart doing something dangerous in her chest. "I was wrong about you, you know. You're husband material."

André scoffed. "Whoa, Fairbanks. Chill. I get that your ovaries are ticking, but—"

"Ugh, please. Don't start an argument just so we can make up later."

He smirked, wrapping her ponytail around his fist and giving a gentle tug. "But it's my favourite game." He leaned in and kissed her cheek. "Eighty-twenty?"

She fought a smile. "Ninety-ten if you get me more potato salad."

"And if I include a sweet bun?"

Grace gave a breathy laugh. "I like your odds."

Next in the Series —>

Sean's story! Preorder Now!

Find special edition e-books and paperbacks exclusively at www. CindyGunderson.com

See the new Campus Confessions series —>

The only thing worse than crossing the line is wanting to . .
.

Living with my boyfriend Logan should have been everything I wanted—until I realized his best friend, Rob Thompson, came with the deal. Rob and I are like oil and water, fire and gasoline, sworn enemies under one roof.

When Logan got selected for World Juniors in Germany, I thought I'd get a reprieve. I could handle the quiet loneliness of his absence. What I couldn't handle was Rob. He's still here, stomping around the house with that cocky grin, pushing every button I have. And somehow, when it's just the two of us, the air feels heavier. Charged.

It's infuriating how he can see right through me, past every wall I've built, calling me out in ways no one else ever has. But as much as I hate him, I can't seem to stay away.

Logan will be gone for two months. Rob will be here every day. And I'm terrified that everything I thought I knew about love—and hate—is about to change.

Start the series now

Cindy Gunderson is a voice actress and award-winning author. Since she has commitment issues, she writes both sci-fi and fantasy, as well as contemporary romance and women's fiction under the pen name, Cynthia Gunderson.

When she is not typing away in a quiet corner of her local library, you can find her traveling with her family, narrating audiobooks, or happily digging in her garden. She loves acting and performing, beating her kids in card games, and playing ultimate frisbee with her handsome husband, Scott.

Cindy grew up in Alberta, Canada, but has lived most of her adult life between California and Colorado. She currently resides in the Denver metro area. Cindy holds a B.S. in Psychology from Brigham Young University.

Cindy's first novel Tier 1 was awarded First Place in Science Fiction at the 2021 CIPPA EVVY Awards and her women's fiction novel Yes, And was honored with the Indie Author Award's first place prize for the state of Colorado, 2023.

Also by Cynthia Gunderson

Yes, And

I Can't Remember

Holly Bough Cottage

The New Year's Party

Let's Try This Again

Sugar Creek Series

One Last Christmas, Love in Audio

Canadian Played Series

Against the Boards, Called for Icing, Stickhandle with Care, On the Power Play, Guarding Home Ice, Offside Attraction, Drop the Mitts, The Dying Seconds

Campus Confessions Series

The Breakaway, The Save

Find signed books and discounted bundles at

www.CindyGunderson.com

Instagram: @CindyGWrites

Facebook: @CindyGWrites

TikTok: @CynthiaGWrites